P9-DNM-405

"Being shot tends to make a man short-tempered . . ."

She held his gaze unflinchingly. Despite his doubts concerning her suitability, Colt found himself drawn to the determination she radiated.

"I can cook, set a proper table, and have impeccable manners. I speak English and Spanish. I hunt, fish, swim, and ride. I'd hoped to find a husband who'd view these qualities as assets, but if you're seeking what society considers a proper wife who'll defer to you in all things, and spend time sitting in a rocker with an embroidery hoop in her hand, you should say so and I'll return to Arizona."

Colt blinked. He didn't know any woman with the pluck to toss down a gauntlet so effortlessly. Life with her would be neither easy nor boring.

CHASE BRANCH LIBRARY
17731 W. SEVEN MILE RD.
DETROIT, MI 48235
313-481-1580

FEB 18

CH

By Beverly Jenkins

TEMPEST
BREATHLESS
FORBIDDEN
DESTINY'S CAPTIVE
DESTINY'S SURRENDER
DESTINY'S EMBRACE
NIGHT HAWK
MIDNIGHT
CAPTURED
JEWEL
A WILD SWEET LOVE
WINDS OF THE STORM
SOMETHING LIKE LOVE
BEFORE THE DAWN
ALWAYS AND FOREVER
THE TAMING OF JESSI ROSE
THROUGH THE STORM
TOPAZ
INDIGO
VIVID
NIGHT SONG

ATTENTION: ORGANIZATIONS AND CORPORATIONS
HarperCollins books may be purchased for educational, business, or sales promotional use. For information, please e-mail the Special Markets Department at SPsales@harpercollins.com.

BEVERLY JENKINS

TEMPEST

AVONBOOKS

An Imprint of HarperCollins*Publishers*

This is a work of fiction. Names, characters, places, and incidents are products of the author's imagination or are used fictitiously and are not to be construed as real. Any resemblance to actual events, locales, organizations, or persons, living or dead, is entirely coincidental.

Excerpt from *Forbidden* © 2016 by Beverly Jenkins.
Excerpt from *Breathless* © 2017 by Beverly Jenkins.

TEMPEST. Copyright © 2018 by Beverly Jenkins. All rights reserved. Printed in the United States of America. No part of this book may be used or reproduced in any manner whatsoever without written permission except in the case of brief quotations embodied in critical articles and reviews. For information, address HarperCollins Publishers, 195 Broadway, New York, NY 10007.

First Avon Books mass market printing: February 2018

Print Edition ISBN: 978-0-06-238904-6
Digital Edition ISBN: 978-0-06-238905-3

Cover illustration by Alan Ayers
Chapter opener illustration copyright © Nikiparonak/Shutterstock, Inc.

Avon, Avon & logo, and Avon Books & logo are registered trademarks of HarperCollins Publishers in the United States of America and other countries.

HarperCollins is a registered trademark of HarperCollins Publishers in the United States of America and other countries.

FIRST EDITION

18 19 20 21 22   QGM   10 9 8 7 6 5 4 3 2 1

If you purchased this book without a cover, you should be aware that this book is stolen property. It was reported as "unsold and destroyed" to the publisher, and neither the author nor the publisher has received any payment for this "stripped book."

I dedicate this book to my friend A. Lynne Wall. She passed away in September 2017 and left a void in the lives of those who knew and loved her. Lynne was a staunch supporter of all things romance and with her passing our genre lost one of its brightest lights. May she rest in peace.

Prologue

My dearest Miss Carmichael,

   You have my deepest gratitude for agreeing to be my wife and the mother to my six-year-old daughter, Anna. As your husband, I pledge my protection and unbridled respect. Life in Wyoming Territory offers little in the way of amusements for a woman of your status but makes up for it in beauty. Anna and I look forward to meeting you and welcoming you into our lives.

Sincerely,
Dr. Colton Lee

Chapter One

Wyoming Territory
Spring 1885

*R*egan Carmichael was tired of riding in the stage-coach. The beauty of the Wyoming countryside with its trees and snow-topped mountains had been thrilling to view at first, but after traveling for three long days in a cramped coach that seemingly had no springs, she longed for the journey to Paradise, Wyoming, to end. Even her excitement at meeting the man she'd come to marry had been dulled by the lengthy trek, and she was certain her bottom would bear bruises for the rest of her days. Her mood was further challenged by having ridden the past day and a half alone. She did enjoy no longer being squashed between the other passengers who'd since departed, but missed the conversations they'd shared. Up top, sat the driver, Mr. Denby, and the guard, Mr. Casey, who due to their duties had no time to lighten her boredom with conversation. The wheels hit another rut on the uneven road causing her to bounce, land hard on the thin leather seat, and her poor sore bottom wailed again.

That it might be months before she saw her family again temporarily took her mind off the uncomfortable ride. She began missing them the moment she boarded the train in Tucson. Her Aunt Eddy and Uncle Rhine. Her dear sister, Portia. The last time she'd been away from home for more than an extended period had been during her studies at Oberlin College, but unlike then Regan wouldn't be returning home. This would be the start of a new life in a place she knew little about other than it was mostly wild and untamed, the two largest cities were Laramie and Cheyenne, cattle raising reigned supreme, and women were given the right to vote in 1869; a national first.

Suddenly, the coach picked up speed. Mr. Denby could be heard hoarsely urging the horses to run faster. Concerned, she quickly pushed aside the leather window shade and looked out. Three men wearing bandanas over their faces were riding hard in their wake. Mr. Casey began firing his shotgun, and the riders, swiftly closing in on the coach, returned fire. Regan snatched up her own Winchester, tore down the shade, and added her weapon to the fray. Seconds later, she no longer heard the shotgun from above.

"Mr. Denby! Are you two okay?" she shouted.

"No! Keep shooting, miss!"

He didn't have to tell her twice.

The outlaws were nearly on them. Even though the careening pitch of the coach played havoc with her aim, she managed to hit the nearest rider, which made him drop the reins, grab his arm, and slump forward in pain. His partner rode past him and positioned himself adjacent to the coach. He took aim at the uncovered window but Regan was already squeezing the trigger on the rapid-fire rifle. The cartridges exploded in his chest and he tumbled backwards off his mount.

The coach thundered on.

The third hombre must have realized the odds weren't in his favor. A grim Regan watched him grab the reins of the riderless horse. He and the slumped man she'd shot in the arm rode back the way they'd come. Whether the one they left behind was dead, she didn't know.

Breathing harshly and shaking, she fell back against the seat. Only then did she acknowledge how terrified she'd been. Her roiling stomach made her think she might be sick, but she thanked her recently deceased neighbor, Mr. Blanchard, for his rifle lessons. Shoot first, puke later! he'd told the then eleven-year-old Regan and her older sister, Portia. The memory made her smile and she drew in a deep breath that calmed her frayed nerves.

The coach slowed, then stopped. When the door opened, an alarmed Regan grabbed the Winchester.

It was the driver, Mr. Denby. For a moment, he stared at her in awe.

"That was some mighty good shooting, miss. Wasn't expecting that—not with you all fancy dressed the way you are."

Regan silently acknowledged the compliment. "Are you and Mr. Casey all right?"

"No. Casey's heart gave out. He's dead."

"Oh no! I'm so sorry."

"I'd be dead, too, if it hadn't been for you. Do you mind riding up top with me so I can put his body in the coach?"

"Of course not."

With her help, Casey's body was placed on the seat. After handing Denby her rifle, she hiked up the skirt of her fancy blue traveling ensemble and climbed the large front wheel to the seat.

"You do that like you've been climbing wagons all your life."

"I have. I drove the mail back home in Arizona Territory."

He chuckled. "Really?"

She nodded.

"You here to visit family?"

"No. I'm a mail-order bride. The man's name is Dr. Colton Lee."

Denby began coughing.

"What's wrong?"

"Nothing. Just a tickle in my throat. Let's get going. We should make it to Paradise before sunset."

He got the horses moving but Regan swore the

coughing fit must've meant something else because when she glanced his way, Denby was smiling.

Before they'd gone another mile, she spied another group of men riding hard in their direction. This time there were no bandanas and their open dusters were flapping like birds of prey. She grabbed her rifle and took aim. "I think the man that got away has returned with friends. You keep driving, I'll try and hold them off."

He let out a curse and slapped the reins down on the horses' backs. The coach picked up speed, but she could tell by the rate they were moving that the poor beasts were tired. "How many men?" Denby yelled. He was unable to see the riders from his seat.

"Eight!" Regan knew there was no way she'd be able to hold her own against so many armed men. She was terrified, but as they got within range she steadied her aim and fired repeatedly. There were three men riding point. She hit one in the shoulder, but apparently, the bullet only grazed him because he slapped a hand over the injury and kept riding. They began returning fire but she realized they were firing in the air. They'd also halted their mounts. Curious, but not drawing down, she waited over her pounding heart.

"What's the matter?" Denby asked.

"They've stopped."

He pulled back on the reins to halt the coach and stood up cautiously. After assessing the riders, he waved his arms as if signaling them and asked her, "Did that rifle of yours hit anybody?"

"I caught the one in the black duster in the shoulder. Why? Do you know them?"

"Yep. It's the sheriff, Whit Lambert."

Her eyes widened. "I shot the sheriff?"

"No, ma'am. The man in the black duster is Doc Lee. You just plugged your soon-to-be husband." And by his chuckles, he apparently found that humorous.

Regan was mortified.

The sheriff and his men approached on mounts held to a walk. Regan couldn't take her eyes off the grim ebony face of the man she'd come to marry. He was tall and lean and sat his big bay stallion proudly. A mustache accented his tersely set mouth. A close-cropped beard dusted his jaw. She was pleased to finally put a face to the man she'd been corresponding with for the past few months, but her main concern was how he'd react upon learning who'd shot him. Regan also noted belatedly that the men who'd attacked the coach were also with the sheriff's posse. Their hands were cuffed and neither looked happy about being apprehended. She assumed the body lying across the back of a black horse was the one she'd shot in the chest.

"Sorry about the shooting, Sheriff," Denby called out. "We thought you were part of the gang that rode down on us earlier. She really didn't mean to shoot the doc."

The tall auburn-haired sheriff appeared as confused by Regan's presence as the men of the posse seemed to be. "You were the one shooting at us, ma'am?"

"Yes."

"I'm Sheriff Whitman Lambert. And you are?"

Drawing in a nervous breath, she gave the doctor a hasty glance. "Regan Carmichael."

The doctor's dark gaze flew to hers. "I'm truly sorry," she replied guiltily.

The sheriff turned to the doctor and although his barely veiled amusement mirrored the reactions of the other posse members, the doctor's jaw was tight with displeasure.

She felt terrible.

"Where's Casey?" the sheriff asked Denby.

"Inside on the seat. He's dead. I think his heart gave out during the gun fight earlier."

The doctor dismounted, wincing a bit as he moved and entered the coach.

"Was it those two?" Lambert asked, pointing to the sullen, dirty-faced outlaws.

"Their faces were covered," Regan replied, "but I believe so. I hit one in the arm and another in the chest."

"That's him back there," he said, indicating the lifeless body. He viewed her with the same wonderment Mr. Denby had earlier.

Denby came to her defense. "You aren't going to charge her, are you? Had it not been for her, I'd probably be dead as Casey. The stage line will probably give her a reward for helping keep the gold I'm carrying safe."

Regan knew stage lines sometimes did such

things, but she didn't need rewarding for protecting herself. She was a woman. Had the outlaws taken the coach, she might have been prey to an unspeakable assault and they may have discovered the large amount of gold coins sewn into the hems of her gowns. She took no joy in having caused the man's death and if she was charged, she knew her Uncle Rhine would provide her the best lawyer his money could buy.

The doctor exited the coach. Ignoring her, he gave the sheriff a terse nod, as if verifying Mr. Casey's demise, before haltingly climbing back into the saddle. His stilted movements made her believe his injury was more serious than the simple graze she'd assumed earlier. Again, she felt awful.

The sheriff said, "You won't be charged, Miss Carmichael, but they will. They've been ambushing coaches up and down this trail for weeks. In fact, they took down a coach earlier today. The driver and guard were wounded and we were out looking for them when we came across them after you and Denby sent them skedaddling. Thank you for your help."

"You're welcome." She was relieved, but so far, Colton Lee had yet to speak to her directly. And as the sheriff and his men escorted the coach the remaining few miles to town, that didn't change.

"Stop laughing and take the damn bullet out," Colt snarled, removing his shirt. The last thing he needed was more of Whit's needling.

"Got yourself quite the delicate bride-to-be there, Dr. Lee. Hold still." Whit used the tip of his big bladed knife to expertly dig into Colt's shoulder, causing him to hiss out a curse in response to the sharp pain.

"Got it." The bloody bullet went into a chipped porcelain basin on the desk. Whit sloshed whiskey over the oozing injury. Colton hissed again and immediately reached for the clean square of white cotton sheeting he'd taken from his medical bag and pressed it against the wound to ease the bleeding.

"Want me to ask her in to sew you up?"

Colton glared.

"Just asking. No need to get surly."

Colt knew Whit was having a good time. Were the shoe on the other foot, he'd be the one poking fun, but it was on his foot and it pinched like hell. What kind of woman shot her intended? Yes, it was an accident but his pride was as wounded as his shoulder.

Whit added, "If you're going to send her back let me know. The way she shoots, I might like to swear her in as a deputy." The two surviving outlaws were locked up in the small jail behind his office.

Colton ignored him, or as much as one could a six-foot-five-inch former cavalry soldier who on better days was called friend. Instead, his thoughts were on Regan Carmichael. What kind of woman had he asked to take the place of his late wife, Adele? What other nonladylike skills did she possess? Had she lied to him about being educated and cultured? A part of him was half-ready to scrap the marriage agreement and send her packing. Colt's grandfather Ben would undoubtedly agree. Whit's humor notwithstanding, Colt found nothing funny about it, and neither did his gunshot shoulder.

*R*egan, who'd been told by the sheriff to wait outside while he patched up the doctor, paced the wooden walk in front of his office. How was she supposed to know the riders were a sheriff's posse? She'd been too busy protecting herself and Mr. Denby to stop firing and politely ask their identities. Colton Lee seemed furious, and on the ride to town hadn't once looked her way. She supposed he was allowed. After all, how many men met their prospective brides via a bullet from her Winchester? She couldn't blame him if he decided to send her packing, thus preventing her from trying to make things right—not that she knew how that might be accomplished.

Word must have gotten around about the shooting because a small group of men were on the other side of the street watching her from in front of the general store. One, sporting whiskers, long white hair, and wearing trousers and a shirt made from deerskin called out, "Did you really shoot the doc?"

Her cheeks burned. "It was an accident."

Another man shouted, "This called a shotgun wedding where you're from?"

They all laughed. She didn't respond.

The door opened and the sheriff stepped out.

"May I see him?" she asked anxiously.

"I think I should probably take you over to Minnie's. She takes in boarders. You'll stay there until the wedding. You can see him later."

That wasn't the answer Regan wanted, so she sailed past him and went inside. Her steps halted at the sight of Lee attempting to drag his union shirt up and over his bandaged left shoulder. Seeing her enter, he stopped and her first thought was that the tall slender Colton Lee was as handsome as an African god. The second thought: the riveting eyes were as foreboding as a gathering thunderstorm. All they lacked were lightning bolts. "I . . . want to apologize. I didn't know you and the others were a posse."

His gaze didn't waver, and again she expected lightning. Instead, he resumed his one-handed attempt to cover his bared left shoulder. She took a step forward to assist him but his silent rebuke froze her in place. Regan swallowed in a dry throat. She noticed him wince again as he finally got the shirt positioned. He used his right hand to do up the buttons, then picked up a blue denim shirt and slowly worked it on.

"Where'd you learn to shoot?" he finally asked quietly.

"A neighbor."

"What else he teach you?"

She took offense at both the question and his tone. Surely he wasn't intimating that Old Man

Blanchard had taught her anything unseemly. "To hunt, shoe a horse. Shingle a roof. Again, I'm sorry for wounding you."

His continued displeasure made her temper rise. In her mind, he was being terribly unfair. Even if he was still angry, he could at least acknowledge her apology.

"I'm not sure we'll mesh," he finally said.

"Neither am I. A grown man should be able to acknowledge a sincerely offered apology and converse in sentences consisting of more than five words. Good day, Dr. Lee."

She turned on her heel and stormed out.

Outside, she found Sheriff Lambert talking with Mr. Denby. All her trunks and valises were off the coach and waiting. "I'm ready to go to Minnie's," she declared hotly. "Wherever that may be."

"Got a temper, too, do you?" the sheriff asked, taking in her tight face.

She glared.

His thick mustache framed his smile. "You may be just the tonic Colt needs."

"The doctor needs a colonic. Not a wife."

Denby hooted.

The sheriff laughed, too, and after Mr. Denby left them, turned his attention to her trunks. "All these yours?"

"Yes."

"You going on safari?"

She gave him another glare, even though she did have a small mountain of belongings.

"Just pulling your leg. Give me a few minutes to get a wagon from the livery and we'll be on our way."

"Thank you."

While waiting for his return, she noticed a man on a bay stallion riding towards the outskirts of town. It was Lee and she wanted to yell after him, "Coward!" Instead she settled for fuming. This was not how she'd envisioned her journey as a mail-order bride would begin.

Chapter Two

While the sheriff drove, Regan sat on the wagon seat beside him and took in the small town of Paradise. They rolled down the rutted dirt road that served as the main street, past Miller's General Store, and a small log cabin with a sign over its door that read TELEGRAPH.

"Can we stop long enough for me to send a telegram to my family?" she asked. "I want them to know I arrived safely."

"Sure can."

People on the walks paused to watch her go inside and she wondered what they thought of her.

The interior was small. Three older men, all sporting whiskers and beards, were seated around a table. In the center was a checkerboard. They all looked up at her entrance.

One of them was the buckskin-wearing man of earlier. He grinned. "You didn't come in here to shoot us, did you?"

Regan dropped her head. Would she ever live this down? "No, sir. Just to send a telegram to my family in Arizona Territory."

"Then I guess we're safe," one of the other men said while studying the board. He moved a black disc, then smiled proudly. "Odell, your move."

Odell was the buckskin man. Bright blue eyes studied the board. He moved his red disc and hopped it over three of his opponent's pieces to the king row. "Beat that, you old possum!"

Regan wondered which of the men was the telegraph operator. "Gentlemen—"

Odell said, "Sorry, ma'am." He walked over to the desk and handed her a piece of paper and a pencil. "Write what you want sent, where it's going, and to who."

So she did and handed it back.

"This has to go through the operator in Cheyenne," he explained. "Their line's been down a few days. I'll pass your message along as soon as things are fixed there."

Regan knew her family was probably worried because it had been over a week since her departure. "How long might that be?"

He shrugged. "Could be a couple days. Could be more, but I'll send it on soon as I can."

One of his buddies said, "Make sure of that, Odell. Don't want her coming back and shooting up the place," and he chuckled.

Regan rolled her eyes. "Thank you, gentlemen." She looked over at the window. A handful of people were staring in at her through the glass. She wondered if this was how it felt to be a circus attraction.

"Your move, Odell."

Regan left the men to their game. Outside, she nodded at the curious onlookers, climbed back on the wagon, and the sheriff drove them away.

Next to the telegraph office stood a bank, a barbershop, and a seamstress shop. On the other side of the street was a dentist's office and Beck's undertaking establishment. She thought about poor Mr. Casey. "Did Mr. Casey have family?"

"No."

"Will someone pay for his burial?" She would willingly offer some of her own gold to ensure he rested in peace.

"I'm pretty sure the stage company will."

"If they don't, would you let me know? I'd like to help."

"Will do. That's very kind of you."

Her thoughts turned to the dead outlaw. Would he be mourned? "Do you know the dead man's name?"

"Jeb Bailey."

"Does he have family here?"

"Yes, a brother named Dun."

"Will you relay my condolences and explain the circumstances?"

"I will."

"And the other two outlaws?"

"Jess Rawl and Abel Corman. Corman's the one you plugged in the arm. They're loners as far as

I know. Both are also wanted by the law in other parts of the county."

The businesses gave way to a small cluster of homes. A few were large, showing off turrets and gingerbread trim like the ones she'd seen in Ohio when she'd attended school at Oberlin, but most were cabins built from timber and stone. "How long has the town existed?"

"Since about 1820. It started as a trading post run by Odell and Doc's grandfather Ben. Odell said they took one look at the valley and called it Paradise. Back then there were only a few cabins, fur trappers, and Indians. Now, about fifty people live in town and a couple hundred more are on ranches and homesteads nearby." He stopped the wagon in front of a small one-story home with a porch on the front. "This is it," he said.

An old woman wearing a long-sleeved brown dress answered the sheriff's knock. Her thinning gray hair pulled back in a severe bun set off a bright-skinned bony face. The garment's frayed cuffs and hem spoke to its age.

"Afternoon, Miss Minnie. This is Miss Carmichael. Doc said she's to stay with you."

She looked Regan up and down with unveiled disapproval. "You're Colt's intended?"

"Yes, ma'am."

"Heard you shot him."

"Accidentally, yes." Regan felt like she should be wearing a sign with those two words written on it.

The brown face soured before she turned to the sheriff. "How long she staying?"

"Until she and Colt settle on a date."

"If we set a date," Regan tossed back, still simmering from their earlier brief encounter.

"You don't think you're good enough?" Minnie sneered.

"I think he may not be good enough."

"Beggars can't be choosy."

Regan ignored that. "How much are your rooms?"

"Thirty-five cents a night."

In response to the ridiculously high price Regan showed no emotion, but thought the place better be fit for a queen. "May I see it, please?"

Minnie grudgingly stepped back so they could enter. The interior was shadowy, and the furniture in the parlor they passed through appeared to be as old as its owner. Regan didn't see any evidence of other boarders.

The room for rent was built onto the back of the house. A quick view showed a thin cot placed upon a wooden platform atop stacked wood. It appeared terribly uncomfortable. Beside it, a listing nightstand held a badly chipped porcelain basin. The ceiling above showed stained wooden beams still damp from a recent rain. Sleeping in the street might be better. "Is this the only room available?"

She responded with a nasty smirk. "Yes."

Regan asked the sheriff, "Is there another place in town?"

Before he could reply, Minnie snapped, "Not for a colored woman."

"Is she correct?"

He gave Minnie a sharp look before replying,

"There may be. Let's go, miss. Sorry to bother you, Minnie."

Outside, Regan climbed back onto the wagon seat. "Should I take her unpleasantness personally, or is she that way all the time?"

"Yes, and yes."

Regan was confused.

"She's unpleasant all the time, and she's the great-aunt of Doc's late wife, Adele."

A chill claimed her. "I see."

He got the horse under way. Regan looked back and saw Minnie standing on the porch watching their departure with hostile eyes.

They were soon outside of town and traveling along a narrow road that cut through a forest of towering pines. The snowcapped peaks in the distance ruled the horizon. Unlike Arizona's red-hued mountains, these were gray and they loomed like ancient gods.

"How well do you know Dr. Lee?" she asked Lambert.

"I'd say pretty well. We grew up together."

"Do you think my injuring him will make him want to call off the wedding?"

She sensed him carefully choosing his words. "You'll have to take that up with him. All I can say is he's fair, honorable, and been a good friend to me."

It wasn't the response she'd hoped for but supposed it would have to do.

As they headed west, Regan thought about the

woman who had been Colton Lee's wife. Had she been well-loved by the people here? Would those who knew her resent Regan's presence, and view her as contemptuously as Minnie? The largest question remaining was whether she and Dr. Lee would be able to move past their disastrous introduction and go forward. From his letters, he'd seemed like a good man. He'd been very up front about his lack of wealth. Many of his patients were unable to pay for his services but he treated them just the same. She'd been moved by his kindness and concerns for his motherless daughter.

The travel-weary Regan spotted a ranch in the distance and hoped it was their destination. The sizable low-slung structure was made of timber and sat atop a small tree-filled rise. To its left were corrals and two outbuildings. "Is that the place up ahead?"

"Yes. The woman who owns it is named Spring."

"Odd name."

"Named after her Shoshone grandmother whose name meant Spring Rain."

"How lovely. And she takes in boarders?"

"Not usually, but she will you."

"Why?"

"She's Colt's baby sister."

Regan blinked. He glanced over, gave her a smile, and refocused his attention on driving the wagon up the path.

As they reached the house, a dark-skinned woman walked out of one of the barns leading a beautiful

Appaloosa colt. Its reddish dappled coat reminded Regan of her sister's mare, Arizona. That Spring wore denims and a man's red-check flannel shirt buoyed Regan's weary spirit because the attire reminded her so much of the clothing she'd worn back home. Spring was lean like her brother. Her thick black hair was braided into a fat plait that reached the middle of her back.

Upon seeing them, she stopped. "Hey, there, Whit. Who's that with you?" Her low-toned voice was a mixture of whiskey and smoke.

He set the brake and got down. "This is Miss Regan Carmichael."

She nodded a greeting Regan's way, then stilled. "You're my brother's mail-order bride."

Regan sighed. "Yes. And if you haven't already heard, I accidentally shot him earlier today. With this." She held up her silver-clad Winchester.

Spring's jaw dropped. "You didn't kill him, did you? Never mind," she said, waving the question away. "If you had, you'd be in jail. How serious is the wound?"

Sheriff Lambert answered, "She plugged him in the shoulder. The bullet's out. He's fine. His pride's hurt more than anything. She needs a place to stay so I brought her to you."

Still searching Regan's face, Spring laughed. "Honey, if you shot my brother, you are welcome to share my home for as long as you like. Get down off that wagon and let's go inside so I can hear the whole sordid tale." She turned to the colt, saying,

"Did you hear that, Paint Box? The pretty lady shot the esteemed Dr. Lee!"

Regan smiled and decided she might enjoy being with Spring Lee.

It took a few trips to get all Regan's trunks and hatboxes inside Spring's cabin. At one point, Spring asked with a laugh, "Are you planning to open a clothing shop? My goodness."

Regan took the good-natured dig in the spirit that it was given.

Once they were done, the sheriff touched his hat and departed, and Regan dropped wearily into a sturdy but comfortable chair made of timber.

"You look pretty tired."

"I am. I feel as if I've been traveling for years."

"Are you hungry?"

"Extremely."

"Will a sandwich do? It's all I can offer for now. Wasn't expecting company."

"Yes."

The beef and soft bread was so good, it took all Regan had to remember her manners and not devour it like a starving ranch hand. She washed it down with a tumbler of cold spring water and was content. "Thank you," she said as Spring took the empty plate from her hand. Now, all Regan wanted was a long stretch of uninterrupted sleep.

"How about I show you where you can lay your head."

"That would be wonderful, and thank you for taking me in."

"You're welcome. I'll hear about you and my brother once you're rested up. I've always loved a good tale."

"You aren't angry at me for shooting him?"

"As long as he's alive and I can continue to bedevil him, not at all. In fact, I'm looking forward to what might happen next. Being out here with nothing to do, folks like a little commotion. It breaks up the monotony."

Regan smiled. "Okay. Let me sleep awhile and I'll share all the gory details."

"Holding you to that. Come on with me, and we'll get you bedded down."

"You live alone?"

She nodded. "Never married. Men tend to avoid a woman known for having her own mind."

A wide grin crossed Regan's face. "The two of us will do well together."

"I think you might be right. Between your Winchester and my Remington, we'll scare most men around here to death."

Regan was still chuckling over that as she settled her cheek against the crisp fresh pillow casing and closed her eyes.

*C*olt unsaddled his horse and turned the stallion out into the pasture. Carrying the heavy gear to the tack room ramped up the pain in his shoulder but he managed it and entered the house. He was thankful for Whit's aid but knew the wound needed to be cleaned properly and wrapped with a fresh bandage. He dropped down onto the sofa in the parlor and drew in a few deep breaths.

"You hurt?"

He looked up to see his grandfather Benjamin standing in the doorway. "Got shot."

Ben's eyes widened and he hurried over to him. "Where? Let me see."

"Shoulder. I'm fine. Whit got the bullet out. I need to clean it again though."

"Here. Let me help."

Colt hated being fussed over but had enough sense to know he needed the assistance. Trying to put his shirt back on without help while under the watching eyes of the hellion responsible had caused more pain than he'd shown.

Ben eased the shirt off his shoulder. Colt glanced down and was not surprised upon seeing the blood-soaked bandage. It would probably bleed for a short while longer.

"Who did this to you?" Ben asked, sounding concerned and angry.

Colt chuckled bitterly. "The woman I'm supposed to be marrying."

Ben froze and stared. "Miss Carmichael? She's here?"

"Yes, along with her fancy, silver-plated Winchester rifle."

Confusion filled Ben's face. "What the hell she shoot you for? Let me get a basin of water so we can clean this up, and you tell me what happened."

"Hot water," Colton called at his back. The shoulder would be stiff and sore enough without adding the risk of infection. Thanks to his late mother, Isabelle, and her insistence upon pampering herself with as many modern amenities as could be shipped to the wilds of Wyoming Territory, there was a boiler connected to the house. Adele had enjoyed the luxury as well. Her sweet face looked down at him from the large portrait hanging on the wall above the fireplace. He'd loved her so. She'd been gone now six years, and his guilt remained as fresh as it had been the day she slipped into death after Anna's birth. Had he been at her side instead of off tending a miner's broken arm, they might not have lost her. He looked away from the portrait, buried the somber memory, and awaited his grandfather's return.

Once the wound was cleaned and a fresh bandage applied, Colt told his grandfather the story and how the encounter with the Carmichael woman in the sheriff's office ended with her berating him.

Ben shook his head. "Doesn't sound like she's the one for you. She may be more trouble than she's worth."

Colt was sure of only one thing. "Her shooting me is going to keep folks around here chuckling for decades."

"True," Ben said, his face set with disapproval. "Where's she now?"

"I had Whit take her to Minnie's. She can stay there until I figure out what I want to do."

"Minnie doesn't want you remarrying."

"I know, but Anna needs a mother. Her only influences as she grows older will be Minnie and Spring. Neither are ideal."

"Spring just needs a husband and some babies."

"Spring's never going to find a husband because she doesn't want one and Anna may not either if I let Spring have more of a say in her raising."

"I agree. Let me go empty this basin."

Ben's exit left Colt alone with his thoughts. He loved his sister, but he worried about her defiant and rebellious nature rubbing off on his daughter. He had no quarrel with women moving into the once all-male bastions like medicine, teaching, and business, nor did he begrudge them a college education. However, like most men in the country, he continued to believe the goal of a well-raised young woman centered on a husband and raising a family. Adele had been a perfect example. Soft-spoken, well-mannered, deferential even upon the few occasions they'd disagreed. But his sister? Spring couldn't spell the word *deferential*, and based on what he'd seen and heard from Miss Regan Carmichael today, she probably couldn't either. His ears still burned from her blunt assessment of who she perceived him to be. And it made him wonder if she'd answered his advertisement because none of the men she knew back home would take her as a wife. She'd sounded so sensible and right in the letters they'd exchanged. She'd impressed him as being educated and refined, but he never imagined that education included being a crack shot. And this neighbor she'd referenced? Who was he? He'd obviously influenced her raising. Was he family? Colt had so many questions. Due to the positive nature of their correspondence, he assumed an arranged marriage between them would be an easy undertaking. Now, things seemed as complicated as a knotted skein of yarn, and he wasn't sure he wanted to do the unraveling for fear of what he might find.

"I think you should send her packing," Ben said, reentering the parlor. "Her shooting might have been accidental but what other accidents will she bring? You have enough challenges being the only doctor around here without giving your name to an unsuitable woman. Find someone else."

Colt slowly ran his hands down his bearded jaw and replied, "That might be easier said than done. I've been placing advertisements in the Colored newspapers for almost a year, and counting the response from Miss Winchester there were only three." One came from a Pennsylvania widow five years older than him with four children, and the other from the Kansas parents of a girl of seventeen, who'd been honest enough to admit their daughter was carrying another man's child. "I'll speak with her tomorrow, then decide whether she stays and gets to meet Anna. I need to reconcile the woman in her letters with the one who shot me today." If he could.

Colt saw the disapproval. His grandfather had

little tolerance for opinions different from his own. Despite his advanced age, the old fur trapper remained as formidable and unrelenting as a Wyoming winter. Few crossed him. Colt did when necessary.

"Right or wrong, I'm prepared not to like her," Ben stated.

"Noted." Being a curmudgeon was another of his grandfather's traits.

A glance at the clock on the mantel of the stone fireplace showed it was time to get Anna from school. If he wasn't tied up with a patient he usually drove over to get her. His wounded shoulder would make handling the reins difficult. "Can you drive to the school? I'll ride along."

Ben nodded and they set out.

On the way, they came upon the sheriff. "Hey, Whit," Colt said, "Miss Carmichael get settled in with Minnie?"

"No. Instead of offering her one of the upstairs rooms, Minnie tried to make her stay in that rundown addition built on the back."

Colt's lips tightened. He'd hoped her stay with Minnie would give them a chance to get acquainted and help deflate Minnie's opinion that his remarrying disrespected Adele's memory. He should have known better. Minnie Gore was as judgmental as she was sanctimonious. "So, where'd you take her?"

"To Spring."

It was not what Colt wanted to hear.

Chapter Three

$\mathcal{W}$hen Regan opened her eyes in the shadow-filled room, it took a few moments to remember where she was. Getting out of bed, she padded barefoot to the large window and looked out. The sun was just coming up over the trees and mountains, and the sky held the pinkish gray streaks of dawn. She realized she'd slept the balance of yesterday away. It wasn't what she'd planned, but she felt less tired so she supposed she'd needed the extended rest. What would the day hold, she wondered. Would she and Dr. Lee be able to put yesterday behind them and move forward? Was he somewhere thinking of her and wondering the same thing? Regan had no answers. The smell of bacon scented the air and in spite of her musings, her stomach growled with eager anticipation, so she set thoughts of the grim Dr. Lee aside for the moment. After making use of the facilities and the washroom, she opened one of her trunks, dug out a pair of denims and a shirt, and left the room to seek out her hostess.

Spring was standing at the stove tending strips of bacon frying in a cast-iron skillet. "Morning, Regan. How'd you sleep?"

"Like a bear in winter."

"Feeling better?"

"Yes."

"Hungry, I'm betting."

"Starving."

"Bacon's almost ready. There're biscuits, and my hens graciously allowed me some eggs."

After filling their plates with the offerings, they stepped outside and ate at a small table set behind the house. The peaceful setting temporarily overrode her worries about her future. "Do you eat out here often?"

"As much as I can. Winter comes early, and once it arrives we're forced inside for years it seems sometimes. Eating outdoors is one of my small pleasures."

Regan liked the idea of that. She liked Spring as well. "I grew up on a ranch that was also a hotel, so if there are chores I can help with, please let me know. I'd like to earn my keep."

"After your fancy dress yesterday, seeing you in denims this morning surprised me."

"You can't muck out stalls in a ball gown."

Spring nodded over her raised coffee cup. "You're not what my brother is expecting, believe me."

"His late wife didn't dress this way, I take it?"

"No. Adele was sweet as pie, but she knew little about life out of doors. She could cook and clean and do all the things a proper wife is supposed to do, but she didn't know a hammer from a pitchfork."

"How'd they meet?"

"At Howard Medical School. Her grandfather was one of the men Colt studied under."

She knew of Howard and its illustrious history. "Was it a love match?"

"Yes. He was inconsolable after her death. I think in some ways, he's still grieving her passing."

Regan was pleased to learn he'd loved her but wondered if he had it within himself to love again. "What's their daughter like?"

Spring paused as if debating her response. She met Regan's eyes. "Truthfully? Anna is unhappy and rarely smiles. My heart aches when I see her."

"Why is she so unhappy?"

"After Adele's death, my brother didn't know what to do with an infant, so he turned most of her raising over to Spare the Rod Spoil the Child Minnie Gore, Adele's aunt. My niece has spent most of her life walking on eggshells so as not to evoke Minnie's wrath."

"I met Minnie yesterday. It wasn't pleasant. The wrath isn't physical, is it?"

"No. Colton wouldn't stand for that, but Minnie fusses at Anna incessantly about staying clean, sitting and speaking properly, using the correct utensils, her diction. There's nothing wrong with having those expectations, but Anna doesn't get to be a child. She's not allowed to go out and play because she'll get dirty. Minnie has discouraged her from having friends because she thinks they'd be a bad influence."

"What does her father say about this sadness?"

"He sees it, but isn't sure how to undo what Minnie has done. He's the only doctor in this part of the Territory, which means he's sometimes gone for days at a time, so Anna's cared for by either Minnie or my grandfather Ben who believes children should be seen and not heard."

"Do you get a say in her raising?"

"No. Colt and Ben think I may teach her to grow up and speak her mind one day. Can't have that, now can we?"

Spring's bitter tone made Regan curious about its cause and her standing with the two male family members. Anna's plight was disturbing. Growing up, Regan and her older sister, Portia, had chores and were expected to be accomplished in all the areas Spring had pointed out, but they were also encouraged to have adventurous, carefree childhoods. They each had their own mounts, swam, explored the nearby canyons, fished, learned to use tools, and were never chastised by the adults for getting dirty. "Sounds like little Anna could use a champion."

"I agree, but it won't be Aunt Spring."

Regan had no idea what kind of mother she might be, but having been abandoned by her own mother, Corinne, and later raised by her loving Aunt Eddy and Uncle Rhine she knew bad from good and considered that to be in her favor. In her mind, every child should be allowed to be a child and not have to walk on eggshells. She realized her own naïveté in thinking she'd simply waltz into this arranged marriage, find the love and adventure she desired, and all would be well. A complicated road lay ahead.

After breakfast, Spring took her on a tour of the place. In addition to the Appaloosa colt Regan had seen yesterday, there was also a beautiful black stallion named Cheyenne and two mares: Sunrise and Lady. Spring greeted the stallion with an affectionate hug and the horse whinnied in response. "I found him up in the mountains when he was a colt. I'm not sure if his mother died or if he got separated from his clan, or what, but he was near death. Brought him home, nursed him back to health, and he's been with me now about six years."

"He's very handsome. Where'd you get the mares?"

"They're his."

Regan's confusion must have shown, so Spring responded, "I woke up one morning a few years back and he was gone. I looked for him for days and when I couldn't find him, gave up. I figured he'd found a clan and I'd never see him again. Broke my heart. But at the end of the summer he returned and had the two mares with him."

"Needed some company?"

Spring laughed. "Apparently. Took me a while to

get the mares used to the saddle, but the three are strong stock. I've been selling the foals and making a good profit."

"I'll need a mount. I didn't want to subject mine to the long train ride." She missed her mare, Catalina, terribly and wondered how she was faring, and if she missed Regan as deeply.

"I don't have any for sale at the moment, but there are a few ranchers who do. Once you get settled in, we can go see them."

"If I get settled in. Your brother might not want to go through with the agreement."

"And you?"

"I'm still willing." In spite of her earlier protestations and misgivings, she hadn't come all this way to turn tail and run simply because he'd seemed prickly and, yes, rude at the outset. Surely there had to be more to him than that.

"If he isn't, you're still welcome to stay here while deciding if you want to go home."

"Thanks." The offer was a kind one. "Now, show me the rest of the place and then put me to work."

Spring showed her the henhouse, the hogs she kept for butchering and sale, the barns, and her large vegetable garden.

"We have a short growing season, but I try and grow as much as I can. I'm pretty self-sufficient."

"How long have you lived here?"

"Be twelve years in July. I'd just turned nineteen when my grandfather demanded I leave his household. I was more than happy to oblige."

Regan regarded Spring's frank eyes and wanted to know more, but didn't know the woman well enough to ask.

As if having read Regan's mind, Spring said, "I'll share that tale another time. Now your turn. Tell me why you shot my brother."

"Livy got a pony yesterday."

Colt glanced up from his breakfast and met his daughter's brown eyes. "Did she?" Livy was a classmate and the closest person Anna had to a friend.

Her gaze dropped. "Yes."

Colt wasn't sure what to ask next. He felt so inept around his child most of the time. He wondered if this was her way of saying she wanted a pony. He and Spring had had their first mounts around Anna's age. "Do you think you might like one, too?"

She shook her head. "Aunt Minnie said I'd just fall off and break my neck."

"Oh." His late wife, Adele, having been raised in the city didn't ride, but he wanted his daughter to learn. He tried a different tact. "I think I could teach you so you wouldn't fall off."

She shook her head again. "Aunt Minnie wouldn't like it."

"I see." He needed to get her out from under Minnie's suffocating thumb. Because of her, his Anna lacked the joy and curiosity he and his sister had as children. They'd had a strict upbringing, too, but learned to hunt and fish and ride. Anna did none of those things. "If you change your mind, let me know."

"I won't," she replied with soft finality. "I've finished eating. May I be excused?"

"Yes. Get your things for school and Ben will drive us in the wagon."

"Is your shoulder still hurt?"

"It is, but it should be better in a few days." He'd explained the injury as an accident, which on the surface was the truth. He didn't tell her he'd been shot.

"Do you have to be a doctor today?" she asked.

"I'm going to my office, but I should be here to have supper with you." The question was her way of asking if he'd be leaving town. His duties were such that sometimes he didn't return home until after she was asleep.

"Okay. I'll get my books." She scooted off her chair and left the table.

He watched her go and wondered if a new wife could transform the now wooden Anna into the vibrant laughing child she deserved to be.

After dropping Anna off at the schoolhouse, Colt gingerly mounted his stallion that he'd trailered to the back of the wagon. Ben would be going home, but Colt planned to ride over to see his sister and her guest.

Ben was still convinced that the Carmichael woman should be sent home. "You sure this is a good idea?"

"If she and I don't suit, we'll part ways and I'll place more advertisements in the newspapers." Even though he wasn't optimistic about receiving favorable responses. "When I leave Spring's, I'll head to my office in town."

Ben gave him a nod and set out. Colt turned his stallion and rode west.

He found his sister shoveling feed into the troughs for her hogs. She paused as he dismounted. "Morning. How's the shoulder?"

He fought to keep the discomfort from showing on his face. He guessed she'd learned about the shooting from either Whit or Regan, or both. "I'll live." He was glad Miss Winchester hadn't aimed lower or he might be as dead as Jeb Bailey and laid out at Lyman Beck's undertaker's place.

Spring asked, "You come to see me or your intended?"

"Is she awake?"

"She's mucking out one of my stalls."

That caught him off guard. "Really?"

"You do know she grew up on a ranch, right?"

"She mentioned that in her letters, but I assumed—"

"That she had hired hands to do the work?"

"Yes."

"She must've worked beside them because she went at it without any instructions from me."

Something else Colt had to reconcile about the surprising Regan Carmichael.

Spring added, "I know my opinion doesn't mean

much, brother, but I think she'd be good for Anna. And you could do a lot worse for a wife."

"We'll see."

"You need someone in your life to challenge your thinking besides your disreputable sister."

"You're more than enough."

She smiled and shoveled more feed into the trough. "How's the old man?"

"Crotchety. Told me he's prepared not to like Miss Carmichael."

"That surprise you?"

"No." His grandfather seemed to have problems with headstrong women. He hadn't gotten along with his mother, Isabelle, either. Watching Spring work, memories rose of the good times they'd shared growing up. He knew she and Ben would probably never bury the hatchet, but he found himself wishing he could find a way to make peace with her so they could be back in each other's lives again. She was his sister. Over the years, she'd cleaned up the scandal-filled mess that had once been her life, and proven her ability to take care of herself. But as her brother, the need to watch over her remained strong.

Leaving Spring to her chores, Colt entered the shadow-filled barn and walked to the stalls. He supposed he shouldn't have been surprised to find Regan wearing a snug pair of denims and a man's shirt as she worked. She hefted the big hay-filled pitchfork and shook it to sift the hay from the clods of manure before tossing the offal into the wheelbarrow beside her.

"Good morning."

She jumped and swung his way, pitchfork tines pointed out like a weapon. "Goodness," she said, lowering the fork. "Don't creep up on a person that way. You scared me half to death."

He hid his amusement. "My apologies."

She nodded an acceptance then went back to work. "You come to send me home?"

Watching how efficiently she went about the task, he saw that his sister was right. Regan Carmichael knew what she was about. He raised his gaze from the denim-covered curves of her behind. "I'm not sure."

She stopped, set the fork's tines against the stable floor, and used her free hand to pull a bandana from her pocket to wipe her brow. Her eyes grazed his shoulder. "How's your wound?"

"Healing."

"So how and when will you be sure?"

"I thought we could talk about that."

"Do you mind if I work while we do? I'd like to finish up here. Should only take a few more minutes."

Colt had expected to have her undivided attention, not compete with sifting manure. He debated leaving and riding to town, but decided against that. This needed to be settled as soon as possible for both their sakes. "Meet me outside when you're done."

"Thanks."

He noted that she didn't even spare him a glance when he departed.

Spring was sitting at her outside dining table. "That was quick."

He sat. "She wants to finish the stall."

Spring's eyes sparkled with amusement. "Made you play second fiddle to horse manure?"

He didn't respond.

"I know you're accustomed to a woman who'll bend and bow, but Regan's not that type. If you're seeking someone more like Adele, you should send Regan home and keep searching."

Colt stared off into the distance. At this point he wasn't certain what he wanted. He already knew how limited his future choices might be. Even though the territorial government was doing everything it could to entice good women to consider making their homes in Wyoming, the response had been low. The cities were small and unpolished; the winters long and harsh. There were few theaters, lending libraries, or fancy dress shops that seemed to ease women's lives, but he had a woman who seemed willing. Did he want to throw her back like a too-small fish because she appeared to lack Adele's sweet deferential nature?

Spring added, "That she isn't already on a train back to her family says to me that she's willing to meet you halfway. Are you prepared to do the same?"

He considered Spring's question. "She and I need to talk first."

A few minutes later, he saw her exiting the barn. He noted the confidence in her stride and the sway in her hips as she approached the pump. Adele had sometimes needed help priming the one at his place, but not Regan Carmichael. Expertly working the handle, she displayed confidence in that task as well. The water spilled out, she cleaned her hands, wiped them dry on the front of her denims, and made her way to where he waited.

Spring got to her feet. "I'll be inside."

He nodded and focused on Regan's approach. By all accounts she was a beautiful woman. Short in stature, she had clear ebony skin and a pair of sparkling black eyes that had snapped at him angrily yesterday in Whit's office. In contrast, they'd been cool and almost distant during this morning's short encounter in the barn. He found himself taking in her figure again. The snug denims emphasized her curves and his mind strayed to their potential wedding night. Like most well-raised women, she'd probably hope her husband did his business quickly, and would only bother her with his needs when necessary.

"Sorry to keep you waiting," she said upon reaching the table.

He stood and gestured her to take a seat. "Your work ethic is admirable."

"Thank you."

She sat and he followed. Colt wasn't sure where or how to begin the conversation, so he simply plunged ahead. "Your letters made me believe we'd be compatible."

"And now?" she asked frankly.

He wondered how long it would take him to get accustomed to her blunt way of speaking. "Now, I'm trying to reconcile the woman I thought you to be from your letters with the woman seated here."

"They're one and the same. I answered your letters truthfully. You never asked if I knew how to shoot."

She had him there, he admitted.

She continued, "I was raised in Arizona Territory, a sometimes dangerous place. My sister and I were taught to carry a firearm for protection."

"By this neighbor?"

"Yes. His name was Mr. Blanchard and by my Uncle Rhine, who insisted we learn. Mr. Blanchard was a dear and honorable man. He died recently. I didn't appreciate you casting aspersions on what I may or may not have learned from him."

Her displeasure was plain.

"My apologies for being disrespectful. Being shot tends to make a man short-tempered."

She held his gaze unflinchingly as if to remind him she'd already offered her apology, more than once. Colt found himself drawn to the determination she radiated. "What else did I fail to ask?"

"What type of work I did."

He paused and studied her. "And that was?"

"I drove the mail wagon from Tucson up country to the mining camps."

He stilled and wondered if he'd misheard her. "So, you lied about having attended Oberlin?"

"Of course not."

"But—" He didn't know what to ask or think. "And your uncle allowed this?"

"Yes. It took me a while to convince him but he eventually agreed."

"But why would a well-raised woman want to do such a thing?"

"It's my adventurous nature I suppose. My sister, Portia, and I are both considered unconventional by the men back home. She enjoys working with numbers and handles my uncle's ledgers for the hotel. I enjoy seeing what's over the next hill, which is one of the reasons I responded to your advertisement. But as I said in my letters, I can also cook, set a proper table, and have impeccable manners. I speak English and Spanish. I hunt, fish, swim, and ride. I'd hoped to find a husband who'd view these qualities as assets, but if you're seeking what society considers to be a proper wife who'll defer to you in all things, and spend her days in a rocker with an embroidery hoop in her hand, you should say so and I'll return to Arizona."

Colt blinked. He didn't know any woman with the pluck to toss down a gauntlet so effortlessly. Adele had been a devoted tabby, but the sheer force of Regan's fiery spirit made her more akin to a she-puma, both wily and untamable. Life with her would be neither easy nor boring, and as his sister stated, he could do a lot worse. "Would you come to dinner this evening and meet my daughter? I know she's only a child but this will impact her as well."

"I'd enjoy that."

"If meeting Anna goes well and you're still willing to accept my proposal, we'll set a date for the wedding."

She responded with a soft smile and it seemed to fill the cloudy day with sunshine. Getting to her feet, she stuck out her hand. That threw him a bit, but he stood, took it, and was surprised to feel the calluses there. They shook, and she said, "We have a deal."

"Ask Spring to bring you over."

"I will."

A part of him was certain he'd lost his mind, but the agreement was made.

After Colton's departure, Spring stepped outside to join Regan and asked, "All's well?"

"As well as can be expected under the circumstances." And she relayed what transpired and asked if Spring would drive her over for the dinner.

"Of course."

"Thank you."

"Oh for heaven's sake. What does she want?" Spring snarled.

Regan turned to see an approaching buggy driven by a woman wearing a fancy green hat and a matching ensemble. "Who is she?"

"Colleen Enright. Widow and local busybody. Probably stopping by to see what gossip she can pick up on you. In her mind, she's more educated, well-mannered, and better dressed than any other woman of color in the Territory, and not afraid to voice it. Maybe once she gets a look at what's inside all your trunks she'll be so devastated she'll move to the Klondike."

Regan smiled.

The widow parked the buggy and stepped down. After adjusting her skirt, she paused, as if allowing the morning to view her and her attire approvingly before walking over to join them. "Morning, Spring. Is this Colt's intended?"

"It is."

The visitor extended a green-gloved hand to Regan. "I'm Colleen Enright."

Regan took the hand. "I'm Regan Carmichael."

Colleen looked Regan up and down. "Denims," she voiced with disapproval at Regan's attire. "You've already turned her into a hoyden, Spring. Shame on you."

"Hoydens of a feather, flock together."

The widow countered, "Colton is a well-respected doctor. His wife should be above reproach in both manner and dress."

Regan didn't want to judge the woman, but couldn't remember ever not liking a person within seconds of being introduced—other than Minnie Gore.

"So, Regan. What an odd name. Where are you from?"

"Arizona Territory."

"I see."

"And you?"

"Originally Delaware," she replied in the snootiest of tones. "My great-great grandfather was a Tory and fought on the side of the Crown against the rebels."

"He was on the losing side then?"

The green eyes sparked with displeasure. "He went on to found his own mercantile."

"How nice," Regan said.

The widow opened her mouth to ask another question but Spring cut her off. "So, what brings you all the way out here, Colleen?"

"I dropped Felicity at the school and since I was in the area, I thought I'd come by and extend a welcome to Colt's intended. I adored Adele. She was such a lady. He was so devastated by her untimely passing no one thought he'd ever marry again. Did you really answer an advertisement he put in the papers?"

Regan sensed the woman's hunger for more details but didn't take the bait. "Is Felicity your daughter?"

"Yes, she just turned seven and she's such a little beauty. Takes after her mother, if I may be so bold. The beaus will be flocking around her like deer to corn once she comes of age. Have you met Anna yet?"

"No."

"Poor little thing. She'll always be in my Felicity's shadow."

Regan had had enough. Yes, the widow was a beauty with her light brown skin, straw-colored hair, and striking eyes, but the person beneath was a steaming pile of fresh horse manure. "Nice meeting you, Mrs. Enright. I have a few more chores to finish."

"But—"

Regan headed for the barn and didn't look back. Once there, she picked up the fork and went back to work. Her meeting with Dr. Lee claimed her thoughts. At least he was now speaking to her. Would all the accomplishments she'd ticked off about herself outweigh his concerns over her being so unconventional? She had no way of knowing. From his letters, she knew he cared deeply for his daughter. That his final decision rested on Anna's opinion, spoke to that as well. A man who wanted to do what was best for his child was one to be admired.

A short while later, Spring walked in. "Colleen's gone."

"Good."

"She rubs me the wrong way, too. Always has."

"How long has she been a widow?"

"Her husband, Erasmus, died four years ago in a Rock Springs coal mining accident."

"His death had to be terrible for her and her daughter. How long had they lived here?"

"Ten years. He came out here to be a schoolteacher, but the town didn't have the money to pay him enough to live on, so he went to the mines."

"She doesn't impress me as a woman who'd enjoy the lack of status tied to that type of work."

"She didn't, and they struggled because she spent most of what he earned on gowns and hats."

"He must have really loved her."

"He did, but it wasn't reciprocal. She was very dismissive of him. Complained openly that she didn't have a fine house and constantly threatened to take Felicity and move back East."

"If she was so unhappy why'd she stay?"

"Because she's in love with my brother."

Chapter Four

Colton spent the rest of the morning in his office seeing to patients like the buckskin-wearing Odell Waters whose gout had flared up again; Manx Solomon who'd learned last week the dangers inherent in drinking while using an axe—he'd lopped off the first digit of his right thumb—and Russ Neville who'd taken to drink in a misguided attempt to kill the pain in the infected molar he refused to let Colt pull.

"Can't you give me something?" Russ whined, holding his hand against his swollen whiskered jaw.

"Yes, a pair of pliers so you can pull it out yourself since you won't let me or Carl Goldson do it." Russ was an old mountain man friend of Ben, and equally as stubborn. Goldson was the town dentist.

"I ain't letting either one of you pull it. It's the last one I got back there."

"The infection is only going to get worse and it can kill you if it gets in your blood."

"You're just trying to scare me."

"Yes, I am. Let one of us pull the tooth, Russ."

He stood up and wobbled a bit from all the drink. "No." And he staggered out.

Colt watched him through the office window that faced the street and saw him head towards the saloon behind Miller's store. He sighed and hoped he didn't find the old man dead soon.

His next visitor was his boyhood friend, the sheriff. "Morning, Whit."

"Morning. How's your shoulder?"

"Stiff but healing."

Whit took a seat in one of the two empty chairs by Colt's desk. "You going to marry Miss Winchester?"

"She's meeting Anna tonight. If that goes well, then yes."

"Good for you."

"And you say that, why?"

"We all need a woman to shake up our lives."

"So, when are you going to find one to shake up yours?"

"I'm still looking over the herd. Haven't found the right filly yet."

"Colleen Enright is always available."

"Not for all the coal in Wyoming. Poor Erasmus. The way she treated that man, I wouldn't be surprised if she paid someone to push him down that chute. Besides, she's got her lariat out for you, or at least she did before Miss Winchester shot her way onto the scene."

"Even without Miss Winchester I had no intentions of giving Colleen my name or access to my bank account, small though it may be."

Colt saw Minnie Gore outside the window heading his way. He hoped his office would somehow become invisible so she'd pass it by, but she pushed the door open and stepped inside. At her entrance, Whit stood and touched his hat in greeting. "Miss Minnie. Colt, I'll stop back later."

After Whit's exit, Colt asked, "What can I do for you, Minnie."

"You cannot marry that Carmichael woman. She'll be a poor substitute for my Adele."

Colt sighed inwardly. "Your advice is noted. Anything else?"

"Are you going to send her away?"

"If she gets along with Anna tonight at dinner, no, I won't be sending her away."

"Then I need to be there, too. I'll not have her poisoning the well where Anna's concerned."

"You aren't invited."

"Why not?"

"Because this is between Anna and Miss Carmichael."

"Anna's my blood."

"Mine as well and she needs a mother."

"She has me."

"I'm thankful for all you've done for Anna, and I know Adele would be pleased as well."

The crone's eyes sparked with resentment. "I'm not enough? Is that what you're saying?"

"I'm saying, I'm thankful you were able to step in when Anna and I needed you most."

Her lips thinned. "I insist on being there this evening."

"No disrespect intended but this isn't a debate, Minnie."

"You're determined to blaspheme my Adele's memory."

"No, I'm determined to do what I think is right for her daughter and mine."

She eyed him angrily. "Carmichael won't be half the wife my Adele was to you."

"I need to get back to my work, Minnie. Thank you for stopping in."

They stared at each other like enemy combatants in war, until she snapped, "This is not the end, Colton Lee."

"Have a good day, Minnie."

She stormed out.

Colton drew in a deep breath and silently applauded himself for not lashing out at her the way his temper demanded. Minnie tried his patience even on the best of days and the idea of him marrying again had been a bee in her bonnet since he began advertising for a second wife. It was his hope that she'd eventually accept the fact that he'd moved on with his life but she seemed unwilling to do so.

He spent the rest of the day in relative peace; there were no medical emergencies, Minnie didn't return, but thoughts of Regan Carmichael kept surfacing like the child's game of peekaboo.

The Paradise cemetery was an open stretch of land on the outskirts of town, and as Colt left his horse, he passed by graves marked with crude stones, weathered crosses, and others bearing no tribute at all. At the Lees' family plot, he stopped before the gray slab atop where his mother, Isabelle, lay. He knelt to brush away the leaves and other detritus that had accumulated since his last visit and a familiar sadness took hold.

He'd hoped becoming a doctor would give him the skill and knowledge he needed to save her, but her cancer had been incurable. The last years of her life had been racked with a pain that left her bedridden and him filled with an abject helplessness. By all rights, his father, Lewis Lee, should be lying in a grave beside her, but he was among the one hundred and seventeen men of the First Kansas Colored killed at Poison Spring in 1864. His remains were never found.

Instead, beside her lay his wife, Adele. The cold granite marker bearing her name and her dates of birth and death was a sharp contrast to how warm and vibrant she'd been in life. It was her he'd come to the cemetery to see. He was on the verge of choosing someone to replace her and even though he still felt unsure about his choice, he wanted her to know that no matter the outcome, she would never be forgotten. In a way, he'd also come seeking reassurance. In spite of Minnie's belief that a new wife would dishonor Adele's memory, having Anna go through life motherless and without proper guidance would be more of a dishonor. She deserved the care and softness only a mother could provide, even one as unconventional as Regan Carmichael.

"I'm doing this for Anna because it's the right thing to do, and I know you agree."

He stood there for a moment longer; remembering, regretting, honoring, then after saying good-bye to them both, walked back to his stallion, August, and rode home.

Ben had picked Anna up from school and Colt found her sitting on the back porch. "Hello, Anna."

She smiled. "Hello, Papa."

"How was school today?"

"Okay. Mr. Adams gave us some sums to work on."

"Are they hard ones?"

"No."

"There's a lady coming to supper today and I want you to let me know whether you like her or not."

"Why?"

"If you like her, I may marry her so she can be your new mama."

Her brown eyes met his, and for a moment she didn't say anything, then asked, "Is she nice?"

"I think so." He wished he knew what she was thinking.

"What's her name?"

"Miss Regan Carmichael."

"Is she old like Aunt Minnie?"

"No."

"Do I have to say I like her even if I don't?"

"No. I want you to tell me the truth."

"Truly?"

"Truly, I don't want to get you a mama you don't like. Mamas are very important to little girls."

"Felicity says her mama yells at her a lot."

"I won't get one that yells at you. Promise."

"Okay. Will she live here with us?"

"Yes."

She went quiet again.

"Do you have any more questions?"

"No."

"Okay. I'll let you know when she arrives."

She nodded and turned her attention back to the view.

A terribly nervous Regan prepared herself for her dinner with Dr. Lee and his daughter. Would the child like her? Although Regan wanted her to, there was no guarantee. Removing her curling iron from the small brazier, she rolled it into her bangs. Once that was done, she gave her mirrored reflection a final look. Her hair was pulled back and coiled demurely at the base of her neck. In her tan, slim-fitting bodice and matching full skirt, she looked fashionable but not overdressed. Limiting her jewelry to a pair of small jet ear bobs, the color of which matched the small row of buttons on her bodice, she hoped to make a good impression.

"Are you ready?"

Regan turned to see Spring standing in the doorway. "Yes."

"Nervous?" Spring asked.

"Very."

"You'll do fine. Anna will love you. My grandfather probably won't, but don't let him scare you. When he growls, growl back."

Regan wasn't sure about that tact but tucked it away. Picking up her handbag and a wrap to ward off the evening chill on the ride back, she drew in a calming breath and followed Spring outside.

Her first impression was that Anna was tiny. She wore a gray smock topped by a blue apron-like overdress. Two long braids framed her small brown face. She was holding her father's hand, and the moment Regan met her dark eyes they immediately dropped shyly to the small brown boots on her feet.

"Anna, I'm Regan Carmichael, and I'm very pleased to meet you."

She glanced up. "Pleased to meet you, too," she whispered, holding Regan's gaze for only a moment.

Regan took in Dr. Lee. He was wearing a gray suit as if this were an important occasion and he looked very handsome. Regan wondered if Anna knew why she'd been invited.

"Shall we go inside?" he asked.

"Yes."

Spring said to Regan, "I'll come back for you at sunset."

Anna said, "You aren't going to eat with us, Aunt Spring?"

"No, lamb. Not this time."

"Oh." It was apparent the child was disappointed.

Dr. Lee said, "I'll see Miss Carmichael back, Spring."

Regan was surprised by that but showed no reaction.

"Okay. Have a good time."

Spring drove off in her wagon and Dr. Lee gestured for Regan to enter the house. Inside, she took in the heavy ornate furniture with its faded velvet and suede upholstering. It was as if someone had stuffed the small parlor with three rooms worth of furnishings, and it made the room terribly crowded. She paused at the sight of the large portrait over the fireplace of a smiling woman in a blue walking ensemble. Beside her were two brown spaniels. Her features were so much like Anna's, Regan asked, "Is that your mother, Anna?"

"Yes."

"She's very pretty. You favor her a great deal."

"I killed her," she confessed softly.

Regan froze and stared wide-eyed at the somber little girl and then at her father who appeared equally appalled.

Regan said, "I'm sure no one feels that way, Anna."

The girl nodded. "Great-Aunt Minnie does. She tells me every time we visit Mama's grave."

Before Regan could respond, her father knelt, took his daughter's small hands in his, and said earnestly, "Anna, you didn't kill your mother. Minnie is wrong to have told you that." It was apparent from his voice and manner that this was the first time he'd heard Anna express this and Regan's heart went out to him.

He added, "And I'll tell Minnie she's never to say such a thing to you again. Ever. I promise."

Anna nodded and he rose to his feet.

A male voice asked, "Is this her?"

Regan turned to see an older gray-haired man whose size and heft reminded her of a grizzly.

Face still showing concern for his daughter, Lee said, "Regan Carmichael, my grandfather, Benjamin Lee."

"Pleased to meet you, sir."

He made a grunt that could have passed for a greeting but only to someone hard of hearing. Regan said, "I'm looking forward to us getting acquainted."

By the terse set of his gray whiskered jaw, it was obvious he wasn't like-minded, but she didn't let his attitude bother her. Anna was the person she needed to win over. Grizzly Ben would have to wait his turn.

"Let's eat," he grumbled. "Food's ready."

The small dining room sported a good-sized table with wood so dull, it apparently hadn't been polished in years. The chair backs were equally dry. Smiling falsely, she took the seat Lee indicated directly across from him and Anna. She hoped the grandfather could cook.

He couldn't. Having grown up with her Aunt

Eddy's excellent cooking flavored with spices and the peppers of Mexico, she found the food disappointingly bland. Back home meals had been a time of laughter and conversation. Here? Silence. The family shared the table like strangers.

Attempting to draw Anna out, Regan asked, "Anna, what's your favorite time of the year? Summer? Spring? Winter?"

Anna cast her father a hasty glance as if seeking permission to speak. He gave her a nod.

"I don't have one."

Regan wasn't deterred. "Personally, I like summer, because after my sister and I did our chores, we could swim in the canyons and ride our horses. We could lie in the grass and read, or look for shapes in the clouds. We'd see lions and eagles. Portia even saw a dragon once. Have you ever lain on your back in the grass and looked for shapes?"

"No, ma'am."

"How about kite flying?"

"No."

"Surely you play marbles?"

Anna chuckled. "No."

"Then we shall have to make an Anna Fun List." Regan stood, leaned over the table, and stuck out her hand. "Shall we shake on it?"

Anna glanced tentatively at her father and her great-grandfather, then finally reached out and took Regan's hand. They shook.

"Good. Now, Mr. Ben, may I have more stew, please?"

Regan shot her intended a smile.

For the rest of the meal, Colton watched Regan Carmichael charm his daughter. Anna wasn't any more outgoing than usual but there was a glow of interest and curiosity in her manner that was new. Regan continued to regale them with tales of catching tadpoles and helping to brand cattle with her neighbor, Mr. Blanchard.

"Anna, did I tell you about the time my sister and I had to jump in Mr. Blanchard's pond to get away from an angry swarm of hornets?"

The wide-eyed Anna shook her head.

So, the Lee family listened as Regan related the tale of Mr. Blanchard attempting to set fire to a hornet's nest built under the eaves of his porch. "My sister and I were holding the ladder he used to climb up to the nest, but when those hornets came pouring out of that hive, we dropped the ladder and hightailed it out of there. They chased us all the way to his pond. We jumped in and ducked underwater. When we surfaced, the hornets were gone but Portia and I were soaked from our boots to our braids."

"Did you get a whipping for getting all wet?"

"No," Regan said gently. "My Aunt Eddy and Uncle Rhine didn't mind if we got wet or dirty if we were having fun. They were just glad the hornets didn't sting us."

Anna appeared puzzled by that. Having grown up under Minnie's rigid guidance, Colt understood why. Ben was watching Regan as if unsure what to make of her. Colt felt the same way.

Anna finally asked her, "So if you were my new mama, I could play outdoors and get dirty?"

"Yes, and I'll probably get dirty with you."

Her jaw dropped. She stared in amazement at Colt and he couldn't suppress the smile that curved his lips. Regardless of how he felt about the adventure-loving Regan Carmichael, instinct said she'd be good for his daughter.

For his part, Ben harrumphed, pushed back from the table, and carried his empty bowl into the kitchen.

Colt met Regan's curious gaze but he didn't respond.

Regan asked Anna, "So what's the first thing you want to get dirty doing?"

He could see Anna thinking it over and he found that surprising as well.

She finally replied, "May I think about it?"

"Of course. It's a big decision. I'd have to think it over, too, if I were you." Regan turned her attention his way. "Do you think your grandfather will allow me to help clean up?"

"No, at least not today. You're a guest."

"I only ask because my sister and I always took care of that back home. Habit, I suppose."

"I see." He had no way of knowing if that was the truth, or if she was trying to worm her way into Ben's good graces as well. She certainly had Anna in the palm of her hand. He turned to his daughter. "Anna, would you keep Miss Carmichael company for a moment? I want to check on Grandfather."

"Yes, sir."

He found Ben outside on the porch smoking his after-dinner cigar and sipping a shot of whiskey.

"Your thoughts?" Colt asked as he came to stand beside him. The mountains glowed red and gold in the setting sun.

"She's going to bring chaos to this house. That's for sure."

Colt agreed. "Anna seems to like her."

Ben's face soured. "And if you marry her, Anna's going to grow up to be as incorrigible as your sister."

"Only if I try and force her to marry someone she can't abide."

Ben skewered him with hard eyes. Colt knew the old man still believed marrying Spring off had been his right, but it precipitated the breach that followed, whether he chose to acknowledge his role or not.

Ben returned his attention to the mountains and grumbled, "She was supposed to do what I told her to."

Colt refused to argue. "Miss Carmichael and I will set a date." Not needing a response, he walked back inside.

"Will she be all right?" Regan asked as they rode towards Spring's cabin. They were both mounted. Anna had been left behind with Ben.

"Yes," Lee replied. "Ben's not much of a companion for a six-year-old but he'll watch out for her and make sure she's safe. When I'm away in the evenings, he usually cares for her."

Regan didn't think Grizzly Bear Ben qualified as a companion for anyone under the age of eighty, but kept that to herself. "I enjoyed meeting her. Do you think she enjoyed my visit?"

"I believe so. She's seldom as curious as she was tonight. Both Minnie and Ben feel children should be seen and not heard."

"And your feelings on that?"

"My mother encouraged us to have opinions, our father didn't. Spring and I lost him during Lincoln's War and our mother in seventy-one. Ben moved in in sixty-eight when she first got sick."

"How old were you?"

"I was thirteen when our father died in sixty-four and Spring was eleven."

"Portia was twelve and I was ten when my mother sent us to live with our Aunt Eddy and Uncle Rhine."

"Was your mother ill?"

Regan responded with a short bitter chuckle. "No. She didn't want us anymore, so she shipped us off like a crate of oranges and we haven't heard from her since."

He stopped his horse.

Regan added, "Portia grieved the loss but I didn't. If she didn't want us, I didn't want her."

"Something else not in your letters."

"True, nor did I reveal that she was a prostitute."

He visibly tensed, studying her in the fading light, so she said, "If you wish to cancel our agreement due to my mother, you are free to do so, but you should know the truth."

"Forgive me for asking what might be a rude question but have you ever been with a man?"

"I gave my virginity to someone I cared deeply for. He was the only one though."

He raised his eyes to the heavens as if seeking strength or patience or both. "You're making this very difficult."

"Would you rather I lied?"

He studied her again and shook his head. "No. Anything else I should know?"

"Not that I can think of." Regan wished she knew him well enough to tell what might be going through his head. She'd always been forthright because she found truth to be a better road than lying.

"A man prefers his wife to be virgin."

"I know that but men can visit women like my mother, and have mistresses with no repercussions from society. I'm not a whore, Dr. Lee. I don't plan to have relations outside my marriage, and I don't expect my husband to seek solace with someone else either."

"So, you'll accept my needs in the marriage bed without complaint?"

"As long as you extend me the same courtesy."

"Good women don't have needs."

She scoffed, "And you call yourself a doctor. Let's get to Spring's before it's full dark, shall we?"

He looked stunned. She thought he was about to say more. Instead, his mouth clamped shut and they resumed the ride.

They completed the rest of the short journey in silence, and it made Regan wonder again if she'd overplayed her hand by being so truthful.

When they reached Spring's cabin, she dismounted. "Thank you for the use of the mare. And I did enjoy meeting your daughter. So, where do we stand now?"

"Anna likes you, so we can have the sheriff marry us tomorrow if that's fine with you."

"It is."

"So, there'll be no misunderstanding, I'm marrying you because Anna needs a mother. I will be faithful to my vows. I will protect you to the best of my ability. But this isn't or ever will be a love match. I buried my heart when I buried Adele."

His bluntness hurt, but she shook it off, or at least tried to and replied, "Understood. I will do my best not to embarrass you in any way and raise Anna to the best of my ability."

"Then we'll do well together."

Her chin high, Regan nodded in agreement. "What time tomorrow?"

"Afternoon. Evening. Your choice."

"How about afternoon, at four? I'd like Spring and Anna to stand up with me."

"That's fine."

"I'll ride over with Spring."

"Agreed. Keep the mare until we get you a better

mount. I'll see you tomorrow." He touched his hat, turned his big bay stallion, and rode off.

As the echoes of his horse's hooves faded into the darkness, Regan thoughts went back to her sister's recent wedding. There'd been musicians, tables groaning with food, cakes galore, and hours of laughter and celebration. Regan's own wedding would probably lack that joyfulness. She'd seen horses change hands with potentially more pomp and circumstance.

I buried my heart with Adele.

His words haunted her as she led the mare to the barn. In spite of her longings to be in a marriage that held as much love as her aunt and uncle shared, she realized hers might not. She also realized how silly she'd been to think of being a mail-order bride as an adventure. Her sister, Portia, warned her that marriage was more than that.

After bedding the mare down for the night, she walked to the cabin to let Spring know she'd returned. Her thoughts then strayed to Anna's heartbreaking belief that she'd killed her mother, and Regan was angry all over again. How dare the aunt place such a heavy burden on the shoulders of a child. It was undoubtedly difficult enough growing up motherless, but being led to believe she was responsible? Regan wanted to shake Minnie until her teeth rattled loose. There was a lot to sort out going forward and she again pointed an accusatory finger at herself for being so naïve in thinking this mail-order bride business would be a cakewalk, but she was determined all would be well in the end.

*C*olt found his daughter awake and lying in bed with her drawing paper and pencils. She liked sketching. Upon seeing him, she set everything aside.

"Everything okay with you, Anna?"

She nodded.

"What are you drawing?"

"Me and Miss Carmichael."

He walked in and sat down on the edge of her bed. "May I see it?" On the paper were two stick figures, one tall, one short. They were holding hands. He smiled. "Miss Carmichael said she enjoyed dinner."

"I did, too. She's pretty."

"You think so?"

"Yes. Even prettier than Felicity's mama. Do you think she's pretty?"

"I do." Which was true. She outshone Colleen like the sun to a candle.

"Is she really going to be my new mama?"

"If you want her to be."

"I do, but Aunt Minnie's going to say no."

He thought back on his encounter with Minnie in his office. "Minnie doesn't get a say. Just you."

Anna searched his face with eyes filled with hope. "Truly?"

"Truly."

She quieted as if thinking on that.

"And honey, Minnie should never have said you caused your mother's death."

"But I did."

"No, you didn't and had I known about it before tonight I would've told her to never say that to you ever again. Your mother wouldn't want you to carry that in your heart about yourself."

He couldn't tell if she believed him or not but he'd be having a talk with Minnie about this. Soon. "I know it might be hard to unbelieve something but I want you to try real hard to not think of yourself that way. Will you try?"

She nodded. "The next time I go visit Mama at her grave, can I go with you and not Aunt Minnie?"

"Sure can. In fact, once Miss Carmichael and I marry, we'll only see Minnie when she comes to visit. Miss Carmichael will be looking after you whenever I'm gone from now on." The guilt he felt inside from knowing how awful Anna must feel was tearing his heart apart. He'd put his child in Minnie's hands not knowing how much she was suffering. He doubted Anna's thinking would change overnight but he hoped their talking about it now would be a start.

"What do you think I should put on my list for Miss Regan?" she asked.

"What list?"

"My getting dirty list."

He chuckled and inwardly thanked God for the adventure-loving Miss Carmichael. "I'm not sure."

"Do you care if I get dirty, Papa?"

"No, honey."

"Granpa Ben might."

"True, but he doesn't get a say in this either."

"Then I'll keep thinking."

He caressed her hair. "You do that." He gave her a kiss on her brow. "You can draw a little longer then go to sleep. Oh, and Miss Carmichael and I are getting married tomorrow, here. She wants you to stand up with her."

He could tell by her confusion she had no idea what that meant, so he explained. Once he finished, she beamed. "I don't think Felicity has ever stood up with anybody."

"Then you'll be one up on her."

Anna beamed brighter.

Vowing to make sure she had the best future he could give her going forward, he stood. "Good night, Anna."

"Good night, Papa. And thank you for getting me a new mama."

Emotion clogged his throat. "You're welcome, honey. Sleep well."

"You too."

Chapter Five

Regan awakened the morning of her wedding day to the tangy smell of what she thought was bacon frying. Getting up, she dressed and went to find Spring, but there was nothing cooking in the kitchen and her hostess was nowhere to be seen. Stepping outside where the tantalizing smell seemed stronger, she followed it to the back of the barn where she found Spring tending a huge hog roasting on a spit.

"Morning, Regan."

"Morning. Nice hog you have there."

"Slaughtered him after you went to bed last night. Getting him ready for your wedding dinner."

That left Regan slightly baffled. "I appreciate the gesture but that's more meat than your brother and niece and I can eat in a month."

"Then it's a good thing other folks are coming over to help."

"What do you mean?"

"I took it upon myself to make this wedding the celebration you deserve. Knowing Colton, he'll say his vows and two minutes later head to his study to pore over the latest medical journal. That's his idea of fun."

"How many people are coming?"

"Not sure but folks around here jump at any chance to get together. Lacy's heading up the rest of the food."

"Lacy?"

"Lacy Miller. She's a little White lady, runs the general store with her husband, Chauncey. She's rounding up all the women willing to cook on such short notice, and she's promised a cake."

Regan was stunned. "Have you talked to your brother about this?"

"Of course not." She turned the spit so the hog roasted evenly. "He'd never agree, but I wanted you to be able to smile when you looked back on your wedding day. We'll have a few fiddlers, toss some horseshoes, eat, drink, raise some toasts, and have a good time."

Regan didn't know what to say. She couldn't imagine Dr. Lee's reaction to his sister turning what had originally been a short quiet parlor ceremony into what sounded like a full-blown hullabaloo. "Be sure to tell him you did this without consulting me."

"Will do. Now, go open your trunks and find a gown to get married in that will send Colleen Enright screaming to the Klondike."

That made Regan smile. She'd been missing her sister, Portia, so much, but now it appeared as if she might have gained an additional one. "Spring?"

She looked up from her basting. "Yes?"

"Thank you."

Smiling, she tossed back a wink. "You're welcome."

*C*olt needed to conduct house calls before the wedding so after getting dressed, he paused for a moment in front of his wardrobe mirror. In his denims, boots, and black flannel shirt, he resembled a rancher rather than a physician, but he didn't mind. The back East members of his profession could keep their fancy suits, vests, and pocket watches. He hadn't studied from dawn to dusk and swept floors at the local hospital to pay for his classes just to appear prosperous. All he wanted in life was to help people heal. That he hadn't been able to save his mother from her cancer or Adele from the complications of childbirth continued to haunt him, but he remained dedicated to his calling and proud to have attended Howard Medical School.

The school, founded in 1867 and named for Civil War General Oliver Otis Howard, changed his life. He began his medical studies there in 1870, and for a mountain boy who'd never been farther east than Cheyenne, the nation's capital city of Washington, with its clanging horse-drawn trolleys and thousands of people had been daunting. He'd never been anywhere so noisy or where everyone seemed

to be in such a hurry. It was also his first time seeing so many members of the race doing everything
from riding the trolleys to working in storefront establishments to owning fine hotels and restaurants.

But the most life-changing event took place in his
anatomy class. It was taught by Dr. Alexander T. Augusta, the first Colored man to be commissioned a
major in the Union Army and the first man of the
race to teach at a U.S. medical school. The first day of
class, Colt was so busy staring with awe and pride,
he forgot to take notes. He'd known men like him
existed but he'd never seen a doctor of color before.
Learning from him, being encouraged by him, and
later training under him at Washington's Freedmen's Hospital reaffirmed his belief that medicine
was indeed his calling.

Now, he was to be a husband to a woman so
unconventional, she sometimes took his breath
away. Had she really branded cattle? He'd done it,
of course, but other than his sister, Spring, he knew
few women able to accomplish such a task without
succumbing to a fit of the vapors.

"Interesting times ahead," he said to his reflection. "Interesting times."

Downstairs he found Anna standing at the big
dining room window looking out.

"Morning, Anna."

"Morning, Papa."

"What's going on out there?"

"Granpa Ben and his friends are scything the
grasses in the field."

Curious, Colt walked to her side. Sure enough, his grandfather along with cronies Odell Waters, Manx Solomon, and Porter James were swinging their blades through the overgrowth.

Anna said, "They're getting ready for the wedding."

"Miss Carmichael and I are getting married in the parlor, honey."

"I think the field is where all the food and eating's going to be."

Colt stilled. "Why do you think that?"

"When Granpa Ben was fixing my breakfast, he was grumbling about Aunt Spring, busybodies, a pig, and cake. Is that what you eat at a wedding? Pig and cake?"

Colt was outdone for a few moments. "I'm not sure. Let me go talk with Granpa Ben and see if I can get some answers."

He headed for the door.

"What do you mean half the town's coming?" he asked Ben impatiently.

His grandfather wiped the sweat from his brow on the sleeve of his shirt. "Your sister's doing. Rode over before dawn, told me what she planned to do, and rode off towards town."

"But I don't want all this," he said, indicating the cleared field.

Ben shrugged. "Too late. Spring thinks you and the Carmichael woman need to go all out, and you know how she is once she sets her mind on something."

Colt blew out an exasperated breath. "This was supposed to be a small family gathering in the parlor."

"Tell that to your sister. More than likely that woman you're so set on marrying wanted something more highfalutin. Told you she'd be trouble."

Colt wondered if Regan and Spring were co-conspirators, but realized it didn't matter. The horse was out of the barn and galloping across the county. In fact, he looked up to see a couple of wagons turning onto the property. One, driven by Lacy Miller, had its bed filled with chairs, trestle tables, and Lord knew what else. "I have house calls to make."

"You eat breakfast?"

"Not hungry. Anna's staying home from school today."

"Why?"

"She and Spring are standing up with Regan at the wedding."

His grandfather grumbled something unintelligible. "Okay. I'll keep an eye on her."

"And I'd like for you to stand up with me."

"Why can't Whit do it?"

"Because he's conducting the ceremony."

"Oh all right."

Buoyed by his grandfather's enthusiasm, Colt went to the barn and saddled his horse. His injured shoulder was still tight and sore but felt better than it had the day before. Thankful for that at least, he rode away.

His first stop was to check in on nine-year-old Silas Taylor. A week ago, the boy and his black-and-white bull terrier, Lucky, had a run-in with an old male cougar the locals had named One Eye because the cat only had one. Due to its advanced age and limited vision, the cougar probably saw the boy as an easy meal, but didn't take into account the fearless Lucky coming to his master's aid. The dog eventually ran the cat off, but not before he and the boy were slashed a few times by its claws. Ben and his friends were planning a hunt to put the big cat down before it attacked again.

"How's he doing?" Colt asked the boy's mother, Geneva, as she ushered him inside.

"The skin around the cuts is still a bit stiff and itches, he says, but the skin's healing."

"Mind if I take a look?"

"No, of course not."

"How's Lucky?"

"Eating all the rabbits my William can bring home as his reward. If it hadn't been for that dog . . ." Her voice trailed off.

Colt agreed. Lucky saved Silas's life.

The red-haired, nine-year-old Silas was lying in bed. When Colt entered, his small freckled face broke into a grin. "Hi, Dr. Lee."

"Hi, Silas." Lucky was lying on a large pillow inside of a wooden crate. "How are you and your brave dog?"

"We're fine. Aren't we, Lucky?"

The dog barked and Colt chuckled. "Is it okay if I check your cuts?"

"Sure."

His mother, standing in the doorway, said, "There's a basin of warm water there for you. I know you like to keep your hands clean."

"Thank you." Colt was a follower of British surgeon Dr. Joseph Lister who touted the benefits of cleanliness and the use of carbolic acid in stopping the spread of infections and disease. With his hands clean, Colt gently freed the bandages covering the three long gashes One Eye had given the boy on the left side of his rib cage. The wounds were still red and angry in appearance, but were no longer draining, which was a good sign. The stitches Colt used to close the deepest cut seemed to be doing well, too. "Are you eating okay?" Colt placed a hand on the boy's brow to check for fever.

"Yes, sir."

"Keeping your hands clean, and away from your cuts?"

"Yes, sir. They itch like the dickens though."

Colt withdrew his stethoscope from his bag and checked his breathing. "Means they're healing." His breathing sounded fine. "I'm going to put some fresh bandages on them, and in another couple of days, we'll see where we go from there." Colt removed a roll of gauze and some cotton pads from his bag.

"Can you check Lucky, too?" Silas asked.

"Sure will. Let me get you fixed up first."

As promised, once he was done with Silas, Colt checked on the terrier. Colt also acted as the local veterinarian because there wasn't one in the immediate area. He checked the short line of stitches he'd placed in the dog's belly. The terrier had lived up to his name because he could've been disemboweled.

Pleased that Silas and Lucky were mending well, he offered them his good-byes and Mrs. Taylor walked him to the front door. "So sorry I'm going to miss the wedding," she said. "I hear your bride's a beauty, and quite the firecracker. How's your shoulder?"

Colt wondered if there was anyone in the Territory who didn't know his business. "My shoulder's fine, thank you for asking."

"My William and I are looking forward to meeting her."

Colt responded with what he hoped passed for a genuine smile and rode off to see his next patient.

*M*en and women were swarming over the Lee property like ants when Spring and Regan arrived. Tents were being set up, the air was fragrant with the smells of roasting meat and food, and she could hear laughter as folks went about the preparations.

"Let's get you inside. No one's supposed to see the bride before the event."

"Spring—"

"You're the closest I'm ever coming to being a bride, so humor me."

"Yes, ma'am." Carrying the gown she planned to be married in, she followed Spring without a further word.

Inside the house, she was led to a room in the back. "This used to be Adele's room."

The small space held a bed, a wardrobe, and a mirrored vanity table. It was about the size of Regan's closet back home and the reality that she was getting married without her loving family by her side instantly made her melancholy, but she shook it off as best she could and hung her dress in the empty wardrobe.

"I'll get someone to bring in the trunks, then I'll get Anna and myself dressed and ready."

In the silence that settled after Spring's exit, Regan glanced around at the room that she supposed would be her own and wondered how Adele felt about another woman being in the lives of her husband and daughter. Regan truly wanted this new life to be successful, even if Colton Lee never grew feelings for her in his heart. Her musings were interrupted by the appearance of Ben and the telegraph operator, Odell Waters, hauling in her trunks.

Ben groused, "You plan on adding a new room to the house to store whatever's in all these trunks?"

She didn't reply. Instead, she asked Mr. Waters, "Has my telegraph been sent?"

"Not yet, but I'm trying every day, twice a day to get it out. Don't worry."

But she did because she'd promised to send word to her family as soon as she arrived. By now they were probably very concerned.

The men had to make two trips, and with the arrival of each additional trunk and hatbox, the room seemed smaller and smaller. When the two men finished she thanked them.

Odell smiled. Ben didn't. They exited, leaving her alone again. Regan began unearthing what she needed from the trunks.

An hour later, Regan studied her reflection in the wardrobe and was glad she'd packed what her sister, Portia, humorously called her "beetle dress." The sweeping skirt was an iridescent blue silk that glowed with beauty and had three-quarters length sleeves. The sapphire bodice had a modest neckline and hugged her frame snugly. Around her throat hung a cameo on a blue velvet ribbon. Small sapphire ear bobs graced her lobes. Her hair was swept up, her face and lips fashionably painted and the way she looked was indeed enough to send the annoying Enright widow fleeing to the Klondike. Regan's real goal, however, was to knock the aloof Dr. Colton Lee to his knees. Smiling at herself, she took a seat on the bed to await Spring and Anna. Her groom didn't stand a chance.

They appeared a few minutes later. Spring, dressed in a blue gown and with her hair up looked nothing like a woman who slaughtered hogs and sold horses. Anna, wearing a little red velvet dress, white stocking, and black slippers looked adorable.

"You look like a princess," Regan said to her.

"Do I?"

"Yes, you do."

Anna smiled broadly at the compliment.

Spring said, "And you, Miss Carmichael, look like a queen. My brother's eyes are going to bug out and roll around on the ground."

"You don't look so bad yourself. The dress is beautiful."

Spring looked embarrassed.

To spare her, Regan asked, "Do you think they're ready for us?"

"Yes. So, let's get going."

*D*ressed in the black suit he usually reserved for weddings or funerals, a terse Colt waited for his bride to appear. He'd been right about half the county showing up, because his fields were over-run with friends, neighbors, and people he'd never met. There was food and horseshoe tossing, dominoes, and poker games. Someone, probably Lacy Miller, had erected a bower decorated with wildflowers. Upon seeing it, Colt rolled his eyes, but was now standing beneath it waiting with his friend the sheriff, Whitman Lambert.

"I thought Ben was standing up with you?"

"I did, too, but he rode off about an hour ago."

"To where?"

"His cabin. Said he needed to set the traps for One Eye. I think he just went to pout because I'm marrying over his objections."

"Here they come!" someone shouted.

The crowd in front of the bower parted and the fiddlers started in on the sweet strains of "Amazing Grace."

Colt turned to see his daughter solemnly walking towards him holding a small bouquet of wildflowers. In her red dress, and her hair threaded through with ribbons, she was so beautiful his chest hurt. He'd never seen the dress before and wondered where she'd gotten it, but further contemplation was cut short by the appearance of his sister. The dark burgundy off-shoulder gown with its fashionable overskirts transformed Spring from a rancher to a woman who'd just stepped out of a back East drawing room. Her raven black hair was pinned up, offering an unhindered view of her stunning face. The fiddlers paused. The locals hooted and hollered. The smiling Spring paused, did a slow turn so everyone could get a good look, and continued her walk to Anna's side.

A hush fell, and as the fiddlers began again, there was Regan Carmichael walking to the bower like a queen to her coronation. Colt stopped breathing.

"My God," Whit whispered. "Would you look at that woman!"

Colt could do nothing but look—at her gown, her hair, her dark beauty, the confidence with which she moved. Her eyes were locked on his and the little smile she shot him immediately made him hard as a post. *Jesus!*

The crowd seemed equally stunned. The silence was so thick, one could hear the wind in the trees.

When she came to stand at his side, a shaken Colt acknowledged her with a nod, and turned his attention to Whit, while the faint, sensual scent of her perfume snared him like a siren's song and added to the heart attack he swore he was in the throes of.

Blessedly, the ceremony was short. She spoke her responses with clarity and ease. He on the other hand, stumbled, causing someone to yell out, "We understand, Doc! Take a deep breath!" Which of course made everyone laugh.

Finally, Whit said, "I now pronounce you man and wife."

His bride turned his way. He knew she and the onlookers were expecting the traditional kiss. Instead, Colt took her hand and pressed his lips against the back.

Spring chuckled. "Coward."

He ignored her, but ignoring the amusement in his new wife's eyes was impossible. It was as though she knew he was struggling with his aplomb and was enjoying herself like a cat playing with a mouse.

For the next few hours, the newlyweds with Anna between them mingled and accepted congratulations. Colt noted how at ease Regan seemed meeting everyone. She laughed, shook hands, listened attentively to everything folks had to say, and genuinely charmed her way from one side of the crowd to the other. To his amazement, she even hiked up that fancy gown to toss horseshoes. And of course, she threw ringers, which made the onlookers roar.

"Quite an interesting wife you have there, Colton." He turned from the horseshoe contest to see Colleen Enright standing beside him. "Can you imagine your Adele conducting herself so—so crudely?"

"Regan isn't Adele, and there's nothing crude about tossing horseshoes." He watched Regan hit yet another ringer. More cheers rang out. Standing by the pit, Anna clapped happily.

Colleen's voice dripped with disdain. "She's standing in the pit in her stocking feet. No lady does that. I would've made you a more cultured wife."

He refused to respond. Instead, upon noticing his sister waving to him, he said, "If you'll excuse me, I need to collect Regan and Anna. I see Spring and Lacy have brought out the cake." He walked away.

When her husband came to collect her so they could cut the cake, Regan was a bit saddened. She loved pitching horseshoes and she'd had fun bantering with her competitors and the people watching. Stepping out of the pit, she brushed the sand from her stockings and stepped back into her shoes. Only then did it occur to her that she may have embarrassed him with her unbridelike behavior. His dark eyes, always watchful, revealed nothing. Anna who hadn't strayed far from Regan's side asked, "Can you teach me to play horseshoes?"

"Sure can. When do you wish to start?"

Anna looked to her father, who replied, "How

about we eat cake first and talk about horseshoes later?"

She nodded enthusiastically.

Regan took one of Anna's small hands, Colton took the other, and they joined the crowd heading to the final event of the day.

Chapter Six

"*I* don't think I've ever seen that many pies," Regan said as she and Colt entered the house after everyone had gone home.

"Neither have I. Lacy must've had every woman in the Territory contribute."

The wedding cake wasn't large enough to feed everyone. To make up for the lack, there'd been dozens of pies of every variety and size. When those gathered had their fill, the reception began breaking up and people said their good-byes to the newlyweds and headed home. Spring offered to take Anna with her for the night, which pleased the child to no end, even though her father looked conflicted. With Ben away, this was the newlyweds' first opportunity to be alone as man and wife. Regan didn't know what the rest of the evening would entail. Since speaking his vows, he'd offered nothing in the way of affection, which she supposed was to be expected. As he'd pointed out, theirs wasn't a love match.

"So, shall I meet you in your room—my room? I assume you'd like to get the consummation taken care of."

Again, the watchful eyes. Again, she couldn't tell what he might be thinking. She did know he wasn't as stoic as he appeared. Her walk to meet him at the bower had knocked him to his knees just as she'd predicted.

Colt had no idea how to move the evening along. Yes, he wanted to seal the marriage, but the awkwardness he felt was so uncharacteristic, he felt like a man who'd never been with a woman before. "I'll come to you in a few minutes."

After she departed, he stood alone in the silence and drew in a deep breath to calm his nerves. The idea that a good women might have urges in ways that mimicked a man was something he still found hard to believe. Everything he'd been taught in medical school and in life contradicted her claim. Good women *did not* have urges. Yet, he couldn't deny his own. All day he'd wanted to brush his lips over her throat and inhale the intoxicating scent of her perfumed warm skin. The saucy smile she'd tossed his way made him want to taste her mouth and fill his hands with her hips while he languidly guided those yards of silk up and down her thighs. He wanted to press his erection against her so she'd feel what she did to him. Willing himself to remember he was a man of discipline and not one to be driven by base desires, he went to join her.

When he entered the room, she said, "I need help getting out of this gown."

"That isn't necessary."

"What isn't necessary?"

"That," he said, gesturing vaguely her way.

"Aren't we consummating our vows?"

"Yes."

"But I'm not to remove my clothing?"

"Good women don't remove their clothing."

After giving him a studied look, she asked, "So, I'm supposed to lie back, lift my dress, and let you rut away?"

Scalded by her bold manner, he somehow managed to say, "That's usually the way it's done."

"Then let's do something unusual because I don't want the gown ruined."

Chin raised, she walked to him and turned her back. "My buttons, please."

Colt hesitated. He took in the line of fabric-coated buttons trailing down the back of her gorgeous iridescent gown and her cool eyes trained his way over her shoulder. In them he saw anger tinged with hurt. The latter gave him pause, but rather than muse over the cause, he complied with her request. The undoing revealed the back of a thin shift dyed to match the color of her gown. When he finished, she stepped out of his reach and faced him. Eyes simmering, she pulled her arms free of the gown and let the silk swish to the floor.

His heart pounded at the sight of her brown legs encased in gossamer-thin white stockings, and the jewel-encrusted garters. As if bent on causing him more havoc, she took hold of the shift's hem and slowly pulled it up and over her head. She may have tossed it aside, but he wasn't sure because he was too busy trying to breathe. The sapphire corset dipped low over the tops of her breasts, accenting the tempting heart-shaped swells and drew his eyes down her slim torso to the matching ribbon-edged drawers hugging the tops of her thighs. He thought she gave him a smug smile, but it vanished so quickly he chalked it up to his imagination. He watched her sit on the edge of the bed and remove her shoes. Lying back, she made herself comfortable. "I'm ready whenever you are."

Colt hesitated. A part of him was appalled by her brazen behavior, while other parts wanted to tear off the tempting corset and have her in every way imaginable. He removed his coat and laid it on the chair with her gown.

"When I was in medical school I had a friend named Artemis James. Night after night while the rest of us pored over our books, Artie was visiting cathouses." He removed his cuff links, set them aside, and folded up the sleeves of his white shirt. "After his visits, he'd come back and regale us with tales of his adventures." By the look on her face, he could tell she was wondering where the tale was heading.

"In addition to feeding our young male fantasies with his salacious details, he also reminded us that a wife would never be as uninhibited as the women he visited." Colt sat on the edge of the bed.

"And I believed that . . . until you." Surrendering to the urge to touch her, he used the tip of his finger to slowly trace the swells of her breasts above the corset. When her breath caught, he leaned over and placed a fleeting kiss first against her lips and then base of her throat. Inhaling the faint remnants of her perfume, he husked out, "You're a scandalous wife, Regan Carmichael Lee."

He straightened and savored the heat he'd kindled in her eyes.

"I know," she whispered with a smile.

Unable to manage his need to touch her, he traced her sassy lips and kissed her again. "Do you wish to have a scandalous husband?"

"Yes."

"Open your corset for me."

Holding his eyes with a boldness that made his erection harden further, she opened the series of frogs one by one and placed her hands behind her on the mattress to brace herself. He eased the halves apart grazing the dark tips of her nipples in the process and heard her breath catch once more. Leaning in he took one into his mouth, enjoying both its hardness and the tiny moan that slipped out, before turning his attention to its twin.

Regan no longer cared that her marriage wouldn't be a love match if he planned to treat her to this kind of bed play. His mouth, touch, and voice were turning her into a human bonfire. The slide of his hands, the tiny nip he placed on her collarbone, the way he watched her react as his palm traveled up her thigh only added more fuel. His finger circled her nipple, before he bit it gently.

"Am I seeing to your needs, Regan Lee?"

His use of her married name was as seductive as his touch.

"You have to say yes, or no. I don't want to be neglectful."

But before she could respond, he slid two fingers wickedly into her heat through the slit in her drawers and her hips rose in response to his beguiling rhythm.

"Yes? No?"

"Yes," she choked out. The heat intensified.

"You're very wet," he whispered. "Another sign of a scandalous wife."

He kissed her, seeking her tongue while his fingers continued their play. Her legs parted wider of their own accord and he deepened the kiss, searing her, sliding his tongue over the fullness of her bottom lip. Her gasps of pleasure rose in the silence. He played, plied, and touched until she found herself on her back, twisting and moaning in shameless uninhibited delight. "I'm going to shatter."

"Are you sure?"

She whimpered.

"Then let's make it memorable." While his fingers continued to drive her mad, his thumb began dallying with the throbbing little kernel at the center of her thighs and her hips rose for more. Granting her unspoken wish, he leaned down, flicked his tongue against it, sucked it in possessively, and she shattered, screaming his name.

After coming back to earth, Regan opened her passion-lidded eyes to see him smiling down. He slid a finger over her still damp nipple. "Memorable?"

She struggled up. "Very." Wanting to give him a taste of his own medicine, she wrapped her hand around the hardness protruding from within his trousers and implemented some plying of her own. He hissed, closed his eyes, and she savored the reaction. She boldly undid the placket and once he was bared to her touch, she savored his warmth and hardness as well.

Colt knew he was close to losing control, and that a few more passes of her small wicked hand would send him over the edge, so he backed away, his eyes glittering with desire, and removed his clothing. Nude, he joined her on the bed and pulled her into his arms. She was such a sensual delight, it came to him that he could have relations with her every day for the rest of his life and he'd still want more of her kisses, her scented skin, the feel of her nipples in his mouth, and the damp heat between her parted thighs. Unable to exist a second longer without having her, he eased himself into her flesh. She was so tight, he almost broke there and then. He lifted her hips to increase their pleasure. Ignoring the pain in his shoulder he began to move. Yesterday he'd been appalled to learn she wasn't a virgin. Now, as she met him measure for measure, he was glad she wasn't. Her inner muscles tightened deliciously, and he knew he'd died and gone to heaven.

"Come for me, Colton Lee," she whispered seductively, running her hands down his damp back and over the rise of his slowly pumping hips. "Show me how scandalous you really are."

The wanton invitation sent him over the edge. The power and speed of his strokes increased until he exploded with a roar. Moments later, she cried out her own completion and together they rode out the storm until collapsing onto the tangled sheets.

For the rest of the night, they consummated their marriage in ways that left them both breathless and dazed. Finally sated, they stripped the bed of the sodden sheets, he pulled her into his side, dragged the quilt up for cover, and they slept.

The following morning, Regan awakened slowly. Her disorientation from being in a strange room soon fled as she remembered, but then realized she was in the bed alone. Sitting up, she listened intently for sounds of his presence. Hearing only silence, she wrapped the quilt around her nudity and went to seek him out. She hadn't been given a tour of the house, so she didn't know who slept where. After placing her ear against the closed doors she took to be bedrooms, searching the small kitchen, and peeking through the windows of the parlor and dining room to see if he might be outdoors, she realized she was alone. Disappointed, she padded back to the bedroom hoping he'd left her a note or some other clue that might indicate his whereabouts, but found nothing. Had he ridden off to a medical emergency? Had last night been nothing more than a legality and they were now back to business as usual? Refusing to believe the latter, she chose the former and decided to wash up and dress.

The kitchen presented a problem. The stove was ancient and outdated in comparison to what she and her family cooked on at home. It would probably take it an hour or more to heat up enough to fry eggs and bacon—if she knew where the food was kept. After a short search, she discovered an equally old cold box outside on the back porch. Inside was a plate of sliced beef, so she took some along with some bread she found, made a sandwich, and called it breakfast. Sandwich in hand, she surveyed the parlor and dining room with its tons of furniture and wondered how much say she'd be given in putting her own stamp on the rooms. She glanced up at Adele's portrait and asked, "Was this your furniture or did you inherit all these stuffy old pieces?"

None of it looked modern and as she'd noted before, the furniture hadn't been polished in quite some time. Polishing it would give her something to do, but again, she didn't know if there was polish or rags in the house or where they might be kept. She also didn't wish to incur Ben's wrath if it turned out to be something he didn't approve of. Regan liked being busy. Sitting in the house alone with nothing to do would drive her batty. She contemplated riding the borrowed mare over to Spring's place to spend the time with her and Anna, but she didn't know the way there well enough yet, and she didn't want to chance getting lost. With any luck, her husband would return shortly or Spring would ride over with Anna. She wasn't anxious for Grizzly Ben's return though. Being stuck in the house with him wasn't something she longed for, so to pass the time, she returned to the bedroom to unpack her trunks.

An hour later, she had nearly everything opened but no place to put or hang the bulk of her items. The small wardrobe held fewer than half her gowns and shoes, and again, she wished she hadn't brought so much. There were day dresses and denims on the bed, face paints, hairbrushes, and combs piled atop the vanity. Hat boxes were stacked beside the wardrobe and the trunk holding winter garments like her coats and heavy sweaters hadn't even been opened. Wondering how she was going to make it all fit, she was standing with her hands on her hips surveying the chaos when she heard footsteps and Anna's voice call out, "Papa?"

Grateful for the company, Regan left the room to greet her.

Upon seeing Regan, Anna asked, "Is Papa here?"

Not wanting them to know how disappointed she felt upon finding him gone, she replied lightly, "No, honey. I believe he's at his office in town."

As if aware of Regan's feelings, Spring looked concerned. "No problems being here alone?" she asked.

"No. Spent the time unpacking my trunks. I may have to move the bed into the hallway though to make it all fit."

Anna and Spring followed her to the room and Anna looked around in awe. "You have a lot of things, Miss Regan."

"I know. Any idea on where I'm to put everything?"

"No, ma'am," she said still eyeing Regan's possessions. "Maybe Papa and Granpa Ben will let you move into Grandma Isabelle's room."

Regan looked to Spring for an explanation. "It was my mother's room, but has been closed up since her death."

"Adele didn't use it?"

Spring shook her head, giving Regan the impression that there was a story tied to Adele's decision, but she didn't ask in case it was something Anna shouldn't hear. "Is it larger than this one?"

"Much," Spring said. "My mother loved her comforts. You might want to ask Colton about it when he returns."

"Okay. In the meantime, I'll just muddle through." She turned to Anna. "Which room is yours, Anna? May I see it?"

"Yes. Papa is next to you, and I'm on the other side."

Regan followed Anna and Spring out to the hallway. Her room was even tinier than Regan's. It held a bed, a wardrobe, and a nightstand. There was nothing that showed it to be the bedroom of a little girl. The walls were plain, the curtains beige, and a brown rug with frayed edges lay beside the bed. Regan didn't see any toys and wanted to ask if she had dolls but didn't. "This is a nice room, Anna."

"Thank you."

Regan noticed the sketch pad and pencils on the nightstand. "You draw?"

"Yes, ma'am."

"May I see?"

Anna handed her the book and Regan viewed the pages. Many were renderings of animals: a fox, an elk, birds. The drawings were rough and looked like they were drawn by a six-year-old, but all the subjects were recognizable. "These are very good, Anna."

Anna then showed her the one she'd drawn of the two of them holding hands. "This is you and me."

An emotional Regan eyed the two stick figures and leaned over and kissed her brow. "May I keep this? I want to frame it and place it on the wall in my room."

"Truly?"

"Yes."

"Aunt Minnie doesn't like for me to draw, so I only do it at home."

"You can draw for me anytime. Will you hold on to this until my room is ready?"

She nodded.

Regan saw the displeasure on Spring's face at the mention of the old woman and Regan agreed with her silent assessment. Regan glanced around Anna's room and wondered if Colt would allow her to brighten up the space. When Regan was young, Aunt Eddy let her paint a sun and clouds on a wall of her bedroom, and she still remembered how much fun it had been. She wondered if Anna might like to do something similar. Regan would also ask him about replacing the drab bedding and drapes with items a bit more cheerful.

Spring said, "I need to get back. Will you two be okay here?"

Regan asked Anna, "Do you think we'll be okay?"

"Yes," Anna replied. She then said to Spring, "Thank you letting me stay with you, Aunt Spring."

"You're welcome, and maybe we can do it again sometime soon."

Regan added, "And thank you again for my wedding day." The day had been memorable and the night even more so, even if she had awakened alone.

They walked Spring out to her wagon and waved as she rolled away.

Standing with Anna, Regan wondered what they might do to pass the time when a shot rang out. It was instantly followed by another. Regan quickly pushed Anna to the ground and covered the girl's body with her own. An eerie silence followed. Over her pounding heart, Regan searched the surrounding landscape for signs of the shooter. "Are you hurt anywhere?"

"No. I'm scared, Miss Regan."

"I know, honey. Just lie still. I hope I'm not crushing you." She needed to get Anna in the house, but didn't want the girl to become a target on the way. Wondering who was shooting at them and why, she continued to study the trees.

To her relief, she saw Spring driving fast in their direction. Regan raised up cautiously. "Stay down, Anna."

Spring jumped from the wagon, rifle in hand. "I heard gunfire, so I turned around. Are you all right?"

"Yes. Someone shot at us." Regan helped Anna to her feet. The small hand in hers was shaking. "You were very brave," Regan told her and hugged her close. "Let's go inside."

*C*olt checked on a few patients then spent the balance of the day in his office reading the latest medical journals and trying not to think about Regan. It was a losing battle. Everywhere his mind turned, she was there. He'd left the house while she was still asleep to keep from awakening her to pick up where they'd left off. He and Adele had never shared such a night. He'd never faulted her for her distaste for the marriage bed and he didn't now. To do so would be disrespectful of her and what they'd meant to each other outside of the bedroom. On the other hand, Regan clearly had no such aversion. She'd been uninhibited, passionate, and as eager to give pleasure as to receive. Colt prided himself on his discipline and ability to keep his wits about him, but she'd left him so witless that all day he'd been fighting the urge to ride home, take her lush little body back to bed, and make her scream his name. The thought made him hard and he ran his hands down his bearded face. The marriage was consummated, there was no need for him to approach her again anytime soon, but the lust in his blood kept reminding him how it felt to sink into her tight warmth, the weight of her soft breasts in his hands, and the taste of her nipples in his mouth. Hardening more in response he cursed silently, drew in a calming breath and told himself everything would be fine—he'd just keep her at arm's length and go about his life.

The clock on the wall showed it was time to head home. It occurred to him that in his haste to escape his new wife, he'd left her to fend for herself. How had she spent the day? Had she eaten? She probably thought him a poor husband to have left without so much as a note. Had he been in his right mind, and not so befuddled by their bed play, he would've been more considerate. He owed her an apology but had no idea what he might say by way of explanation. He certainly couldn't tell her he'd fled because of how bewitching she was.

He gathered his bag and other personal items and left the office. After locking the door and nodding a silent greeting to people passing on the walk, he was about to mount his horse when he saw Spring drive up on her wagon. Regan and Anna were with her.

"Is Whitman in town?" Spring asked. "Someone took a couple of shots at Regan and Anna."

His heart jumped and his gaze flew to his daughter. Quickly approaching the wagon, he asked her, "Are you all right?" He picked her up from the seat and held her against his side.

"I'm all right. Miss Regan said I was very brave."

He took in the terse set of Regan's face. He noted she was wearing a gun belt over her denims. "What happened?"

"Anna and I were outside and someone took two shots at us. Sounded like a rifle. I found one bullet buried in a nearby tree. Not sure where the other one went. Is the sheriff here?"

"No. He's over in Rock Springs. Problems there with some of the miners. He should be back tomorrow sometime." He couldn't fathom why anyone would shoot at them.

She asked, "The man from the stagecoach. The sheriff said he had family here. Do they live nearby?"

"Yes, but—" He paused.

"Would they want revenge because of what happened?"

With all the hoopla surrounding the wedding, he'd forgotten about the death of Jeb Bailey. His older brother, Dun, was hot tempered, mean, and no doubt angry over the death. That she'd asked the question showed she hadn't forgotten.

Anna asked, "Is someone going to shoot us again?"

He looked her in the eyes. "No." There was nothing linking Dun to the incident, but Colt planned to put the word out that whoever was responsible might want to think twice before opening fire on his family again because he would hunt them down. He asked his daughter again, "Are you sure you're okay?"

She nodded and wrapped her arms tightly around his neck. He held her just as tightly. Over her head, his eyes strayed to Regan. "And you?"

"I'm fine." Angry as well, if the fire in her manner was any indication.

Anna wiped at traces of mud on her dress. "I got dirty when Miss Regan was laying on me so I wouldn't get shot."

He glanced down at the stains. "It's okay. You're safe. No one's mad about you being dirty." He placed a kiss on her forehead and turned to his sister. "Spring, thanks for bringing them into town. I'll let Whit know what happened just as soon as he returns." Had Anna been shot—he didn't even want to think about that.

"Papa, can we go to Aunt Minnie's house and get my things?"

Glad to have something else to think about he replied, "Yes. Spring, can I impose on you a few minutes more before we go home?"

She nodded. Colt set his daughter on the seat next to Regan and they got under way.

When they reached Minnie's, he dismounted. "Anna, how about you sit with Regan and Spring. I'll be right back." Colt hoped this would go smoothly but doubted it would.

In response to his knocking, Minnie opened the door and studied him with hostile eyes. "You come to drop Anna off so you can rut the day away with your new wife?"

He didn't flinch. "No, I came for Anna's clothing.

There'll be no need for her to stay with you overnight from now on."

Her surprise was plain. "Why not?"

"As I told you the other day, she'll be in Regan's
care now."

"That child is my blood. You can't cut me out of
her life."

"That's not my intent but she won't be staying
with you. And, Minnie, if you insist upon telling
her she caused Adele's death, you'll never see her
again."

"I told her the truth. She killed my Adele!"

He snapped, "You don't say that to a six-year-old
child." He lowered his voice. "Better yet. Just keep
whatever she has here. I'll replace them. Good-
bye." He stepped off the porch and started back to
his horse.

"Don't you walk away from me! This isn't finished!"

Seething, he stopped and turned. "Yes, it is. I
thank you for helping me with Anna these past
years. Out of respect for Adele and your age, I will
continue to see to your welfare. Nothing more."

Mounting, he told Spring, "Let's go."

Chapter Seven

$\mathcal{O}$n the ride home, Regan took in the granite set of her husband's face as he rode next to the wagon and wanted to applaud him for giving Minnie the dressing-down she'd deserved. That the woman continued to blame Anna for her mother's death left Regan furious. Seeing Anna physically shrink in response to hearing the harsh accusation further increased Regan's anger. If Minnie was never allowed to see the child again it would be too soon.

Anna asked, "Is Aunt Minnie mad at me?"

Spring answered, "Aunt Minnie's mad at everyone, honey. Don't let it bother you."

"But we didn't get my clothes."

Regan said, "We'll get you new clothes."

Anna didn't appear convinced but remained silent.

Regan saw Colt scanning the corridor of tall pines they were driving through and she began doing the same. It was a perfect spot for an ambush. Reaching down, she picked up her Winchester and placed it across her lap. The Colt in her gun belt was good for shooting varmints up close, but the rifle would be better if they needed to deal with a long-range threat.

Anna viewed the rifle. "Is someone going to shoot us again?"

"No," Regan said. "I just don't want my rifle to jump out of the wagon if we hit a big bump."

It was a lie of course, but between being shot at and Minnie's venomous tongue, Anna had endured enough for one day.

When they reached the house, Colton questioned her about where she and Anna were standing when they were fired upon. She walked him over to the spot. His face serious, he looked around. "What direction did the shots come from?"

"West."

"Just one shooter?"

She nodded. "I'm pretty sure."

"You said there were only two shots?"

"Yes. I have the shell I found." And she pulled it from her pocket and handed it over.

He studied the flattened copper shell. "Looks like a Springfield cartridge."

Regan could identify a cartridge from her '76 Winchester but was unfamiliar with the Springfield.

He put the cartridge in his shirt pocket. "Thanks again for protecting Anna. I'm glad neither of you were hurt. Whit and I will find whoever was responsible. I promise."

Holding him to that, she followed him inside.

Later as they sat down to dinner, Regan was disappointed to see Colt place a large bowl of the same bland stew in the center of the table. It must have shown on her face because he asked, "What's wrong?"

She lied, "Nothing."

"You raved over the stew the other evening."

She met his eyes. "I was being polite."

He ladled some into Anna's bowl and Regan asked, "Do you eat this often?"

"Most nights."

It wasn't the answer she wanted to hear.

"We have fish, chicken, and duck every now and then, but usually it's Ben's venison stew. He cooks it. We eat it."

Regan debated whether starving to death would be better than eating the flavorless dish for the rest of her life. "Do you cook?"

"Other than oatmeal and bacon and eggs, no."

She sighed audibly.

Across the table, he asked, "You said you're a good cook, so I assume you think you can do better."

She almost responded with, "Goats could do better," but instead, replied, "I believe so. My aunt is one of the best cooks in the Arizona Territory. I've been in her kitchen since I was ten."

Anna asked in a hopeful tone, "Can you make cake, Miss Regan?"

"Yes, I can. Would you like one?"

"Yes!"

"Putting it at the top of my baking list."

"Thank you."

Regan asked Colton, "Is the general store in town well-stocked?"

"Since I don't know what you'll need, you'll have to see for yourself."

"May I go into town with you tomorrow?"

He paused and studied her. Finally, he replied, "Sure."

She wondered about the hesitation but didn't ask. She still wondered why she'd awakened alone this morning, but didn't ask that either. "Is there anything that gives you hives or you can't abide eating?" she asked him.

He shook his head.

"What about you, Anna? Is there anything that makes you itch or you don't like to eat?"

"Lima beans."

"Do they make you itch?"

"No. Aunt Minnie eats them every day, so I have to, too, when I'm there."

Regan said, "No lima beans then."

"Good!" she whispered.

Regan was pleased that Anna seemed to be shedding a bit of her shell. A few days ago, she spent most of the time staring at her shoes when Regan spoke to her, but Regan knew she wouldn't turn into a carefree happy child overnight, if ever.

Anna asked, "Do I have to go to school tomorrow?"

"Yes, ma'am," her father said. "You missed yesterday and today."

She looked over at Regan, who replied, "Your education is very important. I agree with your papa."

Disappointment settled over her features but neither adult changed their stance.

At the end of the meal, Regan announced, "Anna and I will clean up."

Anna's puzzled face matched her voice. "But I don't know how."

"Quite all right. We'll have your papa show us where everything goes and I'll teach you."

"Is Papa going to help, too?"

The way he froze made Regan smile inwardly. "No, not today. Maybe another time." He met her eyes and she thought she saw relief. He'd admitted having limited cooking skills, so she wondered if he'd ever washed a dish or cleared a table. "Can you show me where the boiler is and how to heat it?"

His puzzled response made her wonder if tending to boilers was something else he didn't think a woman capable of handling, so she explained, "We had boilers back home. I just need you to show me how yours works. If you're away and I need hot water to do wash or so Anna can bathe, I shouldn't have to wait until you return."

The explanation apparently settled the matter because he walked her outside and showed her what she needed to do. She had a few questions as to how long it took the water to heat and where the wood for it was stored. Once she was satisfied with her ability to master the task, she thanked him.

"You ever going to stop surprising me?" he asked.

"I hope not."

For a moment, he studied her silently. "Beautiful women aren't supposed to be as intelligent as you seem to be."

"And handsome doctors aren't supposed to be as plumb dumb about women as you seem to be."

He smiled at that.

In the silence that followed Regan felt desire rise to fill the space between them and she swore she saw it in his eyes, too. "I worried when I awakened alone this morning. Was there an emergency you needed to attend to, or was I so forward last night that you couldn't bear to be with me in the light of day?"

"No. I just . . ." For a moment, he looked away as if drawn by something only he could see.

"So, I was?"

He shook his head. "No, I was surprised by how forward I was."

Regan wasn't sure what to make of that. "I didn't think you were, at all."

"I'm a doctor of medicine. Keeping my head in a situation is what I'm trained to do but last night, I was . . ."

"Scandalous?" she offered.

The look he cut her almost made her laugh. She schooled her features instead. "Did you not enjoy last night—Doctor?" It was the tiniest of digs but she couldn't resist.

"Enjoying yourself?"

"I am, almost as much as I enjoyed last night."

"Anna's inside. You shouldn't keep her waiting." He walked away.

Watching him go, she sighed. For the second time since meeting him, she wanted to yell, "Coward!"

After she and Anna finished in the kitchen, Regan went to her room to try and bring order to the chaos. Colt and Anna were in Anna's room doing whatever it was they did while Anna prepared for bed. Regan hadn't been asked to join them. Telling herself she didn't feel left out, she cleared the bed of the garments covering it and saw the bare ticking of the mattress. They'd slept on it last night after stripping the sheets. She needed replacements but had no idea where to find them.

"Anna wants to say good night."

His voice drew her to where he stood in the doorway.

"Okay."

She watched him scan the crowded room then shake his head tersely, before silently making his exit. Feeling sheepish about the mess, she followed him out.

Anna, in her nightclothes, lay in bed. Regan walked over and said gently, "Good night, princess. Sweet dreams."

"Thank you for not letting me get shot."

Regan caressed her brow. "Thank you for being the bravest girl in the Territory."

Anna smiled. "Will you really make me a cake?"

"Yes, I will. As soon as I can."

"I never had my own cake before."

Having grown up in a household where cake was as common as the sun rising, Regan found the admission so surprising she turned Colt's way. His face was expressionless. "Then we'll have to make sure it's an extra special cake," she said to Anna.

Her father said, "Time to sleep, Anna."

She snuggled down under the thin quilt. "Good night, Papa. Good night, Miss Regan."

They responded and left her alone to her dreams.

He closed the door and Regan said, "I'm enjoying your daughter."

"I think the feeling is mutual."

Regan was pleased. "Where might I find clean bedding?"

His perplexed response made her explain, "We slept on the ticking last night."

She thought that would evoke some kind of response but again, his face told her nothing. "I have some in the chest in my room."

He opened the door and she followed him inside for her first look at his domain. It was larger than hers but not by much. A big four-poster bed made of dark wood anchored the space. There was also a wardrobe, chest of drawers, and a nightstand made of similar wood. Dark burgundy drapes trimmed in black covered the windows. Unlike her own cluttered quarters, the place was neat and clean. He opened a chest at the foot of the bed, removed a stack of folded bedding, and handed it to her.

"Thank you." She added, "Spring said to ask you

about using your mother's room because I need more space for all my things."

"The windows and walls need repairing."

"May I see it?"

"I can't afford the repairs."

"Understood, but may I see it?"

He sighed. "This way."

He led her down a short hallway to a door that opened to another short hallway. She got the impression that this section was an addition to the original structure. At the end of the hall stood a door. He turned the knob and stepped aside so she could enter first. It was dark but a few fingers of light streamed in through the wood-covered spaces she assumed to be windows. The dimness made it difficult to judge the true size of the space. It was also a good distance from the lone washroom. "Maybe this won't work. It isn't close to the washroom."

"It has its own."

Surprised by that, she tried to make out where it might be. "May I remove the wood over a window so I might see better?"

"Hold on."

He left her and returned with a crowbar, a hammer, and a lamp. Handing her the lamp, he used its brightness to make his way across the room. It took him a few minutes to work the wood free but once it was done, the fading evening light streamed in and she looked around. The space was much larger than she'd first imagined. There was an old bed and other furnishings, all covered with a thick coating of dust. "The washroom?"

He walked to a door and opened it. Carrying the lamp, Regan looked inside and smiled at the sight of the claw-foot tub, but not the thick mat of spiderwebs blanketing the tub's interior. A few spiders skittered away from the light. "Are the pipes still connected to the boiler?"

"Yes."

That sealed things. She loved baths but there wasn't a tub in the shared washroom she'd been using. If she could have her own tub, she didn't care how much it might cost her to restore the room. "I've seen enough. Thank you for letting me see it."

She waited while he nailed up the window again, and followed him out.

"As I said, I don't have the funds to fix it up for you."

"But I do," she said gently.

He stopped.

"Is there anyone in town who can do the work?" She wasn't sure how this conversation might play out. He seemed to be a very prideful man. "My aunt and uncle built their hotel from nothing and we all pitched in. I may not know how to do many of the repairs but I can plaster, paint, sand floors."

"And the windows?" he asked.

"Was there glass in them originally?"

"Yes."

"Can we make arrangements to have a glazier replace them?"

"You're serious."

"I am. My sister and I have a substantial amount of wealth in our names, thanks to the generosity of my aunt and uncle. I can pay for whatever is needed."

"And if I say no?"

"I'd ask why?" she replied honestly. When he didn't respond, she assumed he didn't have an answer, or at least not one he was willing to share.

"Let's go outside so we don't disturb Anna."

They walked out to the back porch and once there, she decided the magnificent view of the mountains would always be the calm she'd seek out whenever obstacles challenged her new life. In their own way, they reminded her of home and she turned her mind away from the small pangs she continued to feel from being so far away from her loving family. "Stays light longer here than it does in Arizona."

"Because we're so far north."

"Ah."

"So, do you really have the funds you'd need?"

"I do. I'd also like to use some to spoil Anna a bit. With your approval of course."

"In what way?"

"Fix up her room so it looks like it belongs to a little girl. New bed and bedding. Maybe paint her walls so they're sunnier. Get her some dolls, take her shopping, and buy her new clothes that will make her smile."

"Where'd she get the dress she wore to the wedding yesterday?"

"From Spring. Your sister said she saw it in a shop a few months ago and purchased it. She didn't know if Anna would ever get to wear it, but you should've seen the way Anna's eyes lit up when Spring took it out of the paper and told your daughter it was hers."

"She looked mighty fine in it. I'll have to thank Spring. So, all the clothes and things you want to buy means you want to raise her the way you were raised?"

"No. She'll be raised the way her father and I want her raised, which I hope includes horses, being unafraid of getting dirty—fishing, books, chores, and whatever else she needs to help her grow into her own woman." She looked his way. "What do you think?"

"I have no problems with that plan. I just want her to be happy and not so afraid of making mistakes all the time."

"I want her to be happy, too." She thought back on last night and compared that scandalous, almost playful man with the starchy distant doctor at her side. "And what makes you happy, if you don't mind me asking?"

"Order and peace."

"I'm not well-known for that."

"I'm finding that out." His face was serious but there was something else in the gaze holding hers; a yearning almost. "I've been trying to get you out of my mind all day."

"Hasn't worked?"

He shook his head and said, "No, it hasn't."

"I'm sorry."

"No, you aren't."

She was amused by that. "You're right, I'm not. Every woman wants to be memorable, especially to her husband." *Love match or not.*

"You are that."

"Is that so terrible?"

"I'm still trying to decide," he replied quietly. In his eyes were embers of last night's passion. Waiting to see what he'd do next, she forced herself to stand still. He didn't disappoint. He gently traced her mouth and she rippled in sweet response. Her lips parted and he kissed her slowly. Easing her closer, the kiss deepened. His lips traveled to her ear. "I shouldn't be wanting you this much . . ."

But she was glad he did. That wanting connected them, burning away the control he seemed to value so highly. Kisses that began slow turned feverish. As if last night had not been enough their hands explored each other lazily. He undid her buttons with a heart-stopping slowness and punctuated each newly bared inch of skin with alternating kisses and tiny flicks of his tongue. His mouth on the hollow of her throat and the strong hands that pulled open her corset sent her spinning.

Colt wanted to slowly devour her; her with her perfect breasts and satin skin. Feeding lustily, he found her as sweet in his mouth as before. Her soft gasps of pleasure fed his senses like the lure of a siren and when he undid her denims, slid them down, and turned her to the now rising moon, the gasps rose higher. He took her breasts in his hands and brushed his lips up and down the edges of her trembling throat. "Feel what you do to me, Mrs. Lee." And he pressed the hard proof of desire against the yielding softness of her bared hips. She responded with a series of slow sultry circles that closed his eyes. Savoring the feel of her moving over him so erotically, he undid the front of his own denims. Now, flesh to flesh, her heat against his made him growl and wonder if a man could die of pleasure.

Regan had never done this this way before but it didn't matter. Her body knew what to do and it glorified in its power. Reaching back, she caressed his length. He sucked in a breath, freed himself from her hold, and entered her with one powerful thrust. She cried out in passionate response, and gripped the porch railing in front of her. At first, he teased her with strokes of varying depths, thrilling her when he filled her completely and making her body silently beg for more when he slowly and partially withdrew. Because of the sultry foreplay, she was already teetering on the verge of completion and when he increased his pace, she sensed he was on the edge, too. The next series of thrusts sent an orgasm rushing through her like the powerful waves of a sea and she clapped her hand over her mouth to keep her screams from waking Anna and the countryside. He came a few strokes later, muffling his roar into her shoulder and she relished having caused his surrender.

In the aftermath, as she righted her clothing, she wasn't sure what to do or to say. He seemed equally unsure, then said softly, "I'll see you in the morning."

"Good night," she whispered and left him to the night.

After her departure, a brooding Colton stared out into the darkness and was again left wanting more of Regan Carmichael Lee. She was everything a man could want in a woman: fearless, intelligent, sensual, beautiful, and his plans to keep her at arm's length were not working out very well at all.

Chapter Eight

The following morning, Regan awakened alone in her bed, and smiled at the memory of last night. A knock on the door made her sit up and cover her nudity with the sheet. "Come in."

Colt stood in the doorway and she sent him a smile. It wasn't returned. "There's oatmeal for breakfast. Anna needs to be dropped off at school before we head to town. If you still wish to go."

"I do."

From his distant manner, one would never know they'd done what they had under the stars on the porch last night. She knew he was fighting his desire for her and determined to throw up a wall between them after each intimate encounter, but not why. Was he still grieving for Adele? Did he consider their encounters so unseemly he was shamed by them in the light of day? Regan had no answers. Keeping her irritation from her face, she said, "I'll join you shortly."

He left without a further word.

Tight-lipped she left the bed to wash up and get dressed.

After Anna was dropped off, he headed the wagon towards town. Determined not to let him know how hurt and disappointed she was by his manner, she concentrated on visual landmarks along the route to help her remember her way into town. She spied a tall pine with a split top that looked as if it had been hit by lightning, and committed it and the lay of the land surrounding it to her memory. Farther ahead was a fast-running stream with an outcropping of rock on its left bank. An elk with an enormous rack was drinking there and glanced up to watch them roll by. A short while later, they passed a run-down abandoned cabin. She wanted to ask him about its history, but he'd been so silent, she kept the questions to herself.

When they reached town, he parked in front of his office. "I have patients to see this afternoon, so when you're done at the store, I'll drive you home then take care of them."

"Thank you."

"I'll come around and help you down."

"Not necessary." She got down without assistance. As she set out for the store, she felt his eyes on her back, but she didn't slow.

The store's interior was larger than she'd expected. There were dry goods, farming implements, and a penny candy display. She saw threads, yarn, a Singer sewing machine, and a stand holding local newspapers and back East published magazines like *The Ladies Home Journal*. There was a handful of customers milling about and they greeted her with nods and smiles. Many faces were familiar from the wedding. She didn't remember their names but hoped to be able to do so soon.

The owner, Chauncey Miller, was behind the counter. She'd met him at the wedding, too. He was of average height, had blue eyes like his wife, Lacy, and wore thick, black-framed spectacles. Unlike his wife, he'd been a bit standoffish, but Regan assumed it was his nature and hadn't taken it personally. "Good morning, Mr. Miller."

"Mrs. Lee. How are you?"

His eyes widened for a second at her gun belt. "I'm well."

"What can I help you with?"

"I need a bit of everything, I'm thinking."

"Doc has a tab."

"I'll be paying for the items myself."

He raised an eyebrow.

Seeing that, she paused, asking, "I am allowed, aren't I?"

"Well, most of the wives here use their husband's accounts. I'll need Doc to say it's okay."

That a store owner would balk at taking her money wasn't something she'd expected to encounter. "You're pulling my leg."

"No."

By then every ear in the place was listening; some discreetly while others made no bones about eavesdropping overtly.

She tried again. "Mr. Miller, maybe you're not understanding me. I'm going to pay for my purchases with my money. Mine."

"I understand you, but I need to make sure Doc knows what you're doing so you and he won't be butting heads over what you're spending."

She wanted to throw up her hands. "So, shall I bring you a note with his signature?" she asked icily.

He offered her a tight yellow-toothed smile. "Have him stop by when he gets the chance."

"But I'd like to shop now, Mr. Miller."

"I understand that, but I need to talk to the doc first."

Were Regan a cursing woman the air would've been hot with brimstone. Instead she turned on her heel, left the store, and angrily marched down the walk to her husband's office.

*W*hen she stormed through the door, Colt and the sheriff paused in their discussion about yesterday's shooting.

"What's wrong?" Colt asked.

"I apparently need your permission to use my own money to purchase items from Mr. Miller's store."

Whit smiled but the hot glare she threw him quelled it immediately.

"Did Colton tell you Anna and I were shot at yesterday?" she asked him pointedly.

"Yes, ma'am."

"I assume you're going to start an investigation today?"

"Yes, ma'am."

"Good."

Colt wondered if the rest of the women in her family exhibited the same fire. He thought about last night and turned his mind to calmer waters. "What's Chauncey want from me?"

"For you to stop by at your convenience. He doesn't want us butting heads over you not knowing how much I spend."

Colt asked gently, "Would it help if I told you that most women here don't have their own money, and so rely on their husbands?"

She didn't reply, so he assumed it didn't help.

Colt was certain Paradise's male business owners had never met a woman with her own money, let alone one as wealthy as Regan claimed to be. And knowing her the way he did, Colt was pretty sure she was going to have the place in an uproar before long. To head off the current one, he got to his feet. "I'll talk to Chauncey and be right back."

"Thank you."

Whit moved to the door as well and said to her, "I'm going to ride up and talk to Dun Bailey. I know he's going to say he had nothing to do with yesterday's shooting, but I want him to know he's in my sights."

Her thanks was brisk.

The two men stepped outside and an amused Colt asked, "Scared to be alone with her?"

"After the look she gave me? You bet. And, she's wearing a gun belt. We both know how good a shot she is."

"When are you going to see Dun?"

"Later this afternoon. I need to finish my report on the stagecoach shooting and send it to the company and Circuit Judge Jinks."

"Mind if I go with you?" Colt wanted to be there when he questioned Dun just to gauge his responses.

"No, you're welcome. Will you be here or at home?"

"Home."

"I'll stop by before heading out."

"Thanks."

Whit left to go finish his reports. Colt set out for the store.

When he entered, everyone inside stilled, making him wonder how many of them heard Chauncey's conversation with Regan. By the interest in their faces, he assumed most.

"Doc," Chauncey said by way of greeting. "Your little lady tell you what she and I talked about? She didn't look happy when she left, but I didn't want her running up a bill you couldn't pay."

Although Miller was smiling, Colt knew he was deliberately being offensive. Colt was a small-town country doctor. Many of his patients didn't have the money to pay for his services, so in exchange, he might receive eggs or vegetables, a side of venison or in some cases just a teary thank-you. It was a wonder he could clothe and feed his child at all on the little bit of money he made, but he managed. Chauncey, on the other hand, owned the only general store in the area, which meant he was financially well-off by Paradise standards, and he enjoyed flaunting the status his business provided. The only reason he didn't get punched in the face daily by any number of people was because his wife, Lacy, was so well-loved. "Can we talk in your office?" Colt asked.

"Sure thing."

Once they were behind closed doors, Chauncey smiled and asked, "So, how do you want to handle this? I know being a doctor here doesn't pay well, and as I said earlier, I'm simply trying to look out for you."

"My wife is able to back up anything she purchases."

"Are you sure?"

"Yes."

"Got yourself a rich one, have you?" He gave him a knowing grin. "She going to pay your tab, too?"

"No, I'll keep paying you monthly, the way I always have."

"Oh." He sounded and appeared confused.

"Do you need anything else from me?"

"No." He was apparently still stuck on why Regan wouldn't be paying Colt's bills, too. "Has she been to the bank to talk to Arnold?" Miller asked.

Colt moved to the door and opened it. "No, but I'm sure she will at some point." And Colt wanted to be a fly on the wall when that happened. Arnold Cale was also the town's mayor and his sense of importance topped even Miller's.

As he walked back out to the store, everyone stopped as if waiting for him to divulge the details of his talk with the store owner, but Colt simply nodded good-bye and went on his way.

When he entered his office, Regan asked, "Will the man take my money now?"

"Yes."

"Thank you. I should probably talk to whoever runs the bank, too."

"Yes." He studied her in her snug denims and man's shirt and thought about the lush willing body hidden within. "I don't mean to be rude or nosy, but how much money are we talking here."

Her reply almost made him keel over.

"That's just an estimate," she said. "Portia and I own a portion of the hotel of course, but we also own stock in mining, railroads, shipping, and land here in America, Mexico, and Europe. Aunt Eddy, Portia, and I grew up terribly poor. Uncle Rhine wanted to make sure we'd never go without ever again."

Colt found that admirable. That she had access to more money than he'd have in five lifetimes gave him pause.

"Is my being an heiress something else I should have revealed in my letters?"

"Not necessarily. A less honest man may have married you just for that."

"I know. It concerned me."

Any man she married would gain access to her funds, with or without her consent. It made him think back on his insistence that Anna marry. What type of man might she choose? She wouldn't inherit much of anything from him as her father, but married she'd have no more rights than she had as a child. Would her husband have her best interests at heart? Colt had never thought about her future in quite this way before. His unconventional new wife was making him view the world through a new set of eyes. "Are you going back to the store?"

"I'd prefer not to but since he's the only choice, I suppose I must."

"He can be a pain in the rear."

"How long have he and Lacy been married?"

"Since I was young. Her father founded the place. Chauncey came in as his clerk from back East and her father married her off."

"So, it wasn't a love match?"

He shook his head. "To be truthful, she's never liked him very much."

And as if speaking about her caused her to appear, Lacy stepped through the door. "Regan, I heard what happened with Chauncey. I told him he could have handled it better, but of course, he disagrees. Do you still want to shop at the store?"

"I do."

"Then come, and while you do, I'll tell you about your invitation to the next meeting of the Paradise Ladies Society. The members all want to meet you."

"I'm honored."

Colt didn't show a reaction. He knew some of the ladies to be as sanctimonious and judgmental as Minnie, who was also a member.

"Doc, I'll return your lovely wife to you as soon as we're done at the store."

He nodded.

Regan said, "Thanks for your help, Colton."

"You're welcome."

He watched them depart and wondered what the Paradise Ladies Society would think of his gun-toting heiress wife. More than likely they'd never met anyone quite like her either.

*W*ith Lacy's help, Regan shopped for spices, cake pans, flour, cornmeal, and sugar. She purchased lemons and oranges, coffee and tea, along with frying pans, roasters, and furniture polish. Spying a display of scented soaps, she picked out a lavender bar for herself and one of lilac for Anna. She knew Colt might consider it an inappropriate indulgence for a six-year-old, but after living with Minnie, Regan thought Anna deserved to be indulged. With Anna in mind, she added hair ribbons, paints, two pairs of little boys' denims, boots, and shirts to the growing pile of items on the counter. Chauncey Miller viewed it all skeptically and Regan ignored him. Paging through a catalog, she found a new stove to replace the ancient one at the Lee home and had Lacy order it along with a new icebox.

"It may take a week or so for them to arrive, Regan," Lacy pointed out, writing down the order numbers. "It has to be shipped from Cheyenne."

"That's quite all right. I can wait." She couldn't really but had no choice.

"And since this is their top model, they'll send some men to install it and take away the old one."

Regan noticed the other customers watching her shop. The more items she picked out, the more curious they became. Some even casually stepped up to the counter to get an up close look. Word must have gone out because the store became increasingly crowded as more and more people arrived. Some gave the pretense of browsing while others flat-out stared.

A man called out to her, "Doc know you're spending him into the poorhouse, Mrs. Doc?"

Regan offered a pasted-on smile and added a Bloomingdale Brothers catalog to the pile of goods on the counter and stacked on the floor beside it.

Chauncey Miller announced loudly, "According to the good doctor, she's spending her own money."

A buzz went up and Lacy snapped, "Chauncey, hush."

"Just telling the truth. Isn't that right, Mrs. Doc?"

Someone else called out with a laugh, "Careful Chauncey before she shoots you like she shot the doc."

Laughter.

Regan steamed. She wanted to ask the people if they didn't have someplace else to be, but kept the question to herself. It was a small town and amusements were hard to come by.

She finished her shopping and Miller totaled up what she owed. He called out the sum so that everyone could hear and Regan agreed with her husband's take on the store owner—he was a pain in the rear. As everyone watched and waited to see if she could pay the large sum, a thick silence settled over the scene. She reached down into her boot and calmly withdrew her money pouch. When she slapped three double eagles on the counter, the crowd cheered. She smiled at Miller. His crestfallen face told all. It was his business to sell goods, had he really looked forward to crowing about her not having enough funds? Regan wondered how he'd react were she to tell him she could've paid ten times the amount.

A glance Lacy's way showed her terse face. "You'd think he'd be pleased to have a customer spend so much, but he's never been a smart man."

He glared at her.

She ignored him, except to say, "Get her things crated up, Chauncey, so she can take them home."

She and Regan stepped outside to wait for her purchases and Regan asked about the invitation from the Paradise Ladies group. "We usually meet Friday evenings at the home of Glenda Cale. Her husband owns the bank."

"How many women are in the club?"

"Seven, sometimes eight."

"Is Spring a member?"

"No."

"Why not?"

"They think she has questionable morals."

Regan didn't care for that. "I see. Was Dr. Lee's late wife a member?"

"Yes. In fact, Adele was our secretary. Her aunt's a member, too."

Armed with this new information, Regan wanted to decline the invitation, but being the doctor's wife made some activities mandatory and this sounded like one she couldn't wiggle out of easily. She'd belonged to a women's group back home and had enjoyed it immensely. If she found the Paradise club not to her liking, she'd concoct plausible excuses to miss as many meetings as she could.

*W*hile his wife was possibly buying everything Miller's General Store had to offer, Colt left his office and walked down to the telegraph office run by Odell Waters. It was the gathering place for the old men of Paradise. Many of whom, now in their sixth and seventh decades of life, shared a past tied to hunting, fishing, prospecting, mining, and gossiping. He was hoping mill owner and carpenter Porter James would be there so Colt could ask him about heading up the work needed for Regan's new bedroom. Like Colt, Porter was a man of color, one of the few in the area. Colt also wondered if Odell had any news on his grandfather Ben.

The men in the office greeted him warmly and

as always there was a checkers game going on. Odell was playing Porter. Colt told them why he'd come and Odell shared news about Ben.

"I was up at his cabin yesterday," he said, eyeing his next move on the checkerboard. "He's still mad that you didn't listen to him about marrying Miss Regan, but then Ben thinks everything that comes out of his mouth is gold." He moved his black piece and waited while Porter studied the board.

"I can do the work on the room, if you like, Doc," Porter said. "Know a glazier, too."

He kinged one of his pieces and Odell blew out a breath of frustration. "I hate playing with you."

"I would, too, if I lost to me as many times as you have."

Porter proceeded to make short work of the increasingly glum Odell and when the game was over, Odell gave up his seat to the next challenger, stagecoach driver Moss Denby.

Odell walked over to the telegraph equipment and said to Colt, "Your wife's telegraph finally went out last night. A reply came back about an hour ago." He handed the folded message to Colt who placed it in his shirt pocket.

"I'll make sure she gets it."

Moss looked up from the checkerboard and asked Colt, "Did somebody really take a shot at her and your daughter?"

"Yes," Colt replied tersely. "Whit and I are riding up to the Bailey place later. We don't know if Dun's involved but we'll see."

The outlaws who'd been with Dun's now deceased brother, Jeb, were still in the sheriff's jail and would remain there until the circuit judge arrived. Rumor had it that some of the stagecoach bigwigs would be on hand for the proceedings.

Denby said, "Little lady saved my life. I don't want anything happening to her. Tell Whit if he needs help finding who did it, I'm his man."

A few others threw in their support, too. She'd won many hearts at the wedding with her horseshoe skills and open smile.

"I'll let him know."

Colt left them to their checkers. Passing the general store, he heard a loud cheer go up inside. Knowing his wife and her penchant for chaos, he figured she was probably involved. Shaking his head with amusement, he kept walking. He'd find out what it meant soon enough.

What he found out was that she purchased enough to nearly fill his wagon's bed. "All this?" he asked as he made room for yet another crate handed up to him by Wayne Meachem, one of the store's clerks.

"I didn't buy anything we didn't need," she said, coming to her own defense.

For a man who'd spent his life pinching pennies, he was overwhelmed. There was also a crowd watching the loading. He wanted to tell them to scat but knew they wouldn't. His rifle-shooting, horseshoe-slinging bride would be the topic of discussion at dinner tables all over the county. One of the onlookers called out, "She bought you a new stove, too, Doc. Lacy has to order it though."

His eyes shot to Regan. She met it without flinching. Filled with disbelief, he set the last crate down and they both climbed to the wagon seat. He glanced over. "Is that it? No cows or horses or railroad cars?"

She snorted. "Not today."

"Then I can drive home?"

"Yes, please."

Their eyes held. She still wore a trace of a smile and she sparkled like sunbeams on a stream. In spite of his inner battle, he was becoming ensnared by her exuberant charm and wasn't sure what to do about it. Turning away, he set the team in motion. Applause from the crowd rang out, and like a queen, she waved good-bye to her royal subjects. Amused, he didn't know what to make of that either.

After clearing town, he reached into his pocket. "Odell said this telegraph came for you."

She opened it and read it. When he looked over, her teary eyes set off concern. "What's wrong?"

She wiped her eyes. "Just so happy to hear from my family. I miss them dearly."

"Are they well?"

"Yes. Aunt Eddy wants to know if I need anything."

"Is there anything left for you to buy?"

"As a matter of fact, yes. Miller didn't have chilies, so I'll let her know to send some."

"Chilies?" he asked warily.

"For tortillas. I need black beans, too. Miller just had regular dried beans. I grew up eating the food of Mexico and I miss that, too."

Colt wondered if he'd ever learn all her facets. Having spent most of his life in the Territory, he had no idea what went into the food of Mexico. How were black beans different, he wondered.

"When is the sheriff going to speak to Bailey? Did he say?"

"This afternoon. I'm going with him."

She went quiet for a few moments, then looked his way and asked, "Have you ever killed anyone?"

He studied her seriously set features. "No. There have a been few times I thought my skills should've saved a life but I've never taken one."

"I'd never taken one either before the stagecoach shooting."

"Is it bothering you?"

She nodded. "Taking someone's life isn't a trivial thing."

"No, it isn't. Shows you have feelings."

"I suppose. I had no choice in the matter though, and I feel terrible that it might be the cause of someone wanting to hurt Anna."

"They'll be found."

"I hope so. No little girl should have to experience that." She quieted for a few more moments and then asked, "Could the shots have been a warning for you, instead? Do you have enemies here?"

"Not that I know of, but anything is possible." He hadn't thought about viewing the shooting from that angle. He was again impressed by how intelligent she was. "I'll think on that."

"Please do."

*T*rue to his word, Whit came by the house a few hours later and he and Colt rode out. Their destination was an hour's ride from Paradise. Dun and his dead outlaw brother, Jeb, were sons of Ethan Bailey, a man rumored to have fled to the Territory ahead of a murder charge down in Missouri. The wide, unexplored expanses of America's untamed West were perfect hiding places for those not wanting to be found, and if they kept their heads down, they could live out their lives in relative peace and anonymity. Ethan Bailey had eschewed both, however. He'd been involved in everything from claim jumping and horse theft to drunken barroom brawls. It was the brawling that eventually did him in. Three years ago, he'd been gut shot in a Casper saloon. By the time Jeb and Dun brought him to Colt, it was too late.

The Bailey place was as disreputable as the family's reputation. The small, poorly constructed timber cabin had a listing tar paper roof held down by boulders. Waist-high grasses surrounded it, making it appear abandoned. Colt and Whit reined their mounts to a walk and took the well-worn path cut through the vegetation to the weathered broken-down porch. Two thin mangy dogs tied to the porch angrily announced their arrival. Dun stepped out, rifle in hand. "What the hell you want?" Dressed in dirty, well-worn clothes, and rip cord-thin as his dogs, he was tall, bearded, and had eyes that spat venom. How he supported himself other than doing the occasional odd job for those who'd allow him near their homes or property, Colt didn't know.

"Looking for information on who fired on Colt's wife and daughter," Whit replied.

The feral eyes swung to Colt who met them steadily.

"Know nothing about it. But seeing as how you said she killed my brother, I'd call that justice."

"Only cowards shoot at children," Colt returned coldly. "You know any, Dun?"

"You accusing me?"

"You a coward?"

Whit interrupted. "Where were you yesterday around eleven?"

"Here. Ask my dogs."

His smug smile tightened Colt's jaw.

"Cartridges came from a Springfield," Whit said.

"Dozens of Springfields around here. You can't prove it was mine."

"No, we can't," Colt said. "But spread the word that whoever did it should leave the Territory if they want to keep living."

"You threatening me?"

"If you were the coward who shot at my wife and child, yes."

"Get off my land."

"Gladly."

Colt and the sheriff complied.

Once they cleared the grass and were back out on the road, Whit said, "You can't make threats like that, Colt."

"Talk to me when someone takes shots at your family."

"Point taken."

"Regan wondered if the person might be an enemy?"

Whit looked over. "Do you have any though?"

"Not that I know of."

"Jeb and Dun were pretty mad when you couldn't save Ethan."

"They were, but he was all but dead by the time they brought him to me." He remembered the pain in Jeb's voice as he'd screamed at him to save his pa's life, but the damage had been too extensive, not to mention the blood loss he'd suffered on the long trek from Casper back to Paradise. "Because of Jeb's death, until proven otherwise, I still say it was Dun shooting at Regan and Anna."

"We'll see."

When he returned home, Regan gave him a look of inquiry as she set the table for dinner, but he didn't want to discuss the visit to Dun with Anna about. "How about we talk after Anna goes to bed?"

"That's fine."

"Did you get everything from the store put away?"

"I did."

Anna entered and her attire grabbed his attention. Dressed in a pair of denims and a blue cotton shirt, she resembled a miniature version of Regan. Seeing her, Regan smiled and asked, "Are the denims stiff?"

She nodded. "They make my legs feel heavy."

"They'll soften up after they're washed a few times. If they're uncomfortable you don't have to wear them."

"But I want to."

Colt thought his daughter would wear a saddle if it was somehow tied to Regan. Her desire to emulate her new mother pleased him. The further she took herself out of Minnie's sphere the happier she'd be.

After Anna went to bed, he and Regan went out to the back porch to discuss the visit to Dun Bailey.

"He denied being involved." He went on to describe the encounter and finished by saying, "I know it was him."

"But there has to be proof."

"We'll find it."

She nodded and continued to hold his gaze as if waiting for him to say more. And he had more but no idea how to express it. He remembered how irritated and disappointed she'd been that morning when he hadn't returned her smile. After what they'd shared last night, greeting her kindly had been warranted, but he hadn't. He'd never been one to express his feelings, and even though what he felt for her seemed to be growing and expanding, he was more comfortable remaining the man he'd always been. It was a poor excuse, which left him no happier with himself than she apparently was. She was changing him and he wasn't sure where to stand. "I've some journals to look over."

She replied softly, "Enjoy your reading."

Chapter Nine

*I*n the days that followed, Colt's quiet well-ordered life was obliterated by the comings and goings of Porter James and his crew of carpenters with their accompanying racket of sawing and hammering as they worked on his mother's old bedroom. True to her word, Regan pitched in to help by sanding the floors, applying plaster, and offering to assist with anything else Porter needed doing. The old carpenter was skeptical at first but was soon impressed by her skills, and Colt was glad he wasn't the only one dazzled by all that she was. She even got Anna involved. He came home late one afternoon to find his denim-clad daughter on her knees in the washroom applying a new coat of white paint to the claw feet of the now sparkling clean tub. "Anna?" he said, voice filled with surprise.

She looked up and smiled. "Miss Regan is letting me help."

"I see." There were spots of paint on her nose and left cheek. "Are you having fun?"

"I am. She said we're going to make my room pretty next." She paused and asked hopefully, "Is that all right?"

"Of course. I can't wait to see it."

Another smile lit up her small face.

"Where's Miss Regan?"

"She's outside cutting screens to put on the windows until the glass comes."

"Ah. How was school?"

"Wallace Denby tripped me when I walked by his desk."

Wallace was Moss Denby's seven-year-old grandson and a known terror. "Did you fall and hurt yourself?"

She shook her head.

"Did you tell Mr. Adams?" Adams was the teacher.

"I did. He said he's going to tell Wallace's mama if it happens again."

"Good." Denby's daughter-in-law, Dovie, was the boy's mother and the town's seamstress. Last spring her husband, also named Wallace, abandoned her and their son to take up with a young woman he met in Casper. Dovie had been devastated. "Are you sure you didn't get hurt?"

"I am."

"Okay. I'm going to go see Miss Regan."

She nodded and went back to work.

Just as Anna said, Regan was on the back porch using a pair of tin snips on a large roll of window screening. She looked up as he stepped out of the door.

"Welcome home," she said.

It was difficult to explain how coming home to her made him feel but it warmed the places gone cold since Adele's passing. "I see you put Anna to work."

"I did. I thought I'd find little things for her to help with after school. She'll graduate to tools next."

He didn't know if she was pulling his leg or not. "She asked if it was okay if her room is made pretty next."

"And you replied?"

"I couldn't wait to see it."

She nodded approvingly. With her hands protected by gloves she concentrated on cutting through the wire.

"Do you need help?"

"No, this is the last one, but you can nail them up for me if you'd like."

"I can do that. When's the glass arriving?"

"Mr. James said a few more days. The glazier is in Laramie. He'll send it by wagon. I just hope none of it breaks on the way."

"I saw Lacy in town. She said to remind you that the ladies' meeting is this evening."

She made a face. "I was hoping to fall off a ladder or something so I wouldn't have to go."

He hid his amusement. "Why?"

"They probably won't like me. Lacy said Minnie's a member, and that your sister isn't because of her questionable morals. I like Spring."

He understood their reasoning. The Spring of old had been an embarrassment to her family and to herself. "Maybe it won't be as bad as you imagine."

An eye roll was her reply.

He asked, "How are you getting to town?"

"Colleen Enright was at the school when I picked up Anna. She's a member, too, and offered me a ride. Our first meeting didn't go well, but I took it as her offering an olive branch and agreed."

"That's a good way of looking at it, I suppose." He hoped Colleen would keep her snottiness to herself.

"Did Lacy say anything about my stove?" she asked.

He shook his head.

"It would be nice if it arrived soon. I'm tired of wrestling with this one. I did a pot roast and potatoes for dinner but it took lots of prayer. We can eat whenever you're ready."

Even though she and the old stove fought daily, Colt had to admit her food was outstanding. Ben's stew couldn't hold a candle to what she'd been feeding him and Anna.

"Oh, and this is going to be the last day the carpenters are here until Mr. James returns from Cheyenne. His sister's ill and he's going to go see about her. I'm disappointed he can't finish, but his family is more important."

After dinner, Regan changed into a skirt and blouse ahead of the meeting. When Colleen arrived, Regan gave Anna and Colt her good-byes and walked out to Colleen's wagon.

Colleen looked at the rifle Regan carried. "Why on earth do you need that?"

"In case someone tries to take a shot at me again." She wondered about Spring's claim that Colleen was in love with Colton, and if he was aware.

"I heard about that. Probably someone shooting at something else. Not you."

Refusing to argue, she climbed up and placed the Winchester within easy reach by her feet. "I'm ready now."

Colleen drove off. "At least you aren't wearing those horrid denims. We wouldn't want the mayor's wife to have to turn you away. She's very influential here, you know."

Regan supposed she'd been wrong about the olive branch and should've thrown herself off a ladder. "I know how to dress appropriately." Back home, their hotel regularly hosted wealthy Americans and European royalty but she didn't tell that to Colleen. She said instead, "Tell me about the other ladies in the group."

"There's the mayor's wife, Glenda. She's from Boston. Her family was at Plymouth Rock. Her husband also owns the bank." She glanced over to see if she'd impressed Regan. She hadn't.

"And the others?" Regan asked.

Colleen rattled off unkind descriptions of some of the other women, making Regan wonder how someone living in a territorial backwater could consider herself so superior. Regan decided to form her own opinions after meeting everyone.

"I hear you bought up half of Miller's store," Colleen said.

"Almost."

"That's very unconscionable of you. Dr. Lee doesn't have that kind of money."

"Then it's a good thing I do."

She stared. "Your family's wealthy?"

"Where I was raised, it's considered very gauche to quiz someone about their financial state."

Colleen startled at her brusque reply. Regan guessed no one ever put her in her place. Regan didn't plan on being one of them.

After that, Colleen had no more questions, gauche or otherwise, so Regan turned her attention to the beauty of the mountains.

The Cales lived in one of the large homes Regan had seen on her first day in Paradise. With its turrets and gingerbread trim, it seemed to look down on its more modest neighbors. She hoped it wasn't indicative of the owners.

Glenda Cale with her red hair and green eyes was lovely. She met Regan warmly and took her hands. "Welcome to my home."

Regan estimated them to be about the same age. "Thank you for the invitation."

"So sorry I missed your wedding. My husband and I were in Denver on business. Come in. The ladies are all here."

Colleen spoke up, "I thought I'd offer her a ride with me."

Glenda's bright smile faded to one that appeared

pasted on. "Thank you, Colleen. What a good neighbor you are."

That exchange gave Regan the impression that Glenda was not as impressed with the Widow Enright as the widow was with her.

Introductions were made, and Regan was glad she hadn't taken Colleen's views of the other women as gospel. Colleen had derided seamstress Dovie Denby, and talked rudely about the tall statuesque woman as being so unattractive she'd lost her husband to a younger woman. However, the blond-haired Dovie smiled upon making Regan's acquaintance. "I apologize for my son's behavior at school today. Mr. Adams said he tripped your Anna."

"He did."

"If it happens again, he'll be sitting on a pillow for two weeks. His grandfather wasn't happy hearing what happened either. Welcome to Paradise, Regan."

"Thank you." Regan eyed Dovie's simple white blouse and dark skirt and wondered if she'd done the work herself because the quality of material and the fit on the blonde's six-foot-plus frame was outstanding.

Lacy Miller gave her a grin. "Glad you could join us, Regan."

Seated in one of the chairs, Minnie glared. Nonetheless, Regan acknowledged her. "Good evening, Minnie."

Minnie curled her lip and looked away.

Glenda's eyes flashed angrily at the ill-mannered response but the introductions moved on.

Next, came Lucretia Watson, who was middle-aged, plump, and the wife of a local rancher. Colleen had described her as empty-headed. "Pleased to meet you, Regan," she said smiling. "I'm learning to pitch horseshoes because of you."

"Maybe we can have a ladies' tournament."

Regan saw the horror on Colleen's face in response to the idea, but ignored her.

Lucretia added, "Your Anna and my granddaughter, Olivia, are good friends. The two of you are welcome to visit anytime. I also sell eggs, hens, butter, and cream if you need them."

"Best in the county," Lacy added.

"Thanks for the invitation and I'm looking forward to being a customer."

Glenda then introduced Maud Adams, mother of Anna's teacher and owner of the town's largest boardinghouse. She greeted Regan with an icy nod. Glenda didn't appear pleased by that reaction either. Regan remembered Minnie saying there was no other place in town for a woman of color to rent a room and wondered if race was the reason for Maud's response. Shrugging it off as best she could, Regan took a seat on the red velvet sofa beside seamstress Dovie, and waited to see what the group was about.

Over finger sandwiches and tea, she learned that they engaged in charity work but not regularly. "People are proud here," Glenda said as way of explanation. "They don't like admitting they need assistance."

Maud, who was knitting, added, "It's not our business to butt into people's lives." And she stared straight at Regan. Did the woman regard her as having butted into the lives of the Lee family? She also noted Colleen Enright nodding as if agreeing with Maud's statement.

Lacy weighed in, "Colleen needed help after her husband's death, especially that first winter. She and Felicity might not have survived had she turned her back on her neighbor's charity. Now that she's taking in laundry she's needing less help."

Colleen beeted up and shot fury Lacy's way, as if in spite of agreeing with Maud, she didn't want her plight discussed. The veiled mischief twinkling in Lacy's smile suggested she'd used the example purposefully.

Glenda brought the conversation back. "Regan, were you affiliated with a club back home?"

"I was and we raised funds to purchase readers and supplies for our local school, contributed clothing to the Apaches on the reservation at San Carlos, and supported suffrage by attending rallies and distributing information."

Lacy and a few others appeared impressed. Glenda asked, "How many were in the group?"

"We were small like you are."

"Was it a mixed-race group?" Maud asked with what sounded like disdain.

Regan shook her head. "No. We were all Colored women."

Lacy said, "I'd like for Paradise to have a lending library."

Regan replied, "Is there money to build one?"

"No."

"That might be a project to begin raising funds for."

The women seemed to think that over.

Regan added, "Our group held bake sales, we sold cakes and pies at some of the local fairs, and held raffles."

Glenda said, "When I was a young girl, my mother's group held some of those same activities. I think we might want to discuss this subject further at future meetings. Having a lending library would help Paradise become more progressive."

The others appeared to agree, but Regan noted the knitting Maud's tight lips mirrored Minnie's and guessed they weren't as enthused.

"Do any of the other cities have a library?" Regan asked.

"Laramie County has had one on and off but they can't manage to stay open. At one point, they had to mortgage the books in order to pay their bills."

They went on to discuss other ways they might help their community, like getting the town council to pay Mr. Adams a salary that enabled him to teach more than three days a week. As it stood, parents helped with his pay, provided money for readers and supplies, and even the coal and wood needed to keep the children warm during the winter months. It was a lively discussion and Regan decided attending the meeting had been better than throwing herself off a ladder after all. "So, are women really allowed to vote here?"

Lacy said, "Oh yes. We can vote, sit on juries, and a few have even been appointed justices of the peace."

Dovie added, "We also have the right to own and hold title to land."

"Colored women, too?" Regan asked.

Lacy replied, "Yes. Colt's mother, Isabelle, voted in Territorial elections until she passed away. Adele and Minnie voted as well."

Regan was pleased to hear that but with Jim Crow spreading across the country there was no guarantee the right would continue to be honored.

When it came time to leave, a short stocky man wearing a too tight brown suit and vest entered the sitting room and marched over to Regan as if he were President Grover Cleveland himself. "I'm Arnold Cale, the mayor and owner of the bank. Welcome to Paradise, Mrs. Lee."

A bit caught off guard, she replied, "Pleased to meet you." He appeared to be much older than his young wife. Glenda's face was unreadable.

His beady little eyes took her in. "I hear you have quite a nest egg. You should let my bank manage it. After all, we men know more about finances than you little ladies do."

Regan overlooked the insult and replied calmly, "Thank you for that kind offer, but one of my uncles is an owner of the Bank of California. He helps advise me."

He startled. "The Bank of California?"

She saw him trying to puzzle out how a Colored woman like herself could possibly be related to someone tied to the Bank of California.

"I see," he said finally. "Maybe he could give me some advice." But as if not believing her claim, he asked with a challenging tone, "What's his name?"

"Mr. Andrew Fontaine. I was raised by his brother, Rhine Fontaine, and my Aunt Eddy. At one time, my Uncle Rhine owned much of Virginia City, Nevada."

His eyes bugged out so far she thought they might jump from his face. "Are you familiar with either of them?" she asked innocently.

"Uh, no. I'm afraid not."

He continued to look her up and down as if she were a talking icebox.

She stuck out her hand the way she'd been taught by her Uncle Rhine. "Again, thank you for the offer. A pleasure meeting you, Mr. Cale."

He stared down at her hand. Shaking it, he offered her another bewildered look and hastily left the room.

Glenda sidled up to her and whispered, "Bravo."

Their eyes met, and Regan thought she'd just gained a new friend.

On the drive home, Colleen kept eyeing her with the same bewilderment banker Cale had shown but kept any questions she may have had to herself. While the silent Colleen drove, Regan thought about her husband. He seemed pleased with the way she and Anna were getting along and Regan was as well.

She still had no answers to why he retreated behind a wall each time they were intimate. There was no question as to whether he desired her; she saw it in his eyes. She just wished he'd admit it so they could openly enjoy that aspect of being married.

Realizing she'd arrived home, Regan picked up her rifle. "Thanks for driving me."

"You're welcome," she said curtly.

Regan walked to the door and Colleen rolled away.

The house's interior was quiet when she entered. She poked her head in Colton's study and found him seated at his desk. He looked up from the journal he was reading. "Is Colleen still alive?"

"Barely. She's incredibly rude."

"I know."

"Anna in bed?"

"Yes. Did you really tell her you're going to buy her a set of tools?"

"I did. Is that a problem?"

He shook his head and smiled.

"I like when you do that," she said.

"What?"

"Smile. I don't think you did it very much before I burst into your life."

"*Burst* is a good word."

She left the doorway and crossed to the desk. "What are you reading?"

"*New England Journal of Medicine.* Article on rabies. Dr. Pasteur has created a vaccine."

"Sounds scintillating." Regan thought him scintillating as well and the heat simmering in his dark eyes sparked her desire. "Shall I close the door?"

"Might be a good idea."

As she returned, he pushed his chair back from the desk to make space for her to stand in front of him. He reached out and slid a finger down her cheek. "Doctors don't like being interrupted in their offices."

"I didn't know that. Do I owe you a boon?"

"Maybe." Bold as day he slowly raised her skirt, eased her drawers down her thighs, and had her step out. He set them aside. "You won't be needing these."

Her knees turned to water.

"Doctors do prefer patients who follow orders," he said in a hushed voice. "So, unbutton your blouse for me, please."

Holding his glittering eyes, she complied, fingers shaking a bit. When the last one was freed, he gave her a kiss that stirred her already awakened senses and left her shimmering. He pulled back and traced an unhurried, featherlight fingertip over the crowns of her breasts above her corset, then down the line of tiny hooks.

"Your corset next, Mrs. Lee."

She released the hooks one by one, exposing the thin white shift beneath, and set the corset on the desk. He slowly circled each berried bud before leaning in to greet them, and the warmth of his mouth made her croon and arch back against the edge of the desk.

"You're a very good patient, Mrs. Lee. Now, lift your skirt so I can give you a reward . . ."

She complied and he stroked her heat until she moaned and widened her stance for more. His touch was hot, sure. Her senses sang. When he withdrew, she groaned in protest.

"You'll get more, soon. Promise."

Colton couldn't believe this gorgeous sensual woman was his to seduce and enjoy. He continued to fight the urge to surrender to his growing attraction, but once again, he couldn't deny himself the faceted Regan Carmichael Lee. He wanted her in all ways a man could want a woman. He kissed her again and savored the mouth he swore had been made for him alone. As the kiss ignited his passion he wondered about the man she'd given her virginity to. Had she screamed his name too, had she let him take her in the moonlight? But as his hands began to lazily map and explore, the questions retreated, buried beneath a fierce rising need that held him in thrall. His hunger grew in response to her passion-lidded eyes, so he undid his trousers and husked out invitingly, "Come, sit."

Regan never knew a woman could straddle a seated man. As she slowly lowered herself, every hard inch of him radiated heat that spread like liquid flame, and the glory closed her eyes.

"Do you like this?"

"Oh yes." Guided by his hands, she rode slowly. She wondered if she'd be damned for wanting to spend the rest of her days doing nothing but this, with him. The position let her set the pace, and she enjoyed the way he watched her and the hard slide of him in her flesh. He moved her shift over her breasts, languidly teasing her nipples until they pleaded. When he bit each gently, she arched, crooning. His touch, so delicious, their joined bodies moving in tandem so decadent, desire blurred both time and place. Her greedy rise and fall became her world.

Colt knew he'd take the memory of this to the grave. She was so tight, her silken hips in his hands so enticing, he wanted to spill himself there and then, but he didn't want this to end. Ever. The tastes and feel of her, the scented hollow of her throat, the way she met his strokes, all fed a brewing storm that played havoc with his desire to take her slowly. But she was too hot, too sweet, and the leisurely pace he wanted to maintain failed. Her moans became more vocal, his grip roughened lustily. Needing more room than the chair allowed, he stood. She wrapped her legs tightly around his waist, held his shoulders for balance, and he growled with each deep stroke. Watching her feed on the pleasure sent his desire soaring and when she exploded, calling his name, his own completion flung him to the stars with a roar.

Regan came back to herself, breathing harshly and cradled against his sweat-dampened shirt. He fell back into the chair, still holding her close. "Did I hurt your shoulder?" she asked.

He gently tipped her chin up, raising her eyes to his. "No."

In the silence, they studied each other and there

was a softness in his gaze she hadn't seen before. He placed a kiss on her brow. She snuggled deeper into his hold wondering if lust might pave a path to something deeper. Her sated body didn't care, but her heart, yearning for love, continued to hope.

"I owe you an apology for the way I've acted after the last few times we've done this. I've not been very gentlemanly."

The confession was unexpected and she studied him. "I accept the apology, but may I ask the reasons for your actions?" She'd asked about it before and hoped he'd explain this time.

"Because I can't seem to control myself around you."

"That isn't a bad thing, is it?"

"It is when you're accustomed to handling situations dispassionately. A doctor isn't supposed to allow himself to run amok."

She found his honesty endearing. "Not even with his wife?"

"Not even with his wife, or at least that's what I believed."

"And now?"

He paused as if thinking about the best way to phrase his response. "I'm beginning to believe differently. You're very special, Regan. Even a man as plumb dumb as I've proven myself to be at times knows that. Who would've thought my Anna would be excited about owning tools, or want to learn to pitch horseshoes? Or that I'd want to lay you down on this desk to hear you scream my name again?"

"You do know that underneath all that doctorly reserve you're a very scandalous man."

"So I'm learning."

Silence rose for another moment and he broke it by asking quietly, "Can we make a pact to forget about the shooting and my being plumb dumb, and see where this marriage of ours leads? Just because we don't have a love match doesn't mean we can't enjoy being man and wife."

That he seemed determined to keep his heart at bay was again disappointing to hear, but she kept it from her face. "I'd like that," she replied lightly. "And whenever you wish to lay me on your desk, just let me know."

"I will." He chuckled, then added solemnly, "Thank you for your kindness to my Anna."

She whispered, "You're welcome." She let herself be held for a few moments longer, wishing their times together meant more to him, then said, "I'm going to let you go back to your journals. I'll tempt you into running amok again soon."

He dropped his head and smiled. "How am I supposed to get my work done?"

She shrugged. "I've no idea. Good night, Colton."

"Good night, Regan."

Later, lying in bed, she thought back on their sensual encounter and smiled. She enjoyed making him run amok. Being with him was so different from the few times she'd had relations with Levi Spalding, the soldier she'd given her innocence to. They were both novices and, looking back, their couplings had been short fumbling attempts when compared to the powerful passion she'd experienced with Dr. Lee. Her thoughts drifted to the pact he'd asked for. He hadn't detailed how they'd accomplish this new understanding. Would it come about through their daily interactions? And what about the softness she'd seen in his gaze? Did it mean his view of her was changing without him being aware of it? She had no answers but supposed in the end, time would tell. She'd just have to be patient. Snuggling down as best she could in Adele's aging bed, she closed her eyes and drifted off to sleep.

Chapter Ten

*T*he next morning, Colt entered the kitchen just as Regan pulled a pan of biscuits from the oven with a mitt-protected hand.

"Good morning, Regan," he said easily. "Did you sleep well?"

She placed the pan on the small counter and removed the mitt. "I did. And you?"

He nodded.

For a moment, they drank in the sight of each other and all she could think about was how wanton she'd felt having her legs wrapped around his waist.

As if reading her mind, he warned, "There will be no running amok today."

She faked a pout. "Spoilsport."

Eyes glowing with amusement, he poured himself a cup of coffee. Regan placed the biscuits in a bowl and decided she enjoyed starting her day with his smile instead of the distance he'd employed in the past.

Anna entered. Her attire of denims, shirt, and boots again mimicked Regan's. "Good morning, Papa. Good morning, Miss Regan."

Both adults greeted her in turn.

"Can you take the plates to the table, sweetheart?" Regan asked.

She nodded eagerly and exited with the three stacked plates.

"How about I take the eggs?" Colt asked, gesturing to a bowl on the counter.

"If you would, please. I'll bring the rest."

He complied and Regan followed him out.

As they ate their breakfast, Anna said, "I like the way you cook, Miss Regan."

"Thank you, Anna. Maybe when the new stove arrives, I can show you how to make biscuits. Would you like that?"

"Yes, ma'am."

Regan saw approval in Colt's eyes. "Do you have any fishing poles?" she asked him.

"I do."

"Where's the best place to fish?"

"The river that cuts through Odell's land."

Since it was Saturday and she had nothing planned, she asked Anna, "Shall we go fishing today?"

The little girl responded by looking to her father, who replied, "It's your decision."

She turned back to Regan. "I don't know how to go fishing."

"That's quite all right. I'll teach you." Regan watched Colt butter another biscuit and shook off the memory of his hands doing other things last night, and asked, "Will Mr. Odell mind?"

"No. Just about everyone fishes there. I'll get the poles out of the barn for you."

"Would you care to join us?"

She wanted him to come along but didn't know his plans for the day. She thought this might be a nice way to begin their pact.

"I'd like that."

His reply pleased her and the smile on Anna's face indicated her pleasure as well.

With Colt driving the wagon they set out. In the bed were poles, a basket holding food, jugs for water, and kindling in case they wanted to eat some of the catch for the midday meal. All in all, Regan was looking forward to spending the day with her new family. She also had questions about the beauty of the land. Spring wildflowers covered the countryside in a riot of colors. The ever-present mountains with their snowy caps dominated the view.

"Do these mountains have a name?" she asked.

"Yes. They're called the Bighorns. The Cheyenne, Crow, and Sioux considered them sacred."

"Are the tribes still nearby?"

"Yes, but on reservations. Cheyenne and Sioux were the last to be brought in."

The tribes in Arizona were no longer free either and she doubted they ever would be again. "When I left Arizona, the army was hunting Geronimo. I don't know if he's been recaptured."

"Read about him leaving the reservation in the newspaper here, but so far nothing's been said about him being found."

"A member of his tribe worked on Mr. Blanchard's ranch. His name was Tana. He was very kind to me and my sister, Portia. In fact, he taught us how to jump fences with our horses."

"You didn't fall off and break your neck?" Anna asked from her spot on the seat between them.

"No, sweetie. I didn't."

"Livy has a pony, but Aunt Minnie said I couldn't have one because I'd fall off and break my neck."

Regan looked to Colt and saw him give an exasperated shake of his head. "Your father and I could teach you to ride."

"I'm scared I'll fall off."

"There's nothing wrong with being afraid to try new things. How about we talk about it again sometime soon. I enjoy riding and I think you will, too."

"Okay," she said softly.

Regan wondered how many other fears she and Colt would have to banish before Anna could enjoy her childhood.

They arrived at Odell's place a short while later. His log and stone cabin sat in a clearing backed by pine forest. At their approach, he stepped out onto the porch. Standing with him was Ben Lee. Regan drew in a calming breath and hoped Ben would be more welcoming than he'd been during their initial meeting. "Did you know he was here?" she asked Colt.

"No."

Anna turned to her father. "Do you think Granpa Ben would like to come fishing with us?"

"You can ask him."

She gave a confident nod.

Regan hoped he wouldn't disappoint the girl, but didn't want his grumpiness casting a pall over their fun either.

The deerskin-wearing Odell, with his snow-white shoulder-length hair and whiskers, walked out to meet them. "Morning. You come to take the old bear off my hands?"

Colt smiled. "No. Came to fish."

He eyed their party. "Anna, you're going fishing?"

"Yes, sir."

"Can I come along?"

"Yes, sir."

"Can I bring the old bear?"

"Yes."

"Okay. We'll meet you on the bank."

Colt got the horses moving and Regan did her best to ignore the disapproval in Ben's eyes.

They were unloading the wagon when the two men joined them. She greeted Ben with a nod, but he ignored her. Odell watched the exchange and glared at his friend but didn't intervene. With everything unloaded, Regan scanned the rushing crystal clear water. It brought back memories of the rivers and canyons she and her sister swam in back home. "Mr. Odell, can you swim here?"

"Only if you want to drown. Current's pretty swift."

"Oh," she said with disappointment.

"You swim?"

"Yes."

He smiled. "The more I talk to you, the more I like you. Right, Ben?"

He grumbled.

Odell said, "He's not going to agree because it'll prove he's wrong as always."

Ben groused. "We come here to fish or listen to you jabber?"

"Both," Odell said proudly.

The two shared an easiness that made Regan wonder how long they'd been friends. Determined to show Ben she wanted to know him better, she asked, "How long have you and Mr. Odell been friends, Mr. Lee?"

"Why do you care?" he asked coldly.

Regan drew back as if slapped. "My apology."

Determined not to show her hurt, she pasted on a smile just as Colt snapped, "He's the one who should be apologizing."

Ben rolled his eyes dismissively and asked again, "We fishing, or not?"

Anna looked between the two warring men and cried unhappily, "Granpa, please don't be mean to Miss Regan. If you make her go away she won't be my mama anymore." There were tears in her eyes.

Regan's heart broke. She knelt and spoke to her as gently as she could. "It's okay, honey. Nothing he can do will make me go away. I promise. Come, let's go dig for worms."

"Worms!"

Regan nodded. Ignoring Ben and the sting to her spirit, she nodded thanks to her husband and led Anna down to the bank.

Colt watched them go and once they were out of earshot, he asked Ben, "Happy?"

His grandfather didn't respond.

"Anna adores Regan, and I'll not have my daughter living in fear that her new mama will leave because of you. If you don't think you can respect Regan as my wife and as Anna's mother, you shouldn't come back to the house."

Ben showed his surprise. "You don't mean that."

"If I'm forced to choose between Anna's feelings and yours, hers will win every time."

Watching the exchange, Odell advised sagely, "Change your ways, old man, before you wind up alone. You've already lost Spring; don't lose Colt and Anna, too. I'm going to join the worm hunt. You coming, Colt?"

"Yes. Think about what I said, Ben."

They left him alone.

Colt and Odell found Regan on her knees using a small trowel to dig into the bank. Anna was watching warily.

"I found one, Anna!" Regan cried, and held up a large brown earthworm. "Do you want to hold it?"

"No!" she said, shrinking back.

Regan placed the worm in one of the small baskets and held it out. "Come see. I won't make you touch it, but it's fun to watch them wiggling around."

Colt could tell by his daughter's skeptical expression that this wasn't what she deemed fun. "How about you and I look together?" he asked her.

She gave a quick nod. He took her hand and walked her closer. Anna peered in and eyed the worm silently. It was twisting and turning as it tried to burrow to freedom.

"The fish like them," Colt explained.

"Do the fish eat them?" she asked.

He nodded.

"So, we eat worms when we eat fish?"

Regan replied, "I suppose we do, but we'll cut that part out so you don't have to eat the worm."

The girl looked relieved but no more convinced. While they watched, Regan did more digging and soon there was a small pile of the wrigglers in the bottom of the basket. "I think that might be enough to get us started."

"I think so, too," Colt said. He was again amazed by her pluck. Her knees and hands were covered with mud. He thought back on how hurt she'd appeared in response to Ben, and his anger churned to life once more. Since first meeting her, she'd radiated nothing but confidence, but Ben's strike had left her shaken. Outwardly, she seemed to have recovered but Colt never wanted to see her hurt that way again. "Do you want a pole, Anna?" he asked.

She quickly shook her head. "Can I just watch this time?"

"Sure." He didn't press. She was only six years old. She had plenty of time to get comfortable with new activities like this one.

So, with Anna looking on, Colt, Regan, and Odell baited their hooks, cast their lines into the fast-moving river, and waited for a bite.

It took only a few minutes for Odell to pull up a large bass. "Look at that, Anna!" he crowed. "It's almost as big as you." He tossed it into the basket, baited his hook again, and threw his line back into the water.

Colt followed by catching a fat trout. Anna clapped, and when he and Odell caught three more, she clapped even harder.

Looking over at the still waiting Regan, Colt asked her, "You sure you've fished before?"

"Hush up, doctor man, my worms are just being particular." Her line tugged and she gloated, "See?" and she pulled up an old black wader. Her shocked face gave Anna the giggles. Colt and Odell laughed like loons.

Apparently not minding being the butt of the joke, she worked the boot free and said to Anna, "I think this will make a great dinner, don't you?"

"No," she replied through her laughter.

Odell said, "Probably be real tasty with pepper sauce."

Regan stuck out her tongue, rebaited her hook, and tried again.

Regan finally hooked two medium-sized trout and after that, everyone agreed they'd caught enough.

Odell volunteered to cook. "Anna, you want to help me build a fire and get the fish ready?"

"Do I have to touch worms?"

He grinned. "No. Just bring me the plates and tableware you and your folks brought."

She nodded and hurried over to the items they'd unloaded from the wagon. Colt went with her to carry the kindling needed for the fire.

Colt placed the kindling down near the ring of stones Odell used as a fire pit, and asked, "You want me to start gutting and scaling?"

"No, I want you and the missus to go take a walk and let me and Anna do our jobs." He looked to Anna. "Do you think they should take a walk together?"

The smiling Anna nodded.

Odell said, "Then it's unanimous. Get going, you two. Pretend you like each other's company. Anna will be okay. When you smell the fish cooking it'll be time to come back, not before." He made a shooing motion. "Go."

So, they did.

"Is this his way of playing matchmaker?" Regan asked as they followed the rocky shoreline away from their fishing site.

"I don't know." But the old trapper was definitely up to something and had roped Anna in as a coconspirator.

"Does he have family?"

"His wife died when Spring and I were young, but he had a son and a daughter. They live back East, if I remember correctly." He looked her way and decided spending time alone with his wife wasn't anything to complain about. "How about we find a place to sit?" he asked.

"That's fine."

They walked along in companionable silence and came across a felled tree. Taking a seat, they looked out at the water and the mountains.

"I had fun today, even if I did catch an old boot."

He chuckled at the memory of her astonished face. "Not what you expected?"

"Not at all. Wasn't expecting Ben to bite my head off either."

He sighed. "I'm sorry."

"You can't apologize for someone else's actions, but I appreciate you coming to my defense."

"If it's any consolation, he didn't get along with my mother either."

"What about Adele?"

"He was cool to her, too. He was living at his cabin back then, so we only saw him occasionally."

"I've never had anyone speak to me so rudely."

"I could tell by your reaction. It won't happen again."

"How can you be sure?"

He told her about the ultimatum he'd issued.

"You really told him that?"

He nodded and added sincerely, "I don't want Anna afraid you'll leave her." And he didn't want her to leave either.

"I wouldn't do that."

"Anything is possible, Regan." He sensed she wanted to offer more reassurance, but instead she let the subject drop. "Besides, our pact might fall apart if Ben's allowed to meddle, and I don't want that."

"Neither do I."

Looking into her eyes, memories of last night's encounter rose, bringing back the sight and feel of her riding out her pleasure with her legs around his waist and arching to meet his thrusts. His body stirred with a now familiar desire that refused to be tamed, bridled, or denied. "You have mud on your cheek," he said softly and trailed a finger gently across the spot.

"Anna and I will both need baths tonight. Maybe we'll use the tub in your mother's room since it's restored. Care to join me after? It's big enough for two."

"You're determined to be my personal temptress, aren't you?"

"It's either that or find a job delivering the mail," she whispered.

Unable to resist, Colt brushed his mouth against hers. Sweetness poured into him and he placed an arm low on her back to ease her closer. He kissed her fully, taking a moment to nibble her bottom lip while she ran her hands possessively up his arms and down his back. He dragged her onto his lap and moved his kisses over her jaw and down the silken line of her neck. Her head fell back to offer him more and he felt bewitched. Everything about her called to him like a siren and he could no more resist than he could stop breathing. "Every time you're near I want to touch you."

"I like it when you do."

He undid the top buttons on her red flannel shirt

and kissed the hollow of her throat. "You smell like fish," he chuckled.

"So do you."

He raised his head and savored the smile in her eyes. He traced her lips. "Maybe I will take you up on that bath. I could use one, too."

"Only if you promise to be very scandalous."

Who knew he'd wind up enjoying her company so much? "I'll see what I can do."

The aromatic scent of fish cooking over a fire drifted their way on the breeze.

"I think Odell's ready for us," he said with a hint of regret.

She offered a mock pout. "I was hoping to get a preview of how scandalous you plan to be."

He threw back his head and laughed. "Up, you sassy woman. Let's go eat."

She rose. "I've enjoyed the first day of our pact."

"So have I. Let's plan on more days like this."

"Agreed."

They took a leisurely walk back to the fishing site. Anna, seated on a tarp, looked up from her plate and greeted them with a grin. Odell stood talking to a man in an army uniform. Both men turned their way. The soldier's eyes widened. Colt heard Regan gasp.

The soldier smiled fondly and asked with a laugh, "Regan Carmichael, what on earth are you doing here?"

Chapter Eleven

*R*egan wondered why the Fates were conspiring against her. First, she'd mistakenly shot her intended and now, here stood Levi Spalding, the man she'd given her virginity to.

Odell asked Levi, "You two know each other?"

He nodded. "My unit was stationed near her home in Arizona Territory a couple of years back. How's your family? Your sister?"

Unable to look Colt's way, she fought to keep her tone light. "Everyone's well. Portia recently married."

Odell said, "Levi, meet Colt Lee, he's the doc around here. Colt this is my grandson, Lieutenant Levi Spalding. He and his unit are over in Rock Springs, hoping to keep the miners from going on the warpath about the Chinese strikebreakers. He rode up to see me. He's my daughter's boy."

Colt shook his hand. "Pleased to meet you, Lieutenant. Regan is my wife."

Levi stiffened and his eyes flashed her way before moving back to Colt's. "Congratulations. She's a lovely lady."

Regan hazarded a glance at her husband and wondered if the guilt screaming inside was visible. In truth, she had nothing to be guilty about, but the awkwardness of the situation and his unreadable dark eyes made her feel as if she'd swallowed sand.

Unaware of the intrigue, Odell said, "Come on and grab a plate, you two. Fish is ready."

As they sat eating the fish and potatoes Odell had prepared, Levi asked casually, "So, how long have you and Dr. Lee been married, Regan?"

"Not long." She prayed he'd not bring up what they once meant to each other.

She saw Odell watching her intently before he asked his grandson, "How long have you and Marie been married? Can't remember."

Levi's face went red. "It'll be six years in October."

Six years! She was stunned. During their six-month relationship, he'd claimed to be unattached. Outwardly, she schooled her reaction as best she could. Inside fury burned white-hot. She'd gifted her innocence to a married man!

The meal continued and the men talked about the volatile situation in Rock Springs.

Colt said, "The White miners resent the companies bringing in the Chinese, and they're being targeted more and more."

Odell added, "They hate the Chinese as much as they hated the Indians."

While listening, Regan imagined how she might subject Levi to a slow and painful death. He'd taken advantage of her in ways that made her feel young and foolish. She'd trusted him with her heart and her feelings, only to realize she'd been used. She knew she could be naïve but she'd always prided herself on being a good judge of character. Apparently, she'd been naïve to believe that as well.

She was still brooding when it came time to depart.

Levi said, "It was good seeing you again, Regan."

She lied, "Same here. Give my regards to your wife."

He winced visibly. "I most certainly will when I return home to Virginia."

Colt asked, "How long will your unit be in Rock Springs?"

"Not sure. We'll see how the situation unfolds. Pleasure meeting you, Dr. Lee."

"Good meeting you, too."

The way Odell studied her made Regan wonder if the old trapper had somehow gleaned the truth about her and Levi.

"Sorry Ben's being such a pain in the rear," Odell said. "He went back to his place but he'll come around. Take care of yourself, Regan."

She nodded.

"You too, little Anna. Don't forget to draw me those fish you promised."

"I won't. Tell Granpa I'm sorry I fussed at him."

"I will."

As her husband got the team under way, she noted his distance. She was focused on her own bruised feelings but didn't want it to affect Anna, so she asked her, "Did you have a good time?"

"I did," Anna replied, then turned to her father. "Papa, can I have my own pole so I can fish next time, too?"

"Yes, you can."

"I'm glad Miss Regan asked you to come with us."

"Me too."

Regan looked his way and smiled, but it wasn't returned. She sighed and wondered if he'd somehow figured out her true ties to Levi, too.

When they reached the house, they unloaded the wagon and put everything away.

Regan said to Anna, "Let's get you a bath. How about we use the big tub?"

Her eyes went wide. "Truly?"

"Yes, truly. Go get your bath things."

She ran to her room leaving the adults alone.

Regan looked to Colt. "Is there something we need to discuss?"

"No. I have some reading to catch up on. I'll see you later." And he walked away.

She wanted to yell, "Coward!" Instead she went to help Anna with her bath.

Later, while the sparkling clean Anna drew the fish she'd promised Odell in her bedroom, Regan was in the kitchen preparing a light dinner when she heard the door pull. Drying her hands, she went to the door and found the sheriff waiting on the other side. "Hello, Whit."

"Regan. Is Colt here?"

"He's in his study. Come on in. I'll get him."

She knocked on the door. "The sheriff's here."

"I'll be right there."

He accompanied her back to the parlor and asked Lambert, "Is someone hurt?"

"No. Just got a wire from Judge Jinks. He'll be here Monday to begin Rawl's and Corman's trial." They were the outlaws from the attempted stage-coach robbery.

Regan asked, "Will I be allowed to testify?"

"Not sure, but you should be there just in case."

In many places, Colored people were barred from testifying against those outside the race by laws instituted both before and after the Civil War. She supposed Mr. Denby could be called upon as a witness in her stead, but he'd been driving and hadn't seen much.

Whit added, "Court will be held at nine in the morning."

Colt asked, "Does Dun know?"

"Yes. I just left his place. He said he'll be attending."

Regan decided that even if she wasn't allowed to testify, she'd have an opportunity to see his face.

Whit left shortly thereafter. Colt returned to his office and she went back to the kitchen to finish dinner.

After the meal, she and Anna went outside. They

picked wildflowers, and later stretched out on an old quilt and searched out shapes in the clouds. They saw horses and bears and cats. Their time together helped distract Regan from the lingering hurt of Levi's betrayal and gave her and Anna another way to have fun.

"I like having you for my mama, Miss Regan," Anna said, lying beside her.

"I like having you for my daughter."

"Are you and Papa mad at each other?"

Caught off guard, Regan took in the girl's serious eyes. "Your papa and I just need to talk about some things." Even if she didn't know what the things might be.

"He isn't smiling at you like he was when we were fishing."

"I know. It'll be fixed. Promise."

"I don't want you to go away."

Regan hugged her close and placed a kiss on her forehead. "It's too late to get rid of me now, honey. I'm here to stay." Although she and Anna hadn't been family very long, doing things together, like the dishes and working on the new bedroom, had given them a connection Regan enjoyed. She couldn't imagine not having Anna in her life and looked forward to watching her grow up.

"Can I have a little sister? Livy's mama is giving her one."

Caught off guard again, Regan chuckled softly. "Let me talk to your papa."

"She can share my room once it's pretty."

With the scandalous behavior she and Colt had been indulging in, a child was a likely possibility and she savored the idea of that. "What if it's a little brother?"

Anna seemed to think it over. "I guess that would be okay as long as he's not like Wallace Denby."

Regan laughed. "I agree."

Later, Colt joined her to put Anna to bed. "I asked Miss Regan to give me a baby sister. She said she'd speak to you about it. May I have one, please?"

He looked so stunned, it took all Regan had not to burst into laughter. He finally managed to reply, "Uhm. She and I will discuss it."

"Promise?"

"Promise."

Regan noted he avoided looking her way. He gave his daughter a kiss on the forehead. "Sleep well."

Regan gave her a kiss, too, and after he doused her lamp, the two adults left her to her dreams.

Without a word, he headed back to his study, but Regan decided enough was enough. He'd talk to her whether he wanted to or not. With that in mind, she knocked on the closed study door. Without allowing him the opportunity to turn her away, she walked in.

He looked up, perturbed.

"Our bath?" she asked.

"Tell me about Levi Spalding."

She drew in a calming breath. "He was the man I gave my innocence to."

Jaw hard, he studied her for a silent moment. "And you did all the things we did together—with him?"

"No. Nor did I know until this afternoon that he was married at the time. Either way, I told you about him."

"You did, but putting an actual face to the man— it's different."

"How?"

"It just is."

"You were distant even before you knew what the man meant to me."

He paused.

"I tell you the truth, I find out Levi used me terribly, and you have the gall to have your nose out of joint? Fine. My apologies for being truthful and for disturbing you. Enjoy your journal." She stormed out. She dearly wanted to slam the door but it would've alarmed Anna so she didn't.

Colt blew out a breath. Wondering when he'd lost the upper hand and feeling properly chastised, he felt frustrated, angry, and ashamed. From the moment he'd learned she and the soldier knew each other he'd sensed she was disturbed, but he'd been too busy wallowing in his own jealousy to consider asking why. He hadn't liked the idea of her even knowing the soldier, and now, finding out they'd been intimate made him see red. He didn't want to imagine her with someone else. That the man was not of the race was of no consequence. The simple fact that Spalding had been her first was all Colt cared about and it made him want to find the soldier and punch him in the face. He ran his hands down his own face. Regan Carmichael Lee was making him lose his damn mind. This wasn't a love match, so why was he so upset? By all rights, he owed her an apology. Knowing her the way he did, she'd undoubtedly given Spalding her heart and soul, and to find out today, years later, the man was married had to be devastating. And yet, he, her husband, had placed his injured pride above her feelings. He'd gutted their agreed upon pact in less than twenty-four hours. If she never smiled at him again, it would be too soon. He wanted to make this right, because like Anna, he didn't want her to leave.

Colt rose to his feet. He needed someone's counsel. Remembering Regan's concern the morning he left the house without informing her, he penned a quick note and slipped it beneath her bedroom door. Outside, after saddling his horse, he rode off to see the only person he might be able to talk to about the mess he'd made.

When Spring answered his knock, she asked with concern, "Has something happened? Are Anna and Regan okay?"

He nodded. "They're fine. I need to speak with you." He could tell she was wondering why he'd sought her out at this hour, but she stepped back to let him enter.

"Sit," she said, gesturing to a chair in the parlor. "What brings the illustrious doctor to the door of his disreputable baby sister?"

He blew out a breath and explained.

When he was done, she shook her head. "Poor Regan. She must've been very hurt to find out her trust in that man meant nothing. As for you. She told you the truth. Did you want her to lie to you about who he was?"

"No. I wanted the truth, or thought I did."

"You owe her an apology, Colton."

"I know. But will it be enough?"

She shrugged. "Depends on how low you grovel."

"I don't grovel, Spring."

"You may need to learn."

He looked away. "I'm not one for second-guessing myself. I never had to do that with Adele, but Regan . . ." His words faded into silence. In his mind's eye, he could still see her furious face as she'd swept out of his study.

"They're two different people, Colt. You keep forgetting that. Adele always aimed to please you, no matter what. Regan doesn't impress me as being here solely to make your head larger. She's a woman who walks beside a man, not behind." She paused as if to let the words sink in before continuing, "I'm still trying to understand why you chose to come to me about this?"

"Because you helped me think through whether I wanted to marry her or not, and besides, who else is there for me to talk to? Ben? He was so rude to Regan today, I wanted to take a bullwhip to him. Whit? He's a good friend, but he'd just find the situation amusing. You're it."

"I suppose I should be flattered but you haven't been very brotherly these past few years."

"And why is that, Spring? I tried to help when you were running wild and you told me what?"

"Go to hell," she replied softly.

He nodded. "Yeah, you did."

She looked away. When Ben kicked her out of the house, she'd signed on as a hand with one of the local ranchers and the resulting scandal was still fueling gossip today.

"Spring, I understood why you took up with Mitch. Ben left you no choice, but the rest? The drinking, the carousing. I finally threw up my hands. I had to." He thought about all the years they'd wasted. "I miss you in my life, Spring."

She replied softly, "I miss you, too, brother. I was young and scared and wanted to pay Ben back. I'm sorry for the pain I caused you."

It was the first time they'd talked about those years. "I kept waiting to be told you'd been shot in a brawl or assaulted by some drunken cowhand. I was so afraid I was going to be burying you."

"But I made it," she said softly. "And I'm proud of that, no matter what anyone else thinks."

"Yes, you did."

"But I have to say, I'm enjoying watching you be turned inside out by your new wife."

"Why?"

"It means you're alive again. Feeling again. You've been encased in ice since Adele's passing. I don't think I've ever seen you this befuddled or confused. You're quite taken with Regan."

"I enjoy her company."

"If you want to plant your flag there, fine. But it's more than her company."

"She's done so much for Anna in the short time she's been with us."

"It's also more than Anna."

He mused on that, too, then admitted aloud, "I've never been a jealous man, Spring."

She smiled softly. "I know. Something else adding to my enjoyment. She's got you at sixes and sevens."

He dropped his head into his hands. "This is all so new." He'd spent a lifetime building a well-ordered mind based on logic and discipline; both necessary for a man of the race practicing medicine in a nation where many viewed him as unequal and unqualified. There'd been no place for frivolous emotions like passion and desire. Although he'd loved Adele, he'd not allowed himself to be distracted by such things, and she'd been content with what he had to give. Or had she? That she might not have been was a startling thought.

"What's wrong?" Spring asked.

"Just asking myself if Adele had been as content with me as I assumed she'd been."

"There's no way to tell. And truthfully, you two weren't married long enough for you to know her true feelings."

He pulled his mind away from Adele. He was flailing enough.

Spring said, "Colt, go home. Apologize. Grovel to this woman you only like for her company and see where it leads."

She was right of course. He'd already made a previous apology for erecting a wall after their intimate encounters. He'd just have to do it again and hope it would be enough. He stood. "Thanks for listening. Sorry to disturb you so late."

"That's okay. As I said, I'm enjoying watching you trying not to fall in love with my new sister-in-law."

His eyes flashed to hers.

She chuckled softly. "That is where this is going, whether you want to admit it or not. But you'll figure it out, eventually."

"And here I was just about to ask you to dinner tomorrow."

"May I still come?"

"Yes. I'm sure Regan won't mind. She may not feed me, but she will you." He viewed her silently for a few moments before saying, "Thanks, Spring."

"You're welcome. See you tomorrow."

He gave her a nod and left.

Lying on her bed in the shadowy, predawn silence, Regan's mind slipped back to last night's encounter with Colt. Their agreed upon pact lasted less than a day and she placed the blame squarely on his shoulders. Should she have lied to him about Levi Spalding instead? Some women would have, but as always, she'd let truth be her guide and all she'd gotten in return was frustration.

Last night after her bath, she'd found a note he'd

slipped under her door to let her know he'd left the house and would be returning shortly. An hour or so later she heard his return and his bedroom door close. Although she wondered where he'd gone, she'd been too upset to care. She had no idea which version of himself he'd present this morning at breakfast, and truthfully it didn't matter. She'd never begged for anything in her life and she had no plans to do so to gain his affection. Today would be her turn for distance. She knew it was childish and petty to pay him back in kind, but he'd earned it. And besides, she was still angry.

She revisited their conversation, hearing what she'd said and how he'd responded, and she froze. Was the stodgy, but sometimes scandalous Dr. Colton Lee jealous? Her jaw dropped. She'd been so upset last night she'd failed to consider the reasons behind his attitude. But jealousy didn't make sense. Why be jealous over a woman he didn't love? Wasn't he constantly pointing out that theirs wasn't a love match? Was he starting to care for her in spite of that? She had no answer, but the question was intriguing; not intriguing enough for her to pretend last night's heated conversation hadn't occurred. However, it gave her something to think about as she left the bed to begin her day.

One of the reasons Regan detested the old stove was the oven door. The hinges were rusted and so out of line, the only way to keep it closed was to prop something against it like the small sawhorse being used now. Add to that the small dirty burners and the hour the oven took to reach a reasonable baking temperature. Having to cook on it further soured her already grumbling mood.

"Good morning, Miss Regan. Where's Papa?" Anna asked, entering the kitchen.

"Good morning, Anna. Not sure. Maybe he's being a lazybones this morning." Or maybe he was still sulking.

"May I help you cook?"

Anna's smiling presence warmed Regan like beams of sunshine. "Of course. Do you want to break the eggs into the bowl for me?"

She nodded and dragged the small crate she used to stand on over to the counter. Once on her perch, she very carefully broke each of the dozen eggs into the bowl. "I like helping."

"And I enjoy having your help. It reminds me of when I first began helping my Aunt Eddy. I was a little bit older though."

"How old were you?"

"Ten."

"Did you already know how to cook?"

"Just a few things."

"Did you know how to make cakes?"

Regan chuckled. "No, but Aunt Eddy showed me how."

"I can't wait until I get my cake."

Regan placed fat strips of bacon into the hot cast-iron skillet and peeked in at the biscuits. When she straightened she found Colt watching them from the doorway.

"Good morning," he said.

Anna greeted him with a cherry, "Morning, Papa."

To not upset Anna, Regan forced out a lightly toned, "Good morning," before turning her attention back to Anna. "Let's put some cream in your eggs and some salt and pepper." She watched while Anna slowly poured a bit of cream into the bowl, added the seasonings, and whisked the mixture with a fork. Regan felt his eyes on her.

"Anything I can do?" he asked.

"I think Anna and I have everything under control."

"Okay. I'll go feed the horses and be back."

He left.

She saw Anna watching her intently. The girl didn't say anything but Regan sensed a change in her mood when she resumed whisking the eggs. She knew things weren't right between her parents and Regan wondered if all six-year-olds were so perceptive. Thinking back on her early years with her mother, Corinne, she supposed they were.

"Your papa and I are a bit at odds, Anna, but we'll smooth things out. Promise."

"You won't leave?"

Regan hugged her waist and gave her a kiss. "No, honey. I won't leave. That's a promise, too."

As they ate breakfast, Regan did her best to be pleasant so Anna wouldn't worry. "Did you sleep well?" she asked Colt, passing him the bowl of steaming scrambled eggs.

"I did, and you?"

"I did. I think it was my heavenly bath. Nice warm water. New bar of scented soap. Nothing like a new bar of soap, it suds up so well. I felt so good when I finally stepped out. You should try the tub sometime." It was a dig but an innocent-sounding one.

The way he looked up from his plate made her think the barb hit home. She gave him a sweet smile and turned to Anna. "You enjoyed your bath, too, didn't you?"

"I did. Papa, the soap Miss Regan got me smells like flowers. I never had flower soap before."

"I'm glad you enjoyed it," he said, eyes on Regan.

Regan added, "Mine smells like lavender. Maybe you'll get a chance to smell it sometime."

He coughed.

Pleased, she picked up her coffee cup and took a sip. "Are you okay?"

He wiped his mouth with his napkin. "Yes."

Subtly letting him know what he'd missed last night was a better way of getting his goat than hurling angry thunderbolts, and far more satisfying. She hoped he spent the day imagining her stepping out of the tub nude and wet from the water and what they might have enjoyed had he been there.

He said to her, "I should have asked you first, but I invited Spring to have dinner with us this evening."

"You don't need my permission to have your

sister join us. It will be great to see her. Don't you think so, Anna?"

"Yes. She should come every day."

Amused, Regan replied, "I don't think she'd want to come every day but she's welcome if she does." Regan wondered when he'd issued the invitation and why. Had they patched up their differences? She planned on roasting a chicken for their Sunday meal and adding some vegetables, so she hoped Spring would be content with the simple fare. "Anna, do you know the way to Livy's house? I need to get a hen from her grandmother and some eggs." Colt had been supplying their food needs, but Regan thought it time to take on the responsibility herself. She remembered meeting Lucretia Watson at Glenda Cale's home, and store owner Lacy Miller had touted the items Livy's grandmother sold.

"Yes. She lives near the school."

"I can go for you," Colt replied.

"No, Anna and I will go. I need to begin taking on the household duties and it'll give her a chance to visit with her friend. I'm sure you'd rather be reading your journals."

From his expression, she couldn't tell what he thought of her response. Her plan was to spend time with Anna, so she wasted no time worrying about his take. "Anna, let's get the table cleared and the dishes washed, and we'll go."

Anna hopped up.

Regan left him at the table.

Chapter Twelve

*W*ith her rifle on the floor near her feet, Regan guided the wagon over the rutted road. Having reins in her hands for the first time since leaving Arizona flooded her with memories of home, family, and delivering the mail. The leather reins felt good, and even though the two horses weren't familiar with her, they seemed to sense she knew what she was doing and didn't put up a fuss, strain, or try and turn around and head back to the Lees' barn. Anna was her usual silent self, but Regan could see her studying the clouds. "What do you see up there?"

"There's a lady lying on her side on a sofa."

"Really?"

"And a turtle, an eagle, and a castle. Thanks for teaching me this game."

"You're very welcome. Let me know if you see anything else fun."

"I will." She resumed her watch.

They passed the school shortly thereafter and Anna said, "Keep going and you'll see Livy's road."

The Watson place was about a mile and a half from the school. The house reminded Regan of the Lee place in that it was built of timber and stone but it was much larger. A pack of hounds loped out to meet them, barking excitedly. Anna explained, "They don't bite. The big one's Basil. That's Daisy, Seth, Julia, and Willis."

"Odd names for dogs," Regan said as the pack ran alongside the wagon.

"Livy's granpa named them after Livy's aunts and uncles."

"Oh I see."

When the wagon reached the porch, Lucretia, wearing a worn canvas apron over her skirt and blouse, stepped through the door. With her was her granddaughter, Livy, who Regan had met previously at the school. Livy's grin showed her missing front teeth. "Hi, Anna!"

"Hi, Livy!"

"Hi, Miss Regan," Livy called.

"Hello, Livy. Good morning, Lucretia."

"Morning, Regan. How are you?"

"Good. Wondering if you have a hen or two and some eggs I might buy."

"Yes, on both. Come on, and I'll walk you round back."

Livy asked Anna, "Do you want to see my pony?"

Anna looked up at Regan who said, "Go ahead. I'll find you once Mrs. Watson and I are done."

They climbed down from the wagon. Anna ran off with Livy and Regan walked to the back of the property with Lucretia.

Lucretia said, "Anna is smiling more. Glad to see the change. When she would come with Minnie she wasn't allowed off the wagon. Might get dirty."

Regan sighed.

Lucretia added, "Don't mean to talk out of turn, but I don't like Minnie Gore, nor the way she treated Anna. Doc Lee marrying you is the best thing he could've done for the girl."

Regan wasn't swellheaded enough to agree but did like the small changes she was seeing in her stepdaughter.

"So, you're needing a few hens?"

"And some eggs."

"I have some hens I readied for sale last night."

Lucretia removed the lid of a large copper's barrel. Inside, among large blocks of ice were a dozen or so plucked hens. Regan was glad they weren't strung up individually on a tree branch like stockings on a clothesline. She had no desire to serve her family turned fowl.

Lucretia picked through the offerings and showed Regan two nice plump ones. "I'll take them both."

They then walked to the large henhouse. Regan put a dozen eggs in the basket she'd brought along and cushioned them with the tea towel inside. "I'd like to eventually get a few laying hens."

"I can sell you three or four in a week or two. Rooster too."

Regan was pleased to hear that. Back home, they'd had a large henhouse, so she knew the ins and outs.

"Do you need butter or cream?"

"Both," she said with a smile. Those items were added to her purchases as well, and Regan paid her.

Lucretia pocketed the coins in her apron and on the way back to the front of the house said, "Heard folks talking about the fancy new stove you ordered. Has it come in yet?"

"Not yet, but hopefully any day now. I'm sick of fighting with the old one."

Lucretia added, "I've been thinking about what you said at the meeting. I agree with Glenda about raising money for a lending library. Never learned to read myself but I made sure my children did and Livy does every night. In fact, she's been trying to teach me."

"Good for her and for you."

"I'm wondering if maybe we ladies could raise money during the Paradise Founders Day celebration?"

"When is it?"

"Mid-August."

"Seeing as it's now almost the end of May, we have time to plan. When's our next meeting?"

"Friday after next."

"I think that's a wonderful idea, Lucretia. Let's see what the others have to say."

"And I want to have the ladies' horseshoe tournament, too."

Regan laughed. "Then if the idea is approved, we will add that to our offerings."

Lucretia turned serious. "When I first saw you at the wedding, I thought maybe you'd not fit in here."

Regan stopped and searched her sun-lined face. "Why?"

"Colleen Enright said she'd met you and that you were snooty and put on airs."

Regan's ire rose at Colleen and her gossipy meddling. "And now?"

"I like you. Hoping our girls can visit more regularly, and that Anna can spend the night every now and again."

"That would be wonderful. We'll be redoing Anna's bedroom and once it's finished, I'd love to have Livy spend the night with us, too."

Lucretia nodded. "They're good friends. Race might matter to some folks but not to me and mine."

"Nor to me and mine either." Regan was glad she'd made the trip to see Lucretia. "I hope you and I can become friends, too."

"I'd like that. Not many women around here. Be nice if we could all get along. Looking forward to knowing you better."

"Same here."

"Let's see what our girls are up to."

They found the girls in the barn. Livy was brushing the coat of a snow-white pony while Anna watched from the stall's entrance. Beside her stood a man of average height with salt-and-pepper hair. He eyed their approach and offered Regan a nod of greeting.

Lucretia said, "Regan, this is my husband, Matt. Matt, this is Doc Lee's new wife, Regan."

"Pleased to meet you."

"Same here." Regan didn't remember him being at her wedding.

Lucretia explained why. "Matt was in Cheyenne visiting one of our children the day of the wedding."

He said, "So you're the lady who has my wife wanting to pitch shoes."

"Yes."

"She's getting pretty good at it."

Lucretia beamed in response to the praise.

Matt added, "Livy and I are introducing Anna to Snowbird."

Regan walked closer and ran a hand over the animal's back. "Pretty name for a pretty pony."

Matt said, "She is a beauty, isn't she? Anna doesn't want to get too close, but I told her it's fine to watch from here."

Anna's eyes were riveted on her friend as she worked.

"Snow and I love each other, don't we, girl?" Livy said, giving her pet a hug. "Anna, if you had a pony we could ride together."

Whether Anna found the idea enticing or not was difficult to tell, but she didn't appear afraid and Regan found that encouraging.

After a few more minutes of chatting with Lucretia and her husband, Regan and Anna were accompanied back to the wagon.

Livy said, "I'll see you at school tomorrow, Anna."

"Okay."

Regan offered her thanks to the Watsons and turned the team back the way they'd come.

The clock on the wall of Colt's study showed that Regan and Anna had been gone over two hours and he noted how hollow and empty the house felt. Before Regan came into their lives, he doubted he would have been attuned to it, but now it was noticeable. Her presence gave his home life. There was conversation, not only at the table during meals, but throughout the day. Anna's voice and her laughs and giggles had become almost commonplace. None of that had been normal during Ben's residence.

Thoughts of his grandfather surfaced but he didn't let them linger. His mind was focused on Regan Carmichael Lee. Even a man as plumb dumb as he could be at times was smart enough to know she was still upset about last night. The veiled digs she'd directed his way during breakfast had pierced his hide like darts on a board, and the one about her bath cut deepest. Her talk of the warm water, her scented soap, and how good she'd felt when she left the tub painted a mental picture of her wet and nude that made him shift in his seat to accommodate the rise in his anatomy. That she'd done it deliberately, knowing the effect, made him want to retaliate by pulling her onto his lap and kissing that sassy mouth until she was breathless. To Anna's innocent ears the conversation had been about soap and a bath, but he and Regan knew better. Did he wish he'd handled last night's conversation differently so that she hadn't been hurt? Yes. Had he done so, seeing her in the tub would've been real and not something he had to imagine. He deserved the darts she'd thrown at him, and when she forgave him, he planned to enjoy every lavender-scented inch of her satin skin. But he had to be forgiven first, something he had no control over; forthcoming apology or not.

Hearing heavy footfalls in the house, he rose and found himself face-to-face with his grandfather. "I came to get the rest of my belongings," Ben said gruffly.

"You don't have to leave. Just respect my choices."

"I can't."

"But you don't even know Regan."

"No, I don't, but she's a woman and you can't trust them."

Colt saw anger in the old man's eyes, but there was also a veiled ache that seemed so out of character words failed him. Finally, finding his voice, he said, "How about we sit and you explain what you mean."

They sat and Ben began, "When I first met your grandmother, she was the most beautiful thing I'd ever seen."

Colt froze. Ben had never talked to him about Spring Rain.

"Her tribe lived near the trading post Odell and I built, and every time I saw her, the more I wanted her as my wife. Her parents and the elders were opposed, but I'd traded with them, hunted buffalo and elk with them. They knew me to be respectful of their ways, so she and I became man and wife." Ben quieted then as if thinking back and Colt wondered what he was seeing.

After a few more moments of silence, he continued, "She didn't know English but I knew her language, so we had no problems talking. I built the cabin and we moved in. In those days, I made my living trapping and guiding new settlers into the Territory so I was away for weeks, sometimes months at a time. At first, she didn't complain, but when her people pulled up stakes ahead of the new White settlements, she was isolated and alone." Ben looked his way. "I'd thought I'd done her a favor taking her away from the tribe and making her a civilized wife . . ." His voice trailed off.

"So, what happened?"

"When I found out she was carrying your father, I figured that would help her loneliness, but she still talked about missing the Shoshone—the songs, the stories, the seasonal rituals, the open sky over her head. She hated the slurs people threw at her when she went into town. She wanted to return to her people, but I refused to let her go."

Colt heard anger but also what might have been regret.

"After Lewis's birth, the complaints stopped, but on the morning of his first birthday, I woke up to find him in bed next to me and her gone. I was frantic. I found a wet nurse, left your father there, and went to look for her. There were rumors that she'd gone west to find her tribe, an old trapper I knew said he'd seen her walking north towards Canada. I searched on and off for the next two years, then gave up. I was angry, bitter, and left with an infant I didn't know how to raise, and frankly didn't want to because that's women's work."

Colt found that painful to hear. He thought it might explain why his father had been so distant with him and Spring; he'd patterned their upbringing after the way he'd been raised by Ben.

Ben rose to his feet. "I never forgave Spring Rain for leaving me and never will. Never trusted another woman after that either. Neither should you. I'll get my things."

Colt thought over his grandfather's story. Of course, Ben wouldn't admit that his treatment of Spring Rain had more than likely caused her to leave. Had he loved her? Was he still bitter because he was going through life with a broken heart? Did his father, Lewis, know why he was motherless, or that Ben hadn't wanted him? Why had his parents named their daughter after Spring Rain? Had it been over Ben's objections? Colt had so many unanswered questions. When he heard Ben leave the house, he went to the window and watched him drive the old wagon away, maybe for the final time.

Regan and Anna returned a short while later and he went out to meet the wagon. His dart-throwing wife showed him a cool smile, which he took in stride. "Did you get everything you needed?"

"I did." She handed him a basket. "There are eggs in there so be careful with it."

Anna said, "Papa, I saw Livy's pony. She's white and her name is Snowbird. Livy said if I had a pony we could go riding together."

"What do you think of that?"

"I don't know." She climbed down and Regan followed.

Regan grabbed a small crate out of the bed. "Our hens for dinner. Has Spring arrived yet?"

"No, but Ben stopped in to pick up his belongings."

She stopped. "He's welcome here."

"I told him that, but he's going to live at the cabin for now."

She seemed to sense there was more to the story. "Okay. You can tell me about it later."

She looked to Anna. "Race you to the door, Anna!"

Anna screamed joyfully and took off running. Watching them filled Colt with his own joy. Ben's advice didn't apply here. Regan was a perfect choice. Carrying the eggs, he followed them to the house.

Spring arrived just as Regan placed the two roasted hens on a platter.

"Smells good in here," Spring said, coming into

the kitchen through the back door. "Brought you some bacon." She placed the package on the counter.

"Thanks. How are you?"

"Fine. You need my help?"

"No. You're a guest. I'll put you to work next time. Go see your niece. She's very excited about you joining us."

"I'm excited to be here. What have you been feeding my brother to make him offer the invitation?"

Regan chuckled. "Not your grandfather's awful stew, that's for sure."

"Lord, I despised it. Another reason I was happy to leave, but you and I can talk later. Going to go see Anna."

"Thanks again for the bacon."

"You're welcome."

Once Spring left, Regan resumed her preparations.

They had a leisurely meal filled with laughter and conversation. Each time Regan looked up, she found Colt watching her. There'd been no words between them about last night so far and she hadn't encouraged any. She'd see what the rest of the day held.

Spring said, "One Eye was prowling around my place last night after you left, Colt. Ran him off with my shotgun."

"Who or what's One Eye?" Regan asked.

Colt explained about the one-eyed mountain cat, adding, "Ben and Odell were supposed to be hunting him and setting traps after the attack on Silas and his dog, Lucky, a few weeks back." He then told her about nine-year-old Silas and his brave dog.

"And he's recovering?" Regan asked hopefully.

Colt nodded. "The dog, too."

Regan was glad to hear that.

His sister said, "I stopped over at Odell's on my way here to let him know. He said the traps are out, but that cat is smarter than a lot of people. So far he's avoided them."

Anna asked, "Will One Eye eat Livy's pony?"

Her father shook his head. "Her granpa has too many dogs. I don't think One Eye wants to tangle with them."

This was the first Regan had heard about the animal. That Colt hadn't mentioned it before led her to believe she wasn't in imminent danger driving back and forth, but she'd keep her eyes open.

After the meal, Regan brought the pie she'd made for dessert to the table. They dug in, and Spring groaned, "My goodness this is good, Regan."

"Thanks."

Anna piped up, "As soon as the new stove comes, she's going to make me a cake."

"Be sure to invite me over when she does," Spring said.

"I will."

With dessert finished, Spring pushed back from the table. "I need to stretch my legs after all that glorious food. Think I'm going to take a walk. Anna, would you like to come along?"

"Yes!" she replied excitedly.

"We'll be back in a little while," Spring said to Regan and Colt.

Their exit left Regan and Colt eyeing each other across the table. Regan sensed her sister-in-law had intentionally left them alone.

"Can I help you clean up?" he asked.

She shrugged. "Sure."

In the kitchen, she poured hot water from the pot on the stove into the tub to wash the dishes. "I'll wash. You dry."

He nodded.

They worked silently. His movements with the plates were awkward and clumsy. She'd wondered if he'd ever done this before and she supposed she had her answer.

"I owe you a very big apology, Regan."

She paused. His features were as serious as his tone. "I asked for the truth and when you gave it to me . . ."

"You didn't want it?"

"No."

"I will never lie to you, Colt. Being truthful means a lot to me."

"I understand. Now, my truth." He paused then added quietly, "The idea of you being with another man ate at me. I was wrong to turn those feelings on you. I'm sorry."

Regan sifted through her responses. She wasn't one to hold a grudge, but on the other hand, she hadn't deserved his ire. "Thank you for the apology."

"I shattered our pact."

"Yes, you did."

"My apology for that as well."

She nodded acceptance.

"Are you willing to try again?"

She wondered if he'd ever opened himself up this way in the past, but realized it didn't matter. He was doing it for her and she needed to appreciate the olive branch he'd extended. They'd never make this marriage work if she slapped it away. "I am."

"I'll do better." The firm declaration offered a quiet promise that made her eyes sting. "I don't want you to leave."

"Then let's go forward."

"Agreed."

Frantic knocks on the front door caught their attention and Colt immediately went to investigate. Regan followed.

Colt asked the young woman at the door, "Addy? Is something wrong?"

"I need you to come and see my daughter. I think she's dying."

"Let me get my bag. You can tell me what happened on the way."

He ran to his study.

Regan waited with the young woman. The red-rimmed eyes in her pale soiled face showed her distress.

"I'm Regan Lee, Doc's wife. I'm so sorry your child isn't faring well."

"Thank you," she whispered.

Colt came hurrying back and said to Regan, "I'll return as soon as I can."

"Godspeed."

Addy mounted her horse. Colt mounted his and the two rode east.

Chapter Thirteen

$\mathcal{S}$pring stayed to keep Regan company, and later, after they put Anna to bed, the two women sat out on the back porch to pass the time. As dusk fell, Spring asked, "So, have you and the good doctor kissed and made up?"

The question took Regan by surprise. "You know about the argument?"

"Yes. Colt came to see me last night. He was pretty upset with himself."

"He should've been, but the answer to your question is yes, to the latter, and no to the former."

"One out of two isn't bad."

"I wondered where he'd gone last night."

"I was surprised to see him quite honestly. He never seeks me out for advice."

Regan thought back on the sincerity of his apology. They might have kissed afterwards had he not been called away. "Apparently, you advised him well."

"I mostly listened, and I think that was all he really needed. He's in love with you."

Regan paused.

Spring continued in an easy tone, "Not sure he knows it yet, or is ready to admit it, but he is."

"No, he isn't."

"He is, so it would be nice if you were in love with him, too."

Regan was sure Spring was pulling her leg so she chuckled. "Don't tease me this way."

"I'm not teasing you, Regan. My illustrious doctor brother is so in love, he's drowning in his feelings, and I'm enjoying knowing he can't get back to shore and save himself."

She scanned her sister-in-law's dark eyes. "Truly?"

Spring nodded. "You're good for him."

Regan sat back against the porch chair and thought about the surprising revelation. Spring knew Colt far better than Regan. Did she want her assessment to be right? Her heart knew the answer. "Why are you telling me this?"

"Because I want you to keep doing whatever you're doing that's making him change. I haven't had dinner here in years, and I attribute today's invitation to you."

Regan dearly wanted to ask what caused the family breach. She knew it stemmed from Spring refusing an arranged marriage, but the details had yet to be shared. "Are we sisters enough yet for you to explain to me the story behind the estrangement?"

When Spring didn't reply, Regan said apologetically, "I'm sorry. I don't mean to be rude. I shouldn't have asked."

"It's okay. I'm trying to decide if you'll think less of me after the telling. Many people here still do."

"I can't imagine anything that would put me in that camp."

Spring gave a bitter chuckle. "Remember you said that."

Regan waited.

"Ben tried to marry me off to an old codger he knew in Cheyenne. I refused. We argued about it for weeks. When I stuck to my guns he said either agree or leave. So, I left, but I had nowhere to go. Odell let me stay with him for a while, but I knew I couldn't live there forever. Mitch Ketchum was a neighbor and a horse wrangler. When I was younger I'd sometimes ride over to his place and clean stalls, curry the mounts, do little odd jobs just to have some coins in my pocket, and to be able to ride. He had the most magnificent animals and I loved horses even then. I told Mitch about my blowup with Ben and asked if I could work for him, maybe keep his books and work with the horses when it was needed. He sort of smiled and asked what else was I willing to do."

Regan's heart stopped. Darkness had fallen and she couldn't see Spring's face but she didn't need to.

"I was nineteen. Both my parents had passed away. Colt was in Washington. My grandfather didn't want me. I had no place to live and nothing to offer but myself, so I followed him to his bedroom, gave him my innocence, and I went to work for him the next day."

"Oh, Spring."

"For the next few years I rode with him and his hands all over the Territory bringing in wild horses, and he rode me whenever he got the urge. To make myself feel better about being his whore, I drank, caroused in saloons, played poker, got in fights, and swaggered through town like I owned the place. I generally did everything a well-brought-up lady had no business doing. The gossips couldn't stop talking. Ben was furious. Colt tried to get me to see reason, but when I pushed him away, he eventually threw up his hands. But I saved my money and when I had enough, I bought my place, told Mitch I was done, and have been free ever since."

"Does he still live nearby?"

"No. He died in a rock slide five years ago."

Silence followed.

Regan thought over Spring's story and better understood why her family and the people in Paradise considered her a pariah, but Regan didn't think less of her. "My mother, Corinne, was a whore."

Spring stiffened and stared at her in the dark.

"When I was ten and Portia was twelve, Corinne met a man who offered her a chance at a different life. He didn't want to raise children he hadn't sired though, so she put us on a train to her sister in Virginia City. We never heard from her again."

"Oh my goodness, Regan."

"Portia and I survived, and so did you." She looked over. "You have nothing to apologize for. I'm going to enjoy calling you sister."

Spring took Regan's hand in hers and squeezed it gently. "As will I. So, now, answer my question, sister. Are you in love with my brother?"

Regan laughed softly. "I'd hoped you'd forgotten about that. Okay, I confess. Yes."

"Hallelujah!"

Regan didn't need light to see Spring's smile.

The stench of rotting flesh hit Colt the moment he entered the Meachems' small cabin. Having encountered the smell of gangrene while training at the Freedmen's Hospital in Washington, it was something he'd never forgot. "Where is she?"

"This way."

The Meachems were among the poorest in the area. They farmed, but not very successfully. Addy's husband, Wayne, clerked at Miller's store, and she swept floors for any business that would hire her.

Addy led him into the tiny windowless bedroom where the stench was thick as smoke. Her four-year-old daughter was lying on a thin pallet against the wall. Near her stood the tall gangly Wayne, and his parents, Fred and Mirabelle. The entire clan had come to Wyoming three years ago. Wayne offered a terse nod of greeting but Colt noted the hostility in the faces of his parents.

Mirabelle snapped at Addy, "Is that where you rode off to? I told you Betsy doesn't need a doctor!"

Wayne said, "Yes, she does!"

His father countered, "He ain't touching that child."

Colt knew bigotry when he saw it and the father's blazing eyes were clear. He ignored it and turned his attention to young Betsy lying deathly still beneath a thin tarp. According to Addy on the ride over, she'd pulled a pot of boiling water down on herself from the stove and her legs and feet were scalded.

Colt moved closer to the pallet only to have Wayne's ancient father step in his path.

Addy screamed through tears, "Get out of the way, old man!"

Mirabelle declared, "She'll be fine. We don't need him."

Wayne warned, "Step out of the way, Pa!"

Probably due to all the shouting, Betsy's eyes sluggishly opened for a moment then drifted closed again. Wayne stepped between Colt and his father and glared at the older man until he relented and moved aside. Colt knelt beside the pallet. He hesitantly lifted the tarp and the sight and stink of the rotted black flesh roiled his stomach so badly he had to draw in deep breaths to keep from losing his dinner. Gangrene covered the girl's thin legs from toes to knees. "Bring me a lamp."

"No oil," Addy whispered.

His lips tightened. Truthfully, he didn't need

additional light to know that the child was at death's door. He placed a hand on her forehead. She was hot as a stove. He removed his stethoscope from his bag and pressed the cup against her chest. Her breathing was shallow and faint, but her heart was racing like the engine of a runaway train. After putting the scope back into the bag, he silently surveyed the adults: the distraught Addy, the teary-eyed Wayne, the anger on the faces of his parents. "Why'd you wait so long to let me know she'd been burned?" he asked quietly. Addy said the incident had happened ten days ago.

Mirabelle sneered. "Because any fool knows how to treat a scalding. If I keep putting potato shavings and yeast on her legs for a couple more days, she'll be good as new."

Rage filled Colt. It was not the first time he'd encountered folk remedies that did more harm than good. Had he been summoned the day she was burned, more than likely Betsy would already be good as new. Instead . . . he stood. The weight of what he had to tell her parents felt like a ton of boulders crushing his chest. "Addy and Wayne, I need to speak with you outside."

Addy began to sob audibly, and even in the shadows, the plea in her eyes was plain. "Please, Dr. Lee, do something! I don't want to bury my baby. Please!"

Wayne draped his arm across her shoulders, hugged her close, and kissed her forehead. "Come on," he told her, voice thick with tears. "Let's go outside."

Mirabelle and Fred stood silent.

Colt rode home with Addy's screams of "No!" puncturing his heart. There was nothing a doctor could do to save Betsy's life short of amputation, and even if her parents had the funds to make the trip to Cheyenne to find a surgeon, she wasn't strong enough to survive the journey. He was left sad and angry. Sad because a child would be buried soon, and angry because bigotry and ignorance were contributing factors. Addy's screams of pain would resonate inside himself for a long time.

Finally home, he unsaddled his horse, bedded him down in the barn, and walked slowly to the house. The light shining from the parlor was like a small beacon and he silently thanked Regan for its glow. He assumed she and Anna were asleep but when he entered, she was seated at the dining room table writing.

She looked up. "How's the child?"

He shook his head, set his bag on the table, and sat.

His pain must've been visible because she whispered, "I'm sorry."

"So am I." He told her about the scalding. "Had I known earlier, they wouldn't be planning her funeral. Her grandmother treated the burns with potato shavings and yeast."

"I've never heard of that. It doesn't work, does it?"

"No, and neither does flour or bandages soaked in turpentine or any of the other concoctions people sometimes swear by. They usually do more harm than good. Some are comical though. I once had a man come to my office wearing a pair of his wife's underpants around his neck."

"What on earth for?"

"It was supposed to cure his stiff neck. When the stiffness didn't go away he came to ask me if he'd tied them wrong."

She laughed out loud and hearing it brightened his terrible evening. "What are you doing?" he asked, indicating the stationery and ink.

"Writing to my sister. I miss her. I feel as if I owe her a dozen letters. I want to let her know how I'm doing."

"And how are you doing?"

"Better."

He knew she was talking about their marriage. "Good. Did Spring stay long?"

"She did. We're going to be good sisters."

"I like that you two get along."

"We do, too." She studied him for a moment and asked, "Are you hungry? There's pie left."

He shook his head. "No, I'm going to bed shortly. I'm tired, and the court hearing is tomorrow."

"I know. We'll see if I'm allowed to testify. I'm sorry again about the child."

"Addy and her husband, Wayne, are good people but I doubt they have the money to bury her."

"If I go to the undertaker and offer to pay for the casket, do you think they'll accept it?"

The question caught him by surprise.

She continued, "My Uncle Rhine used to tell us, those who have a lot should help those who only have a little. I know it won't ease their pain but they'll be able to bury her with dignity. They don't have to know it came from us."

He noted she said *us* and that made his heart swell. "You're an amazing woman, Regan Lee."

"I can't cure anyone the way you do, but I can help in other ways."

"Thank you," he said. "We'll see what the undertaker says tomorrow after court."

"Okay. You go on to bed. I'm going to finish this. I'll see you in the morning."

He wanted to hold her in his arms for the solace he knew it would bring him, but he didn't know how to ask, so he said simply, "Good night."

Before going to his room, he quietly opened Anna's door and looked in. There she was, sleeping in the pale glow of the moonlight streaming through her window. He couldn't imagine having to bury her. He knew some parents chose not to attach themselves to their children because so many died early in life from diseases like tuberculosis and yellow fever. But he cherished his Anna, and if his love was the deciding factor in how long she lived, she'd outlive time. He closed the door softly and went to bed.

The next morning, Colt and Regan dropped Anna off at school and headed to town. Instead of her usual attire of denims, Regan was dressed in a fashionable gray walking suit topped by a matching pert little feather-tipped hat. She'd be representing her family, and in the eyes of some, her race, and so wanted to present herself properly. "Will you point out Dun Bailey to me when he arrives?"

"I will."

The proceedings were to be held inside the bank. Regan hadn't seen banker Arnold Cale nor his wife, Glenda, since the Paradise Ladies Society meeting but his condescending manner remained fresh in her mind. She still had a good amount of unspent gold so doing business with him wasn't necessary yet.

In town, Main Street was packed with vehicles. On the walks, groups of well-dressed men and women hurried in the direction of the bank.

"Are all these people in town for the hearing?"

Colt eased the wagon into a spot near his office. "Yes. Court day is like a visit from the circus."

Regan remembered the crowd she'd drawn simply by shopping. She supposed a court case offered even more excitement. She waited for Colt to come around and hand her down.

"You look very nice, Mrs. Lee."

"Thank you, Dr. Lee."

He extended his arm, she placed her hand on it, and let him escort her towards the bank. On the way, she thought about Spring's startling revelation. Was Colt really in love? She'd lain awake for quite some time last night thinking about it. She had her doubts but again reminded herself that Spring knew him much better than she did. Even so, she had no plans to ask him. They'd renewed their pact and she didn't want to be the one responsible for making it go up in flames by quizzing him over something he might not be ready to express.

To her surprise, the area around the bank was filled with vendors hawking everything from popped corn and flavored shaved ices, to meat pies, funnel cakes, and small hand pies filled with stewed fruit. A Chinese man in traditional clothing wandered through the crowd selling fans. No one seemed interested however. A few even glared at his passing. Regan was accustomed to seeing people of his race at home and in San Francisco but hadn't seen any Chinese in Paradise. All over the country his people were being targeted by violence. She hoped he'd be allowed to sell his wares in peace. A few feet from the bank's door, a young man sawed away on a fiddle, filling the air with a lively tune. At his feet was a tin cup for contributions. Regan thought the Paradise Ladies Society might have missed a golden opportunity to raise funds for the lending library.

"This reminds me of a fair,'" she said, taking in all the activity. "I don't think I've ever seen anything quite like this. Not for a court hearing."

"Folks here take their fun wherever they can find it."

"Will it be warm inside the bank?"

"More than likely."

"Then I need to purchase a fan." She found the man, purchased two fans, and after receiving his smiling thanks, went inside.

The interior was hot and noisy. There were two tables set up at the front of the space and facing the tables were a large number of chairs set up in rows. Although the proceedings weren't scheduled to begin for another hour, most of the seats were taken. She and Colt greeted and nodded their way through the throng. Happening upon two empty chairs towards the back, they sat and settled in to wait.

A short while later, Whit entered with the cuffed prisoners and the outlaws were met with a torrent of boos and catcalls from the crowd. Walking with them and the sheriff was a short man in an ill-fitting green-and-gray checkerboard suit. His pomaded hair and waxed mustache made him resemble a circus barker. She leaned over and asked Colt, "Do you know who he is?"

"Tolson Veen. Lawyer from Cheyenne. He takes a lot of outlaw cases. Loses a lot of them, too."

"Then why hire him?"

"Because he's cheap and there's always a chance he may win."

"That doesn't sound like a smart strategy."

"If outlaws were smart, they wouldn't be outlaws."

She chuckled softly. His smile peeped out.

Mr. Denby and his seamstress daughter-in-law, Dovie, came in and took the two empty seats in front of Regan and Colt. The four of them were chatting when a sudden hush descended over the crowd. Regan craned around the Denbys to find the cause.

"Dun Bailey," Colt said.

Regan watched as the thin-faced Bailey spoke with the lawyer, Veen, then turned his attention to the crowd. He scanned faces as if searching for someone. When his eyes settled on her and stopped, she knew she was the someone. He looked her over with an iciness so chilling she unconsciously drew back and that apparently pleased him. Giving her a mocking smile, he walked over to the wall and stood next to the large window to wait for the hearing to begin.

"If he's trying to scare me, he did a good job," she admitted to Colt.

"Ignore him. He knows I'll shoot him where he stands if he does anything other than look."

Surprised, she realized he was deadly serious. It was a side of him he'd never shown. She remembered him saying he'd never taken a life, not that he wouldn't.

The crowd continued to grow and now that all the seats were occupied, the latecomers lined the walls. Colleen Enright looked put out that she didn't have a place to sit, but Lucretia Watson's husband, Matt, stood and offered her his. Lucretia didn't appear pleased. The widow, dressed in green again, gave him a sweet smile, stood for a moment as if to make sure she was seen, then sat. Dovie turned to Regan, gave her an eye roll, and Regan chuckled. The temperature inside had risen, too. Regan unfolded the fan she purchased and used it to move the air.

"Is the judge here yet?"

"Yes, that's him talking to Whit."

Judge Jinks was a heavyset man with white hair and a tired face. His wrinkled black suit and vest matched his weary features.

"Is he a fair judge?"

"Yes. He's curt, sarcastic, and doesn't suffer fools. He and Veen don't get along."

"You've seen them in cases before?"

"Yes. It's one of the reasons so many people are here. The judge can be very entertaining, Veen's no match."

"Is he fair to our people, too?"

"I don't know. I've never seen him handle a case with our people."

While the judge and Whit continued their conversation, banker Arnold Cale entered along with three men dressed in expensive suits. His hovering and the concern on his face gave the impression that they were men of importance, so much so he made three people in the front row give up their seats so the men could have them.

"Stage line bigwigs, I assume," Colt speculated.

Mr. Denby turned around and said, "Yep."

Regan hazarded a glance over at Dun Bailey and found his cold eyes waiting. Having gotten over her initial fright, she refused to be intimidated and met his gaze without flinching, then smoothly turned away.

Whit left the table and made his way back to where Regan and Colt were seated. He didn't look pleased. "Regan, the judge wants to speak with you."

Regan thought she might know why. Every eye in the building watched her walk to the table where the judge sat waiting. The three stage line bosses were at the table as well, along with the outlaws' lawyer.

The judge said, "You're Mrs. Lee?"

"Yes, sir."

"Unfortunately, you're not going to be allowed to testify here today."

She nodded grimly.

One of the stage line bosses seethed in a quiet voice, "She's our only eyewitness. She has to testify."

"I understand that, but if this goes to trial, more than likely, her testimony will be thrown out because of her race."

"This is ridiculous," another one of the bosses said angrily.

"Yes, it is," the judge agreed. "But such is the state of our country. My hands are tied. Sorry, gentlemen."

Regan waited.

"Sorry to have taken up your time, Mrs. Lee."

She didn't say she didn't mind, because she did. Being denied something as simple as telling the truth in a court of law due to the color of her skin was infuriating and humiliating. She took in the faces of the stage line representatives. They were visibly upset, too, but she wondered how they felt about her people when it didn't directly impact their profits. "Good luck with your case, gentlemen."

All eyes again turned her way as Colt joined her and they exited the bank.

Outside, she said, "I still want to see the undertaker about the casket, unless the country takes issue with that, too."

He draped an arm across her shoulders, gave her a supportive squeeze, and placed a solemn kiss on her brow.

She was so furious, tears stung her eyes. "Will things ever get better for our people?"

"I don't know. For every step forward, we're forced to take two steps back."

"And the Supreme Court is helping with those backwards steps." Two years ago, the Supreme Court handed down an 8–1 decision that found the 1875 Civil Rights unconstitutional. Not only did the ruling forbid Congress from enacting measures to address discrimination, it allowed states to legally overlook such practices. Regan had no idea how or when the country would live up to the promises of the Constitution but she and everyone she knew were sick of the ill treatment.

Mr. Beck, the undertaker, was overwhelmed by Regan's generous offer to pay for Betsy Meachem's casket and paused to wipe his eyes with his handkerchief. "Wayne came in this morning before work to ask about prices. When I told him how much, I could tell by his face it was more than he could pay. I offered him a much cheaper version made of cardboard he could pay for over time, and he agreed."

Regan refused to let the child be buried in a cardboard box as if she had no more value than a pair of shoes. "How long will it take before it's ready?"

"A day at the most. Just need to have my carpenter nail the boards together. I'll let Wayne know later today that it was donated anonymously."

"Thank you."

Two days later, Betsy Meachem was buried in the Paradise Cemetery. Most of the town turned out to pay their respects. As Regan stood beside her husband and watched the dark wood casket be lowered into the ground, she hoped little Betsy would rest in peace.

Chapter Fourteen

A few days after Betsy's funeral, Regan was standing in the parlor trying to decide which pieces of the old overstuffed furniture to keep and which to give away. She looked up at the portrait of Adele hanging above the fireplace. "What do you think?"

Whenever she was in the house alone, she often conversed with the first Mrs. Lee. It was silly of course, but it was her way of remembering that this had been her home, too, and that she'd been loved. She knew many women would've taken the portrait down as soon as the ink dried on their marriage papers, but Regan didn't feel threatened by Adele's painted presence.

She was further contemplating her furniture decisions when the door pull sounded. Walking to the opened screened door, she came face-to-face with a young man in a dark suit standing on the porch. Parked out in front of the house was a large wagon. Its signage showed it was from the stove company.

Filled with excitement, she asked, "Is that my new stove?"

The man looked her up and down. "I'd like to speak to the lady of the house, please."

"I'm she."

He chuckled. "No, the real lady of the house. The woman who employs you."

Regan paused, eyed him up and down in the same manner he'd done with her, and replied, "Ah. I understand now. You want my mistress?"

"Yes. I do. So, run and get her for me, please."

"Will do!"

Sighing at the ignorance of some people, she walked into the kitchen. She stood, counted to one hundred to give herself time to find her mistress, and returned to the man on the porch.

At her approach, his jaw tightened but before he could express his impatience, she said coolly, "My name is Mrs. Colton Carmichael Lee, and *I'm* the mistress of this house. Is the stove on that wagon the one *I* recently purchased through Miller's store?"

His face turned red and he stammered, "Uhm, yes. Uhm. My apologies, Mrs. Lee. I thought—"

"We both know what you thought, but we'll move past that, shall we?"

"Oh yes, ma'am. I'm so sorry. I-I . . . if you'll show me where you want the new stove placed, we'll get started on setting it up."

Regan held the screen door aside and he entered.

An hour later, the old stove had been hauled away and in its spot stood the brand spanking new replacement, manufactured under the name Acorn. It had six cook plates for her pots, a good-sized oven, a warming closet attached to the side, and it burned wood or coal. It cost her a bit under ninety dollars, but it was well worth the money. Now, she could do some proper cooking and, most important, bake Anna's cake. The new icebox was outside on the porch and it, too, helped turn the ancient kitchen into one more suitable to her needs.

Tired after being up all night helping a rancher's mare birth a breeched foal, Colt trudged into the house that afternoon with only one thing in mind: sleep. A heavenly smell drew him into the kitchen where he found Regan seated on a stool with a bowl of something in her lap. Whatever was in the bowl was being whipped to death by the long-handled wooden spoon in her hand. She looked up and her smile was a balm to his weariness. "How'd the foaling go?" she asked.

"The colt was breech so it was a long night."

"Colt and mare okay?" she asked, still whipping away.

"Yes. What are you doing?"

"Making icing for Anna's cake."

Seeing his confusion, she inclined her head to direct his attention. "Meet my new stove."

He turned and his jaw dropped.

"Isn't she beautiful? I named her Portia after my sister, which may be a mistake seeing as how Portia can't boil water."

Colt continued to stare at the huge stove that dominated the small kitchen. He took in the shiny black top with its six circles where he assumed the pots would be placed, the stovepipe, the oven with its glass window, and the rest. He couldn't get over the size. "What's this bustle-looking contraption on the side?"

"Warming oven so things like bread don't get cold while the rest of the meal finishes up."

"Should I sit before I ask how much it cost?"

She grinned while she continued to whip away. "Maybe."

He made a show of gripping the counter's edge. "Okay, tell me."

She did and his knees buckled. "But," she added, laughing at his antics, "because of how it's constructed, it will help heat the house this winter."

Colt thought that a great side benefit, but he was still trying to recover from the number she'd quoted. She'd paid for it with her own funds and he was glad it made her so happy, but to a poor as a church mouse country doctor, ninety dollars was an extremely large sum of money.

She set the bowl on the counter and dipped the tip of a smaller spoon inside to taste the icing. "Problem?"

"That's a lot of money, Regan."

"I know, but to be able to bake a cake for a child

who's never had one, I would have paid twice that price."

He had no comeback. He remembered Spring saying he was in love with his mail-order bride, and he realized she was right. How could he not be with a woman who'd repeatedly proven herself so kind and caring? "I may not be a churchgoer but I know how blessed Anna and I are to have you with us. Thank you, Regan."

"That's very sweet of you to say."

"I meant it." He hadn't kissed her or held her close in what felt like ages and the urge to remedy that was strong. Basking in the beauty of her small face, he ran a slow finger down her cheek and her eyes closed in response. Encouraged, he gently brushed his mouth over hers and whispered, "I've missed kissing you."

"I've missed it, too."

No further words were needed. Easing her close, he wrapped his arms around her, reveling in her softness against him, her lips parting beneath his, and the sigh of pleasure she gave. Their tongues mingled. The taste of the icing she'd sampled elevated her sweetness, and he was in heaven once again.

The sound of applause made them part and turn to see a smiling Anna.

He chuckled. "How'd you get here?" School didn't let out for at least another hour.

"Livy's granpa drove me. Mr. Adams got sick so we had to go home. I like that you're kissing."

He took in Regan's amused face.

Anna added, "It means you're happy again. Livy says when her mama and papa are happy she hears them jumping on the bed at night. Are you going to jump on the bed?"

Regan placed her forehead on his chest and her shoulders shook with silent laughter. Colt was so caught off guard, he was speechless. Regan backed out of his arms, wiped at her tears of mirth, and said, "Look what came today, Anna."

Her eyes widened with awe. "The new stove! Do I get my cake?"

"Yes, ma'am!"

She ran to Regan, threw her arms around her waist, and jumped with joy. "Thank you!"

"You're welcome."

While he looked on, his two ladies retrieved the cake layers Regan had set out on the porch earlier to cool. As they worked together to spread on the icing, he noted Regan's patience and Anna's serious face. With her new mama's guidance, she was going to grow into a force of nature and he looked forward to seeing her blossom.

Colt overcame his weariness enough to enjoy the first dinner cooked on the new stove and watch Anna delight in her cake. He also watched his wife and imagined jumping on the bed with her. It felt like ages since they'd done that, too.

"Miss Regan?" Anna said.

"Yes?"

"My cake is really good. Thank you for making it."

"You're very welcome."

"Livy said I should call you Mama, instead of Miss Regan."

Colt fielded Regan's gaze and he gave her a shrug.

Regan said, "What do you want to call me?"

"I want to call you Mama."

He heard emotion thicken Regan's reply. "I'd like that, and that makes you a very special little girl. Do you know why?"

Anna shook her head.

"Because you'll have two mamas. One in heaven and one here. Most people only have one."

Colt wondered what he'd done to deserve such grace. It was a perfect response.

The door pull sounded.

He started to rise, but Regan said to him, "You sit. I'll go. And if it's someone needing your help, they'll have to wait until tomorrow. You need rest."

"Regan?"

"I mean it."

Amused by her fierceness, he shook his head.

She returned with Colleen Enright, her daughter, Felicity, and Minnie. Hiding his irritation, he stood. "Ladies."

Colleen gave him the flirty little smile she always had for him. "I saw Minnie at the store. She asked if I'd drive her over to visit, so I said of course."

Regan replied, "How nice. We're having dessert. Would you like to join us for cake?"

"We would. Thank you." And she took a seat. Felicity, dressed in a worn blue smock, sat beside her. Minnie's attention was focused on Anna, who appeared to be avoiding the eye contact. Before Colt could gently encourage her to greet her great-aunt, Minnie lit into her.

"Anna Lee! Look at me and say hello. I raised you better than that."

The rebuke tightened Colt's jaw. Regan looked shocked then her eyes narrowed ominously.

Anna met her eyes. "Hello, Aunt Minnie."

"That's better," Minnie fumed and took a seat.

Voice cool, Regan said, "I'll get some plates. Anna, would you come help me, please."

Anna rose.

"Anna!" Minnie barked. "When someone makes a request, you're to say, 'Yes, ma'am' or 'Yes, sir.' Have you forgotten everything I taught you?"

"No, ma'am."

Colleen and her daughter appeared to be enjoying the berating. Colt wasn't. Regan's glare showed she wasn't either.

Regan said gently, "Anna, honey, go on in the kitchen. Take Felicity with you and show her the new stove. I'll be there in a minute."

"Yes, ma'am."

Once the girls were gone, Regan walked over to Minnie and said, "Please don't browbeat Anna that way. We all know manners are important."

"Then why aren't you enforcing them? She needs—"

"Stop!" Regan snapped and Minnie jumped in her chair. Colleen's eyes popped.

"Don't browbeat her. And if you can't honor my request, Colleen can take you home."

"How dare—"

"She's a child!" Regan pointed out, voice rising. "Not your whipping post!"

The furious Minnie turned to Colt as if expecting his support, but he had nothing to offer.

Regan said, "I'll get the girls."

After she went into the kitchen, Minnie complained to him, "You should've taken my side instead of letting her speak to me so disrespectfully."

"Why are you here?"

She drew back at his blunt question then gathered herself. "I'm moving back East. I want to take Anna with me."

"Safe travels." He had no plans to even dignify that ridiculous request.

"I insist that we discuss this."

"There's nothing to discuss."

"She'll be better off with me."

For the life of him, he didn't understand why she believed he'd place his daughter back in her care. He knew she missed Adele and a part of him wondered if she was simply lonely, but he discounted that because she never showed Anna any affection or gave the impression that she enjoyed the child's company.

Regan returned with the plates and the girls. She appeared calmer but remnants of temper simmered in her eyes.

After cutting the cake and placing the slices on

the three plates, she passed them around along with forks. A woeful Anna stared down at the tablecloth. Colt wanted to rail at Minnie for stealing her joy; she been so happy earlier. Regan was watching Anna, too. Seeing his wife's anger, he hoped Minnie left before Regan set her hair on fire.

Felicity ate a couple of bites, looked Anna's way, and asked critically, "Why are you wearing boy's clothes?"

Anna, dressed in denims and a shirt like her mama, snarled, "They're not boy's clothes."

"Well, my mama said—"

"Hush!" Colleen said quickly. Having drawn Regan's attention, she tittered, "This cake is very good, Regan."

"Thank you."

Apparently sensing how close she was to incurring Regan's wrath, Colleen said, "Hurry and finish your cake, Felicity. We need to get home." She smiled at Colt. "Minnie brought her things, she plans to stay a few days."

He shook his head. "We don't have the room. You can drive her back to town."

Minnie's eyes blazed, but in the face of her actions today, that she believed she'd be welcomed, particularly uninvited, was laughable.

Colleen's lips tightened angrily. He guessed she hadn't planned on making the return trip, but it didn't matter. He was way too tired for this foolishness.

A few minutes later, the guests were headed

to the door. Colt, Regan, and Anna offered polite good-byes. Minnie, for all her fire and brimstone about proper manners, left without a word. None of it mattered.

After their departure, Regan pulled Anna close and kissed her brow. "Don't let that old buzzard upset you. Come, let's get the kitchen cleaned up." And to Colt, she ordered, "Go to bed."

He didn't have to be told twice.

At breakfast the next morning, Regan noticed Anna's subdued manner. Since the wedding, she'd become quite a little chatterbox during meals; asking questions, relating how her school lessons were going, and what she and Livy thought of the antics of Moss Denby's grandson, Wallace, during class time. But this morning, she picked at her oatmeal and didn't have much to say.

"Are you not feeling well this morning, Anna? Should we have your papa take a look at you?"

She slowly circled her spoon in her bowl. "Do I have to go to school today?"

Colt replied gently, "But you like school. Why don't you want to go?"

She sighed. "I just don't want to."

Regan said, "We'll need a better reason, honey."

She sat closedmouthed for a few more moments. When she looked up there were tears in her eyes. "Because Felicity is going to tell everybody about Aunt Minnie yelling at me, and they're going to laugh."

Regan's heart broke. One more transgression to add to Minnie's slate of sins.

"They're not going to laugh," Colt said.

"Yes, they are," Anna countered.

Regan didn't want to contradict Colt out loud but she agreed with Anna. Regan knew from her own experience how cruel classmates can be. In Virginia City, the children at her school somehow learned her mother, Corinne, was a whore and she and Portia were called foul names, made fun of, tripped, and shunned. But they never cried; they fought, and meted out their share of black eyes and split lips to both boys and girls. When the parents began adding to the nastiness with slurs and threats, Aunt Eddy took them out of school and hired a tutor to teach them at home. Regan didn't want to encourage her daughter to fight, and she was certain Colt would be appalled if she did, so she said, "If they do laugh, tell them your mama yelled at Aunt Minnie right back."

Anna's eyes widened with shock. "You did?"

"Yes. While you and Felicity were in the kitchen."

"Truly?"

"Truly. And I told her if she kept being mean to you, she'd have to leave."

The eyes grew wide as plates. She looked to her father for verification. He nodded. "She was as mad as a mama bear."

Anna's smile lit up the room.

Regan said, "You didn't deserve being yelled at that way. So, if Felicity does start gossiping, you tell her what I just said."

"Yes, ma'am," Anna replied firmly.

An hour later, Colt and Regan dropped their daughter off at school. As they drove away, he said, "I hope she does okay today. If I never see Minnie again, it'll be too soon."

Regan agreed.

He looked her way. "Last night, while you were getting the plates, she said she's moving back East."

"Hallelujah. I hope she left this morning at the crack of dawn."

"Told me she wants to take Anna with her."

Disbelief made her shake her head. "We're not going to allow Anna to visit her for five minutes to have tea, let alone live with her on the other side of the country. Maybe Colleen actually bumped into Minnie at the saloon and Minnie was drunk."

He laughed. "You're so outrageous."

"No more outrageous than Minnie thinking we'd agree to such a ridiculous idea." She scooted closer and hooked her arm into his as he drove. She was as content as a kitten.

"I have a surprise for you."

"Animal, vegetable, or mineral?"

"What?" he asked smiling.

"Animal, mineral, or vegetable? Those are the three questions you ask when someone says they have a surprise."

He viewed her with amused skepticism.

"You've never heard that?"

"No, but it doesn't matter, because if I tell you it won't be a surprise."

She showed a mock pout. "You're no fun."

"If I pull into those trees up ahead, I bet I can make you change your mind."

She stilled. Scanning the trees, she took in his mischief-filled eyes. "You're on."

Regan loved it when the scandalous side of her doctor husband came out to play. His kisses. His hands. The way he slowly undid the buttons of her shirt. How the heat of his mouth made her gasp and her nipples harden. But impaling herself as he sat on the seat and riding him languidly in the hidden quiet of the trees was best of all.

Afterwards, he drove the wagon out of the trees and back to the road. "Did that change your mind?"

Cuddled against his side, sated and still pulsing, Regan replied, "Yes."

"Thought it might," he said, sounding very pleased with himself.

"You're such a humble country doctor." She thought back on the settings of the past few times they'd been intimate. "Do you think we'll ever use a bed again—not that I'm complaining."

"I'll put it on my list."

The drive took them into an area she'd never visited before. The land was flatter, wide open, stands of wildflowers of all colors and sizes spread themselves like a carpet, while the ever-present mountains framed it on both sides. "You sure you can't tell me what the surprise is?"

"Yes, Mrs. Curiosity, I'm sure. And no more pouting. We don't have time to make another stop in the trees."

"How about on the way home?"

He shook his head with amusement.

Regan was enjoying being with him. This was the first day of their new pact and she felt as though this one would last. He seemed content, too, and he hadn't thrown up any barriers after their passionate romp in the trees. She again wondered if Spring was right about him loving her, but she was content with the present.

The wagon took the road through the open halves of a large metal gate emblazoned with the figure of a rearing mustang and the words *Sweet Heart Ranch.*

"Can you tell me who owns the ranch? Or is that part of the secret, too?" Up ahead stood a large two-story cabin built from timbers that gleamed like gold in the sunshine.

"A rancher named Ed Prescott."

"Is he a friend?"

"Yes. He and Whit and I grew up together."

"Did I meet him at our wedding?"

"No. He doesn't do much socializing but he's the rancher that owns the mare with the breeched foal."

By then they'd reached the house and she couldn't help but marvel at the design and beauty. There was a wide front porch across the first level, and up top three small porches—one on each end, and one in the center that she assumed led to various rooms inside. "If we ever build a new place I want it to look like this one. This is stunning."

He parked. "It is. Lots of folks are jealous of it though. They think a man like him doesn't have the right to own and live in something this fine."

"Why?"

"When you meet him, you'll understand."

A curious Regan got down from the wagon. She was still taking in the magnificent structure when a man stepped out on the porch. He was tall, dressed like a rancher, but his face and the long braid down his back spoke to his heritage. He was Native.

Chapter Fifteen

*A*s he stepped off the porch and walked to the wagon, his eyes assessed her curiously.

Colt did the introductions. "Regan, my friend, Edward Prescott. Ed, my wife, Regan Carmichael Lee."

"Pleased to meet you," he said.

"Pleased to meet you as well. You have a beautiful home." As Regan learned later, Ed Prescott was a member of the Bannock tribe, which had roots in the Shoshone Nation.

"Thank you. I hear you know your way around a Winchester."

She dropped her head.

"Thanks for leaving him alive," Ed continued. "I shot him once, too, but with a bow."

"Why? What happened?"

Colt explained, "We were playing a game we made up called Buffalo and Brave. His grandfather had an old buffalo hide. One of us would put on the hide and crawl around pretending to be the buffalo. The other would be the brave trying to bring it down with an arrow."

"And he shot you?" she asked with disbelief.

"He got lucky. Shot me in the thigh. Fortunately, the hide blunted most of the force."

Ed picked up the tale. "I was dancing and singing in victory. When my grandmother came out to see what all the commotion was about, old buffalo there was on the ground rolling and moaning."

"What did she do?"

"Snatched my bow away, smacked me on the back of the head, and took the arrow out of his thigh. She didn't let me touch that bow for a month."

Regan wasn't sure whether to laugh or be appalled.

Ed added, "He and I had many adventures growing up, but we'll save them for another time. Did he keep secret about why you're here?"

"Yes, and I'm about to burst."

"I'm surprised. A woman with your beauty would make a man spill everything he knows."

"Stop flirting with my wife."

Regan saw humor and warning in the look Colt had trained on his friend.

Ed told Regan, "He tends to be a grouch at times."

"I've noticed that."

"Stop encouraging him," Colt told her, smiling. "Let's get to why we're here, Prescott. Lead the way."

Ed led them behind the house where an open meadow stretched for as far as she could see.

Corrals and barns were a short distance away, but the rest of the open land held horses; two dozen or more of all sizes, ages, and colors. Fascinated, she scanned the scene. "Are all these yours, Ed?"

"Yes. My family has been selling and trading horses for generations."

Some were grazing. Two knobby-kneed colts with shiny chestnut coats romped and raced. A big roan drank from a line of troughs.

Ed said, "Colt told me you ride and need a mare."

"I do," she said, watching the beautiful animals.

"Take your pick. My wedding present to you."

She thought he might be pulling her leg. "Please don't tease me."

"I'm not." Although they'd just met, his smile appeared genuine.

She looked to Colt.

"He wouldn't lie to you, Regan."

She hadn't had a horse of her own since leaving Arizona. The prospect of being able to choose from Ed's herd added to her excitement, but she was humbled by his generous offer. "This is a wonderful surprise. Thank you."

"You're welcome."

"Are they all broken to the saddle?"

"The older ones are."

"May I have some bribes? Apples, carrots—whatever you have."

"Yes. Hold on." He hurried to the barn and disappeared inside.

While he was gone, she wrapped her arms

around Colt's waist, raised herself on her toes, and gave him a kiss. "Thank you. I feel like it's my birthday, or Christmas."

"As long as you don't ride back to Arizona."

"Not a chance."

"Good. Not sure what I'd do if you did."

His serious tone made her go still. Was he saying what she thought he was?

He whispered, "I think I've stumbled into a love match, Mrs. Lee."

She placed her cheek against his chest and held him as tightly as he held her. Happiness filled her heart. All she felt for him was now free to savor, enjoy, and grow.

"Excuse me." Ed was back with a small basket holding apples and carrots. "Save that for later. You're supposed to be picking out a horse."

Amused, Regan reluctantly stepped out of the embrace and took the basket.

Colt asked, "Do you want help?"

"Maybe in a bit. Are you in a hurry to return home?"

"No."

"Okay, because I'd like to take my time."

"As much as you need."

Leaving them, she walked to the middle of the meadow and sat down in the grass. With the basket in her lap, she waited to see which horses were curious enough to see what she was about. After ten minutes or so, the two chestnut colts stopped racing long enough to walk over. They were too young to be ridden, but not to take the carrot she offered. Smiling, she let them munch and noted a few of the other horses raised their heads to watch. Once the colts consumed the offering, they galloped off to resume their play. A brown-and-white palomino whose coloring brought to mind her sister's mare, Arizona, walked over. Regan thought the animal might be a good candidate. She looked healthy and strong. The mare took a bite of the apple, but when Regan slowly rose to her feet to examine her more closely, the mare raced away. A couple more mares paid her a visit, took the bribes only to race away as well, and disappointment began to set in. Although Ed had offered his assistance, her pride kept her from signaling for help. Suddenly, a mare she hadn't noticed before trotted over. She was a beauty with a dark cinnamon coat, black legs, mane, and tail. A light brown patch spanning the length of her nose resembled an elongated star. She ate the carrot bribe and didn't flee when Regan stood, which she took as a good sign. Regan gently rubbed her neck. "Hello, Star. Do you want to go home with me? I promise to take good care of you and we'll go on lots of adventures."

The horse turned her head, eyed her, walked a short distance away, and then reared. A surprised Regan startled, but held her position. As the mare galloped off and stopped to glare, Regan gave thanks that the sharp hooves hadn't come down on her head. "If you don't like adventure just say so!" she called out.

But to her elation, the mare raced back, and this time let herself be touched without complaint. "Were you testing me, Star?" Regan asked. "Will you let me make sure the bones in your legs are strong and straight the way they should be?" When she ran her hands slowly over each black leg, the mare allowed it. Regan spent a few more moments evaluating her and letting the horse become accustomed to her touch and voice.

Ed and Colt must've seen the progress she was making because they walked out to join her. Ed was carrying a saddle.

"Found your candidate?" Colt asked.

"Maybe."

Ed asked, "Do you want me to saddle her?"

She rolled her eyes and took the saddle.

Colt chuckled. "I could've predicted that reaction."

Ed said to her, "Okay. I'll just move out of your way."

Going about the task, she continued speaking to Star in quiet reassuring tones. Once the last few cinches were done and checked, she put her foot in the stirrup and mounted. The mare danced a bit, but Regan kept her under control with a firm but gentle hand. "Does she jump?"

Ed asked, "Jump?"

"Yes, fences, creeks, potatoes on the ground?"

Ed looked stunned and confused. Her husband was trying not to laugh at his friend but failing.

Regan turned the horse away. "Never mind, I'll

find out." With a kick and a yell, she and the horse set off. She rode the mare at a medium gallop at first but as they became more attuned, she felt Star straining to increase the pace, so Regan leaned in like a jockey and let the mare have her head. Star's strides lengthened. Moving together as one, they pounded around the field a few times then headed for the fence that separated the meadow from the road. "Do you like to jump, Miss Star? Can we take that fence?" Regan asked. She knew that if Star balked at the last minute, they could both be injured, but she sensed the horse had no fear. She was right, they sailed over the fence with ease, and Regan yelled her joy. Star landed solidly on the other side, and they continued, galloping hell-bent for leather up the road.

With Star trailered behind the wagon on a lead, Colt drove his horse-riding woman home. "You know you almost gave me and Ed a heart attack when you jumped that fence."

Snuggled close to his side, she said, "I'm sorry."

"No, you're not. Between the fence and watching the mare rear at you, it's a wonder both of us are still alive."

"She was just testing me."

"Well, you tested us for sure."

"Mr. Blanchard traded horses when Portia and I were growing up, so we learned a lot from him. Some horses hate jumping. Not Star. I could feel it as soon as she began to run. And she loved it. She had her eyes locked on that fence, her ears were back. I'm going to love riding her."

"Good, but try not to scare me into my grave, would you, please?"

"Yes, sir, and thanks so much for the surprise."

"You're welcome."

"I enjoyed meeting Ed."

"He enjoyed meeting you, too. In fact, once we got over the shock of you clearing that fence and could breathe again, he asked if it was okay to kill me, so he could marry you."

He liked the sound of her laugh. After Adele's death, he never imagined finding another woman to fill his heart, but he had. "Can I be truthful with you?"

"Yes."

"I never thought I'd love another woman after Adele passed away."

She met his eyes and he wasn't sure what she was thinking. "I don't mean to offend you talking about her."

"You don't. You loved her and you don't have to forget her just because you're married to me now. She gave you a beautiful little girl who will probably grow up and look exactly like her and that doesn't bother me. I'd be very mean-spirited to try and erase her memory from you or from Anna."

So surprised by her words, he stopped the team. "Do you mean that?"

"No, Dr. Lee, I'm telling you a lie," she groused sarcastically. She cupped his cheek. "Of course I meant it. If you want to leave her portrait hanging over the mantel until we're old and gray, so be it. In fact, she and I speak all the time."

He laughed. "What?"

"Sometimes when I'm in the house alone, I hold conversations with her. They're one-sided of course, but I value her opinion. We've been discussing getting rid of all the stuffy old furniture and we're trying to decide which pieces to keep."

He threw back his head and laughed loud and long. After recovering he took in the remarkable woman at his side, and once again thanked the angels for bringing her into his life. "I love you very much, Regan."

"I love you, too."

"What's she doing now?" Anna grumbled, watching Regan check the underside of Star's shoes.

Colt explained, "She's looking for any stones Star may have picked up on their ride."

"Is she going to play with her horse all day?"

He hid his smile. He and Anna were outside by their small barn. Regan and her new mare were just returning from a short after dinner ride and it sounded as if Anna was jealous that a horse seemed to have taken her place in Regan's heart. "This is the first day she and Star have been together, so your mama's really happy about having her. She still loves you best though."

The look on Anna's face didn't change.

"Livy talks about Snowbird all the time," Anna said.

"Riders love their horses like family sometimes."

"Are you and Mama going to ride together?"

"Probably, but not today. We'll take you with us when we do though." He longed to suggest she reconsider letting him get her a mount of her own, but didn't. She'd come to it in her own time when she was ready. "Was Felicity mean to you at school?"

"No, she wasn't there today."

As a doctor, he hoped she wasn't ill, but as a father he was glad she hadn't shown up.

"Hello!"

They turned to see Odell approaching. "Hey, Odell."

"Hey, Doc. How are you, Anna?"

"I'm fine, sir."

He stopped beside Colt and seeing Regan leading Star to the barn, he asked, "New mare?"

Colt nodded. "Yes."

"Fine-looking animal. One of Prescott's?"

"Yes. A wedding present."

Odell smiled approvingly.

"What brings you by?" Colt asked.

"A couple of crates from Arizona and telegrams for Regan. Runner brought them over from the Laramie train station this afternoon. I'm headed home, so thought I drop everything off on my way."

"Appreciate it. You need help with the unloading?"

"I do. Anna, did you draw those fish for me like you promised?"

"I did. Do you want to see?" she asked, more excited than she'd been all evening.

"Sure do."

"Anna, you fetch your drawings and I'll help Mr. Odell with your mama's crates."

She ran off and Colt followed Odell back to his wagon.

After the two large wood crates were carried inside, Odell left for home with Anna's promised drawings, and Regan watched anxiously as Colt used a crowbar to pry off the top of the first crate. While he worked on the second one, she and Anna pulled out the newspapers and towels placed inside to keep the contents safe on the journey from Arizona. What they unearthed made Regan jump for joy. "My saddle!" She lifted it from the crate and beamed. The way the black leather and overlaying silver accents gleamed, it must have been reconditioned and cleaned.

Colt said, "That's a mighty fine saddle. Leave it to you to have one of the fanciest ones in the Territory."

She ran her hands over its familiar structure. "It's really quite plain compared to some of the ones owned by the vaqueros."

"So, it's Mexican?"

"Yes. My aunt and uncle gave it to me for my eighteenth birthday. What do you think, Anna?"

"It's really pretty."

Colt removed the top on the second crate and she and Anna made short work of the packing. Inside was tortilla flour, a variety of dried chilies, spices of all kinds, bags of black beans, yards of beautiful fabric that could be used for anything from drapes to reupholstering chairs, her favorite rolling pin, and a large tin of orange oil for her hair. And at the bottom, two letters, one from her Aunt Eddy, the other from Portia. Regan wiped away her tears.

Anna asked with concern, "Why are you crying, Mama?"

"Because I'm happy and because I miss my family so much."

Anna looked to her father for help.

"I'm okay, Anna. It's just that everything here reminds me of them. Don't worry." Regan gave her a kiss. "Maybe in the spring, we can all go to Arizona or they can come here. I wrote them all about you."

"You did?"

"And I know they're anxious to meet you." She looked to Colt. "You too, good doctor."

"Looking forward to meeting them as well."

"Anna, let's take all this to the kitchen and put it away. Tomorrow we make tortillas!"

Later, after Anna was asleep and Colt was in his study reading about a medical convention he planned to attend, Regan sat at the dining room table to read the letters and the telegram she'd received. She opened the telegram first and was surprised to see that it was from her Uncle Andrew in San Francisco. It read: *Regan. Received query from banker Arnold Cale. Accused you, a colored woman— his words—of pretending to be my niece. Wanted you arrested. Sent him back very sharp reply. Any problems going forward let me know. Love, Uncle A.*

So, Cale hadn't believed her, to the point that he

wanted to turn her over to the law. In a way she understood his suspicion, she was a Colored woman but due to slavery there were many mixed raced families in the country. She'd spent a considerable amount of coin at Miller's store. Did he think she'd stolen it? She could only imagine his face when he received her uncle's reply. She thought tomorrow might be a good day to visit the esteemed banker and ask if he'd prefer she place her money elsewhere.

She then turned to her letters. The one from her Aunt Eddy was a short note that sent her love, and a request that Regan let her know if she needed anything else. She also sent assurances that she and Uncle Rhine were doing well and that they missed her. But it was Portia's letter that gave her pause:

Dear Sister Mine,

I hope you and your doctor are well. Kent and I are doing fine. We're having a house built on Mr. Blanchard's land, and I can't wait for it to be finished so we can move in and make it our home. How are you? I hope this adventure you set out on has borne fruit and your doctor adores you. Kent and I combined our honeymoon in San Francisco with the Colored Women's Suffrage meeting we were planning before you left for Wyoming and it was a grand affair. Frances Ellen Watkins Harper spoke and she was a rousing articulate force of nature. We jumped to our feet more times than I can count to applaud her stirring words. On a more disturbing note, I saw our mother while in the city as well. She looked me in the face, startled, and walked by me as if she'd never seen me before. I was heartbroken. I've no idea if she lives there or was visiting. Aunt Eddy was incensed by Corinne's snub and is hiring a Pinkerton to ferret that out. I know you said you consider Corinne dead to you but I believe that you, like me, long to at least speak with her. I will let you know if anything comes of this. In the meantime, know that I love you and miss you. Please write to me soon. Portia.

Regan read the part about Corinne again and sighed.

"What's wrong?"

She looked up into Colt's concerned eyes. "My sister saw our mother in San Francisco."

"And?"

"Although Corinne recognized her, she walked past Portia as if she didn't."

"Sorry to hear that."

"My aunt plans to hire a Pinkerton to find her, but I don't agree with that. Corinne made her choice. She didn't want us. We'll carry that hurt for the rest of our lives, but arranging a meeting with her as Portia wants won't change anything, at least not for me. Aunt Eddy gave us enough love for three lifetimes. I don't need Corinne."

He put a hand on her shoulder and squeezed it gently. "Other than that, is your sister and her new husband well?"

She nodded. "They're having a house built."

"Are you sure you're okay?"

"I am. I'm just sad that Corinne broke Portia's heart again. I don't know why my sister doesn't accept the situation and move on."

"Maybe she's hoping for a reconciliation."

"You're probably right, but it isn't going to happen. That she treated Portia like a stranger shows what she thinks of us. There will be no reconciliation." Regan rose to her feet and slipped her arms around his waist and he hugged her tight. She didn't need Corinne. She had his love, Anna's love, and the love of her family in Arizona. "Thank you for loving me," she whispered.

"Always." He lifted her chin and said firmly but gently, "Always."

She fit herself against him again. Content.

Chapter Sixteen

The next afternoon, Regan went to pick up Anna from school and saw the children outside playing tag while Dovie Denby, Colleen Enright, and Lucretia Watson stood talking with the teacher, Mr. Adams. He was a tall, string bean of a man with dark collar-length hair and a dour face centered by a long thin nose. As Regan walked over to join them, she noted his tersely set features and wondered what the conversation might be about.

"Today's my last day of teaching here, Mrs. Lee."

Regan paused and scanned the women's unhappy faces. "May I ask why?"

"The council won't increase my salary, so I agreed to an offer from a school in Cheyenne."

Regan was saddened by the news. She didn't know how the other children felt but Anna enjoyed having him as a teacher. "Is there anything we can do to change your mind?"

He shook his head. "I sent my acceptance last

evening. I don't like leaving the children this way, but my services are worth more than the pennies Paradise pays me."

Regan remembered being told about the council's miserly attitude towards the school at the ladies club meeting.

Dovie said, "Thank you for putting up with Wallace Jr."

He smiled. "Your son's a handful but very smart. Keep his mind occupied. He'll go far one day."

"Do the children know?" Regan asked.

"They do and look how terribly broken up they are."

Watching the lively, ongoing game of tag the women chuckled. Lucky the dog, barking and running, appeared the saddest of all.

Lucretia said, "Thanks for teaching our children. The council may not appreciate you, but I certainly do."

Regan and the others agreed.

He smiled softly. "You're very kind. I hope the council will come to its senses and pay your next teacher fairly. I need to get going. Lots to do. Goodbye, ladies." And he went inside the schoolhouse.

Lucretia asked, "Now what?"

Dovie said, "I'm going to the council meeting this evening and give those men a piece of my mind. How do they expect to grow this town with no schoolteacher? I'm sure Glenda will have something to say about this as well. I'll let her know when I get home."

"Can anyone attend the meetings?" Regan asked.

"Yes," Lucretia replied. "I'm going to go, too. You should join us, Regan."

"I will."

They looked to Colleen, who replied, "I'll see what my evening brings. Felicity's going to grow up and be so pretty, more education isn't going to matter. She'll have no problem finding a husband."

Regan stared as if she'd grown three heads.

Dovie's jaw dropped for a moment. After shaking her head in apparent disbelief, she said, "Lucretia and Regan, I'll see you later." She called to her son and walked to her wagon.

Regan closed her own mouth and wanted to lecture Colleen on how the world was changing, the strides women were making, and what new opportunities their daughters might access in the next decade, but didn't. It wasn't her place. Instead, she, like Dovie, offered her good-byes, called Anna, and drove home.

Colt was there when they arrived. While Anna went to her room to change out of her school clothes, Regan told him about Mr. Adams's departure.

He sighed. "That's too bad. He's the third one we've lost in the past two years."

"Dovie and Lucretia are going to the council meeting this evening to try and convince them to pay a new teacher more. I decided to join them. Surely they can be made to see reason."

"Don't get your hopes up. Cale and the others are notoriously shortsighted."

"I'd thought about taking Anna, so she can see how government works, but decided she would

260   *Beverly Jenkins*

probably be bored and who knows how long the meeting might take."

"Until next week if Cale and Miller start pontificating."

"Who's on the council besides them?"

"The undertaker Lyman Beck, rancher Randolph Nelson who also heads up the Republicans, and Heath Leary."

"I don't think I've met him."

"You haven't. He's a gambler. Owns the Irish Rose, the saloon behind Miller's store."

That was surprising.

"You go to the meeting, Anna and I will stay here. Maybe we'll ride over and see Spring."

The meeting was held at the bank. When Regan entered she was reminded of the court hearing and the part she didn't get to play, but put it out of her mind as her eyes swept the room. She recognized Arnold Cale, Chauncey Miller, and undertaker Lyman Beck. The man seated next to Beck had a sun-lined, weathered face that said rancher, so she assumed him to be Republican Randolph Nelson. To Nelson's right sat one of the handsomest men she'd ever seen. Jet-black hair, eyes that matched. The smart tailored suit and frilled white shirt were the attire of a gambler. The smile he shot her was one that had been stealing women's hearts since the day he was born. Not wanting to be caught by whatever web he was spinning, she spotted Dovie,

Lucretia, and Glenda seated near the front of the room and went to join them.

Glenda said, "It's good seeing you again, Regan."

Shaking off the effects of the gambler, she replied, "Same here." She glanced around. Other than her new friends there were only four people in the room—all men. "Where's everyone?" she asked.

"These meetings are never well-attended," Lucretia explained.

"Unless there's something sensational like last year's proposal to keep the Chinese from moving in," Dovie added bitterly.

"Did it pass?"

"No," Glenda said. "It was tabled, but other towns are weighing similar measures."

Regan thought back on the man she'd purchased the fans from the day of the court hearing and wondered where he lived. The local papers out of Cheyenne and Laramie were filled with slur-laden headlines and inflammatory editorials accusing the Chinese of stealing jobs from the Territory's White miners. Rather than spew their anger at the Union Pacific Railroad for hiring them, it was directed at the Chinese workers instead.

Arnold Cale's voice brought her back. "Let's get this meeting under way."

What followed was a dry recitation by Council Vice President Chauncey Miller on what transpired at last month's meeting: a proposal to raise money for a town hall that was tabled; a proposal to allow Miller and Leary to expand their buildings that was approved. A proposal to give schoolteacher Kerry Adams a raise in pay that was denied.

The mayor looked out at the women and said, "I'm assuming you ladies are here to tell us again how wrongheaded we are for not approving the raise?"

Dovie stood. "Yes, and to ask who on the council is going to teach our children now that Kerry Adams is taking a teaching position in Cheyenne?"

Regan noted Nelson's shocked face. "When's he leaving?"

"Today was his last day."

His jaw tightened. "Did you know about this?" he asked Cale.

Cale fidgeted a bit. "He mentioned that he might be, but I thought he was bluffing."

"He was a good man."

Dovie agreed. "He was. So, now what?"

Before anyone could respond, Glenda stood and asked, "How is Paradise supposed to attract the people needed to use this new town hall you're so fired up about building when you don't have a school?"

Miller said, "Who said you need a school to build a town?"

"Schools bring families, Chauncey. Families build towns. And stores."

His eyes blazed but Glenda didn't appear the least bit intimidated.

Her husband said, "Now, Glenda, let's not be disrespectful."

"I'm not being disrespectful by speaking what everyone already knows, Arnold."

He opened his mouth to reply, but Dovie cut him off. "This is not a difficult decision, gentlemen. Either you want Paradise to prosper or you don't. And if you don't, I'll be moving my business and son to a place that does."

"Hold on," the gambler said in a distinct Irish brogue. "I'll not have you moving away from me, Boudicca."

Dovie hissed, "You don't get a say in what I do, Heath Leary."

"So you keep telling me, love."

Dovie blew out an exasperated breath.

Regan had no idea who or what a Boudicca was but she was caught by Leary's affectionate tone and the way the two gazed at each other as if they were the only people in the room. A curious Regan turned to Lucretia who leaned over and whispered, "He's real sweet on our Dovie. She's sweet on him, too, but won't admit it."

Undertaker Lyman Beck spoke for the first time. "I must admit, I voted no on the raise. I didn't see why we needed to pay Adams more. I only went to the third grade and I've done pretty good for myself. However, I've been telling my daughter what a nice town we have, hoping she'll move here from Indiana, but she has three children. She won't come now if we don't have a teacher."

Dovie said, "And neither will anyone else with little ones."

Cale asked the men seated around the room, "What do you think?"

One with a beard that rivaled Odell's replied, "How do the ladies propose we pay a new teacher what they think he'd be worth? Council shouldn't be asking folks with no children to do it."

Lucretia turned around in her seat. "Ed Sterling, you have five grandchildren in Cheyenne. Why'd your daughter Lindy and your son-in-law move away from here?"

He grumbled, "We didn't have a schoolteacher."

"Exactly. It's why most of my children moved away, too. Between my children and yours, the town lost good tax-paying families because Paradise won't offer steady learning."

Glenda added, "The Territorial government is begging people to settle here so we can gain statehood, but miserly decisions like this will continue to hold us back."

"Miserly!" Miller snapped. "Arnold, send your wife home. I'll not be insulted this way."

Glenda countered, "But you can insult me by asking my husband to send me home? I'm not a child, Chauncey."

Her husband wheedled, "Glenda, please be civil."

Arms folded, she sat back in her seat and seethed.

Cale said, "My apologies, Chauncey."

Glenda snapped, "Don't you dare apologize for me, Arnold Cale, I'm not your child either."

He turned beet red.

Regan had no idea the Paradise women were so forceful.

Making a point of avoiding his wife's glare, Cale said, "I propose that if you ladies can get fifty people in town to sign a petition to pay a teacher more than we paid Adams, the council will take it under consideration."

Dovie replied sarcastically, "If we get the signatures you'll consider it? Why not be truthful and simply say you aren't going to act on this because that's what you mean."

Leary weighed in, "Boudicca, if you get the signatures, the council will act, not just consider. You have my word."

Dovie didn't appear convinced, so he repeated, "You have my word."

Regan wondered who she had to bribe to learn the story behind Dovie and the Irish gambler.

Nelson added, "You ladies have my word, too. There's going to be a territorial college opening next year. If the legislature believes education is important, we should follow their lead. In fact, I'll help gather signatures."

Miller stared angrily. The mayor threw up his hands.

Regan wondered why even require the signatures if that was the case, but she supposed it was a way for the council to save face.

Lucretia asked, "And in the meantime, who'll teach our children?"

When no one answered, Regan stood. "I will."

All eyes turned her way.

A confused Nelson looked her up and down. "And you are?"

"Regan Carmichael Lee. Dr. Colton Lee's wife."

"Pleased to meet you."

"Same here." Regan began having second thoughts almost immediately. She'd never taught school a day in her life, and wondered if she'd ever learn to control her impulsive nature.

Miller asked derisively, "What makes you think you're qualified?"

"The completion certificate I earned at Oberlin College," she returned flatly.

Leary eyed her with smiling wonder. "Have you ever taught school, Mrs. Lee?"

"No."

Beck asked, "How much do you want to be paid?"

"Nothing."

The men stared. The women smiled.

"I'll start as soon as the ladies and I look into what the classroom needs."

And with that, the meeting was adjourned.

Outside, Glenda said, "We need to meet and hash out this petition nonsense."

Further discussion was interrupted temporarily by the men leaving the building. Cale and Miller edged past without a word. Beck at least offered a polite good night before walking towards his undertaker business.

Nelson paused for a moment to say, "Thanks, ladies. I know the mayor and Miller won't agree, but I'm glad you were here tonight, and I'll get those signatures. I'll also ask around about a good teacher willing to move here." He tipped his hat and moved on.

His departure left gambler Heath Leary standing with them, a presence Dovie seemed determined to ignore.

"Boudicca," he began.

"How many times have I asked you to stop calling me that?"

"Probably as many times as I've dreamt of making love to you."

Jaws dropped.

A bright red Dovie said, "Go away."

He bowed. "If you insist. But know this. I will marry you, Dovie. Soon."

Giving the women a solemn nod, he crossed the street and walked off towards the saloon.

Once he was gone, Dovie ran her hands down her cheeks and whispered, "Glory!"

Glenda chuckled. "I'd pay any man to worship me the way he worships you."

"He's unsuitable, Glenny. He's a gambler. He owns a saloon."

Lucretia said, "And so madly in love with you, he can't see straight."

Dovie sighed.

Regan weighed in. "Since I'm new to all this—who or what is a Boudicca?"

"A Celtic warrior queen who fought the Roman Empire," Dovie explained. "According to him, our statures are similar."

"Isn't that delicious?" Glenda swooned. "Arnold would never be that poetic."

"It's not poetic," Dovie gritted out.

Lucretia said, "Take it from someone who's been

in love with the same man her entire life. It's poetic and passionate, Dovie. You could do a lot worse."

"And she has," Glenda pointed out. "His name was Wallace Denby. Remember him, Dovie? Your husband? Bounder? Left you for a girl who can't spell her own name?"

Dovie shot back, "Thanks for the reminder, Glenda Cale. Good night, everyone. Let me know when we're meeting." And she stalked off.

Lucretia said, "You were hard on her, Glenda."

Glenda appeared chastened. "I know, and I'll apologize tomorrow. I just want her to have the love she deserves. You have love, Lucretia. Do you, Regan?"

She thought of her love for Colton. "I do."

"And I have Arnold. No love match for me unless I can turn myself into gold for his bank vault. Wallace broke Dovie's heart and her spirit. Heath's willing to give up the saloon for her. How many men would turn their back on their livelihood to be with a woman?"

Regan's Uncle Rhine had, and even though she knew nothing about Leary, if he was willing to give up his business, she believed his feelings for Dovie must be true.

Glenda said, "Let's meet at my house on Friday."

They agreed and parted.

*B*ack at home, Regan bedded Star down for the night and found her husband seated in the darkness on the back porch.

"No problems on the way?" he asked.

She took a seat beside him on the old weathered sofa. "No." She knew he continued to worry about the shooter being on the loose and she did, too. "Did you and Anna visit Spring?"

"We did. Anna fed the piglets."

Regan chuckled.

"And you owe me a kiss for being gone so long." He slid her over onto his lap.

She laced her arms around his neck. "Just one?"

"For now."

So she kissed him, putting as much sweetness and love into it as she could as penance for her prolonged absence. She drew away reluctantly. "Better?"

"One more."

"Such a greedy doctor man."

"Guilty."

They shared another, this time longer and it was infused with enough passion to make hands roam languidly and desire awaken and spread. As his lips brushed her jaw, she said through the rising haze, "I want to tell you what happened at the meeting."

"In a minute."

But time was lost as buttons were undone and hot kisses trailed over bared skin cooled by the night's breeze. Her shift was eased down so he could play and suck and nip. When he'd dallied enough, she was on her feet, facing the moon with her denims pooled down around her boot-covered ankles, soaring with anticipation over what would come next. Behind her, his palms slipped beneath the tail of her shirt, moved possessively up her spine, then swept down slowly over the smooth curves of her hips. His hands circled her, fingers teasing the damp vent between her thighs until her breath rose on the air. "Are you ready for me, Mrs. Lee?"

But he didn't need an answer. His hardness entered her softness and she purred wantonly. It was the second time he'd taken her on the porch this way. As before, his strokes began slowly, gently, letting them savor the rhythm like the opening strains of a lulling sonata, until love-fed lust snared them both. Gentle burned into carnal. Her cries mingled with his growls, his hands tightened on her hips and they rose and fell with the thundering cadence of the age-old dance. She broke first, he exploded after. Sated, they slid boneless to the porch floor and he held her against his chest in the darkness while they tried to catch their breath.

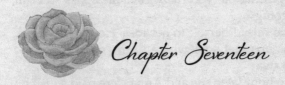

Chapter Seventeen

The next morning after breakfast, Regan walked out to the barn with her husband who was on his way to his office. "I'm not sure what to cook for dinner. Is there anything special you'd like?"

He mounted his horse. "Besides you?"

She laughed. "Didn't you get enough last night?"

"No and neither did you."

He was right of course. He could make love to her until the cows came home next May and she'd still want more. "We really need to use a bed."

"Still on my list. Your plans for the day?"

"Anna and I may ride over to the schoolhouse to see what supplies might be needed." Last night, after they recovered from their lovemaking, she told him about the council meeting.

"You sure you want to teach?"

"No, but I gave my word. Besides, how difficult can it be?"

"Remember you said that when Wallace Jr. has you pulling out your hair. Give me a kiss so I can get going."

She raised herself to her toes. He leaned down. Their lips met somewhere in the middle, and he rode away.

An hour later, she and Anna were paid a visit by Livy, her mother, Julia, and grandmother, Lucretia. Regan and Julia had never met, so Lucretia did the introductions.

"Pleased to meet you," Regan said.

"I'm pleased as well." Julia had her mother's dark hair, plump figure, and her father, Matt's, gray eyes. "My sister, Daisy, just had a baby, and my husband, Paul, and I have been in Fort Collins helping her and my brother-in-law. They have three other children. I have my own coming in a few months," she added, smoothing a hand over her blossoming belly.

"Anna said you were carrying. Congratulations."

Lucretia crowed proudly, "That'll make grandchild number twelve."

Julia shot her mother a grin. "Since there's no school today, Livy and I are wondering if Anna might like to come and spend a few days with us?"

Seeing Anna's wide-eyed joy, Regan asked, "Would you like that?"

"Yes!"

Regan laughed. "Julia, can you and Lucretia wait a few minutes while we pack her a bag?"

"Sure can," Julia replied.

A short while later, Regan waved good-bye as Lucretia and Julia drove off with Livy and Anna giggling away in the wagon's bed.

With Anna gone, Regan decided to pay a visit to the school anyway and maybe swing by Spring's before riding home. She then wondered if she'd need a key to get inside the building. Wishing she'd thought to ask Colt or Lucretia about it, she decided it didn't matter. If the door was locked, she'd return the next day. Either way she and Star would enjoy the ride.

As she and Star set out, Regan kept one eye out for the ambusher, but didn't let it keep her from enjoying the endless blue sky and wild open country that was now her home. She saw hawks and elk, cattle grazing in the distance, meadows carpeted by wildflowers, and streams running clear and pure. She loved Wyoming, and as soon as she was able, planned to write her family and invite them out for a visit, so they could fall in love with the Territory's beauty, too.

Arriving at the schoolhouse, she found the front and back doors locked. Sighing, she remounted and turned Star towards Spring's place. Halfway there, she spotted a child sitting in the meadow. As she slowed her horse, she realized it was Felicity Enright. Glancing around for Colleen but not seeing her, Regan rode over to find out if something was wrong. "Felicity? Are you okay?"

She nodded.

"Is your mama with you?"

She shook her head.

Regan noted the sadness in the child's face. "You're a pretty good piece from home, honey. Does she know you're out here by yourself?"

Felicity picked at the heads of the clover surrounding her and for a moment, Regan thought she wouldn't answer. Finally, she glanced up. "Yes. She makes me come here when she gets company."

Regan was confused. "What kind of company?"

"Men company. When they come at night, she makes me go in my room. She said they give her money so she can buy food."

Regan held the girl's gaze and tried not to jump to conclusions, but saw the seven-year-old version of herself reflected in Felicity's hollow-eyed stare. Her heart broke, not only for the child, but for Colleen, too, if she was indeed prostituting herself to make ends meet. "Do you have to walk back by yourself or will she come and get you?"

"She comes and gets me."

"Do you mind if I wait with you? I don't like you being out here alone."

"She won't like that. I'm not supposed to tell anyone."

"I'll say I just rode up."

"Don't tell her I told you about the company."

"I won't. I promise."

Receiving a barely discernible nod, Regan dismounted and sat by her side.

In the silence that followed, Regan let the cool breeze and the sight of the mountains still her anxiety. She wanted to ask questions, voice concerns, but mostly longed to share her own experiences growing up under similar circumstances, but held off because she continued to hope there was another explanation for what Colleen was doing.

A short while later, Colleen drove up in her ancient buggy and Regan and Felicity got to their feet. Colleen's surprise at Regan's presence quickly changed to irritation. "What are you doing here?" she asked Regan before turning to her daughter. "Get in the buggy," she demanded. "The next time you go wandering off, I'll take a strap to you."

As the child complied, the slump in her shoulders made Regan want to take a strap to Colleen.

"Every time I turn around she's wandered off," Colleen explained and appeared uncomfortable. "Did she say why she was out here?"

"No. I just rode up. I was on my way to see Spring when I came across her."

"Okay, good. I need to get her home."

They drove off and a concerned Regan watched until the buggy with its frayed canopy and wobbly left wheel disappeared around a bend in the trees.

When Regan resumed her ride to Spring's ranch she couldn't stop thinking about Colleen and her daughter. Regan had never been a gossiper so whatever Colleen was doing or not was her own business, but witnessing the unhappy Felicity walking to the buggy weighed heavily. And apparently, it showed on her face. Spring was sitting out back when Regan arrived and the first thing her sister-in-law asked was, "What's wrong?"

Regan sat down in an empty chair and poured some water into a tumbler from the pitcher in the center of the table. "I'm not sure."

"Is it tied to my brother?"

"No. It's about Colleen and her daughter, Felicity, and I need to ask you about something that we have to keep between us."

Spring paused. "Okay. What's the question?"

"Is Colleen a prostitute?"

Spring studied her for a long moment before replying, "Not that I know of, but what makes you ask?"

Regan told her about the encounter with Felicity.

Spring blew out a heavy breath. "We both know how tough that is, but life must be especially hard for Colleen if that's what she's doing."

"I agree, but to yell at her daughter the way she had and accuse her of running off, when she was the reason Felicity was there, was uncalled for."

"Maybe the child wasn't telling you the truth."

"I'm not sure a seven-year-old could conceive of a lie that damning. She reminded me of myself at that age."

"That's sad."

"It is." Memories of those awful years with her mother tried to rise but Regan tamped them down.

Spring said coolly, "Colleen's not been kind to me since she moved here. She took what the gossips fed her and sneered at me just like they did.

Hearing this makes me want to laugh and point, but not at Felicity. She's done nothing wrong."

"No, she hasn't."

"Should I ask around? I still have ties to a lot of the ranchers and their hands."

Regan shook her head. "It's really none of my business."

"I'm going to ask anyway. Discreetly, of course, because frankly I want to know. And if it's true, I'll get a kick out of knowing she's wallowing in the same mud she dragged me through."

"That's not nice, Spring."

"No, but it's the truth."

Regan refused to judge Spring so she asked about something else she wanted to know. "Who holds the key to the schoolhouse?"

"The mayor I believe. Why do you need the key?"

Regan told her.

"You're going to teach school?"

"Yes. Why are you smiling?" she asked, smiling, too.

"I'm just surprised, I guess. Colt said the teacher was leaving and that you and some of the women went to the council meeting. How'd it go?"

Regan told her about the petition.

"If Nelson says he'll support you, he will. He's always been a man of his word, and with him behind you, the other ranchers will sign on, too—if only to get Cale's and Miller's goats."

"Really?"

She nodded. "The two aren't well-liked, but they

got elected because none of the big ranchers have time to play politics, and no one else is interested. There're rumors that Nelson may run for mayor next time around. Many people are hoping he will."

"Why didn't Colt tell me any of this?"

Spring shrugged. "Probably doesn't view it as important. Too busy with his nose to the doctoring grindstone, which everyone appreciates because he's very skilled at what he does, but he's not much on rumors, gossip, or politics."

Regan thought that a reasonable explanation.

"You're really going to teach school?" Spring asked as if needing confirmation again.

"Yes. It's not like I have anything pressing to do right now so I'll fill in until we find a replacement. Mr. Nelson promised to help with that, too."

Spring raised her tumbler in salute. "To success. Let me know if you need my help."

"I will."

Regan rode home. With Anna away, she and Colt could have a nice cozy evening. She envisioned dinner, a relaxing bath, then donning one of the tempting nightgowns she'd yet to wear for him from her bridal trousseau. Maybe they'd even make love in a bed; not that she had any complaints about the other places they'd used, but being able to spend an entire night alone with her husband would be a dream come true.

When she reached the house, his stallion was tied to the post out front. She paused at the sight of the bedroll behind the saddle and went inside. "Colt?"

"In here," he called from his bedroom. She entered and found him packing a bag.

"Where are you going?"

"Rock Springs. Where's Anna?"

"Lucretia invited her to visit for a few days since there's no school." She watched him open a chest and begin withdrawing medical supplies and placing them in his doctor's bag. "Has someone been hurt in Rock Springs?"

He nodded. "The White miners are massacring the Chinese. Same madness going on in Green River and Almy. Whit's gathering a posse and has asked me to come along."

Her heart stopped. "How long will you be away?"

"A few days? A week? I'm not sure. Union Pacific is sending a special train that'll take us from Cheyenne to there." He paused his preparations to walk over and ease her into his arms and against his heart. "You'll take care of yourself while I'm away?"

"Yes. Don't worry. Anna and I will be fine."

He ran a slow finger down her cheek. "It would've been nice to spend a few days with just the two of us."

"I know, but we'll get another chance. Just don't let those bigots hurt you."

"I won't." He kissed her then, a long, sweet parting that let her know just how much she was loved.

He backed away and picked up his bag. "I love you, Regan."

"I love you, too."

And he was gone.

*W*hen Colt and the others stepped out of the box-car in Rock Springs, there was a line of soldiers standing between them and a loud angry mob of men he guessed to be miners who were armed with clubs, hatchets, pickaxes, shovels, and everything else capable of causing bodily harm. It was impossible to tell whether the rage was directed at the soldiers or Colt and the lawmen but he was glad the soldiers were there. As he and Whit and the rest of their party rounded the train and walked to the car holding their mounts, the air was thick with the scent of smoke and the sweet, almost sickening stench of something else.

"What's that smell?" The man's name was Jordan and he'd accompanied County Sheriff Joe Wilson as a member of his four-man posse.

"Death," Colt told him. Jordan froze. Colt stepped up into the car and led his stallion down the plank while the noise of the mob continued.

One of the soldiers peeled away from the main group and rode over to where Colt and the others waited on their horses. It was Odell's grandson and Regan's former lover, Levi Spalding. Upon seeing Colt, he startled then offered a terse nod. Colt nodded in return and swallowed his aversion to the man who'd lied to and taken advantage of his wife. Spalding introduced himself, and Whit and the two county sheriffs did the same.

Spalding said, "Thank you for coming. Most of the violence is over now but there are still some Chinese hiding out in the countryside and we need your help finding them so they can be kept safe. There's been enough death."

"Do you know how many are dead?" Whit asked.

"Officially, around twenty-five, but we're still finding bodies. The homes and businesses of the Chinese were looted and burned to the ground. Miners threw some of the injured into the burning buildings."

"Lord," one of sheriffs said and Colt agreed.

Spalding turned to Colt. "Dr. Lee, there's an infirmary set up and they could use your help."

"Tell me where to go."

"I'll have some of my men escort you. I don't want you riding alone."

Colt appreciated that. More than likely he was one of the few men of color within miles, and with the violence still festering he'd be an easy target. Accompanied by four of Spalding's men, Colt rode off.

He was glad for the escort. On the slow ride through the center of town, dirty, feral-eyed men tracked their passage. Slurs rang out, more than he'd ever had flung his way. A few of the watchers were brave enough or drunk enough to approach their small party only to be deterred by the soldiers' raised rifles. Colt didn't realize he'd been holding his breath until they left the area behind.

The infirmary was two large tents set up in what the soldiers told him had once been the city's Chinatown. There'd been five hundred residents; miners, cooks, laborers, and over seventy buildings, including a house of worship overseen by a priest. But due to the killing and burning, not one building was left standing. Piles of burned and charred wood were all that remained of the barracks built for the Chinese miners by the Union Pacific Railroad, and the shacks the Chinese businesspeople had erected themselves. The thick silence was eerie and the smells of burning and death strong. Nodding at the small contingent of soldiers on guard outside, Colt entered the tent he'd been escorted to. Inside were dozens of injured Chinese lying on cots packed so tightly together there was little room to maneuver between them. Men with their heads swathed in bandages lay nearly on top of others whose bare torsos showed bandaged ribs. By the blood staining some of the dressings, some had been stabbed or shot. Considering the events, such wounds were expected, but what wasn't were the thin silver needles stuck in arms, shoulders, and other parts of the men's anatomies. Having never seen such a thing, a surprised Colt wondered at their purpose.

A Chinese man, dressed in the traditional black shirt and loose-fitting trousers, looked up when Colt and the soldiers entered. He eyed them suspiciously for a long moment before rising and making his way through the maze to where they stood. Glancing down at Colt's black bag, he asked, "You're a doctor?"

"I am. Dr. Colton Lee from Paradise. The soldiers asked me to assist."

"I'm Dr. Crane from Green River. Thank you for coming."

"You're welcome." Colt had heard there was a Chinese doctor in Green River, the only one of his race in the Territory, but knew nothing about him.

One of the soldiers said, "Dr. Lee, we'll rejoin Lieutenant Spalding. If you need anything let the guards outside know." And they departed.

"I was just getting ready to take a break. Care to join me?"

Colt noted the exhaustion in Crane's face. "Sure."

Behind the tent were two charred wooden benches next to a fire that was heating an enormous pot. A man was stirring the contents with a long piece of wood. "Soup," Crane explained as he and Colt sat. "Vegetables courtesy of the governor and the army. The least they could do."

"Do you have anyone assisting you with the patients?"

"Other than a few volunteers, no. The two doctors who live here helped during the height of the killings but when the mob threatened them, they left."

Off in the distance, Colt saw two Chinese and a small group of soldiers digging.

"Graves," Crane said. "Until the soldiers arrived this morning, we were told we had to bury our own."

"The lieutenant said you're still finding bodies?"

"Yes. When I arrived, they littered the ground here. Some intact, others were without heads, limbs, genitals. We had to run off dogs to retrieve others." He was silent for a moment as if remembering the carnage. "These Americans are savages," he whispered bitterly. He met Colt's eyes. "But then your people already know this."

Colt nodded. The United States was only twenty years past the horrors of slavery, and although his father's side had been free before Emancipation, his mother's side had been free for only a generation.

The man stirring the pot handed Crane a steaming bowl of the soup and said something to him in a gentle tone. Crane took the offering. "He's encouraging me to eat."

The man spoke again and Crane translated, "He said if I fall our people will be lost."

Colt wondered if there were any other doctors willing to risk the wrath of the mob to help, but assumed not.

Colt was handed a bowl of soup, too. He thanked the man, and he and Crane consumed their portions silently.

For the next twelve hours, Colt and Crane treated burns, stitched gashes, set and plastered broken arms and legs, and did the best they could with the limited supplies on hand. Colt learned that Crane had been trained in traditional Chinese medicine, and in White medicine in France. He also explained the theories behind the needles. "Some are placed to relieve pain. Chinese healers have been using them for centuries, much to the skepticism and derision of the White doctors."

Colt watched as Crane gently worked one into a spot on a man's arm. Colt admitted being skeptical, too, but upon checking the patient later, noted the man appeared more comfortable.

It was well past dark by the time they decided to get some sleep. "I'll take the first watch," Colt said. "You've been at this almost two days straight. If something happens that I can't handle I'll wake you."

Crane nodded, took one last look at the tent filled with his countrymen, and stepped outside to bed down.

Whit stopped by the following afternoon with details on the negotiations between the miners, the Chinese, the governor, and the railroad representatives. "They put all six hundred Chinese miners in Evanston on a train and are sending them to safety in San Francisco. None of them want to stay in the Territory and who can blame them?"

Crane said, "That's good news."

Colt agreed.

"There's even been a few arrests."

Colt thought that even better news.

But the hope of that afternoon turned to ash later that day when the Chinese learned they'd been victims of a cruel hoax. The train supposedly taking them west from Evanston to San Francisco had in fact been traveling east, and when the boxcars opened they found themselves in Rock Springs. The Union Pacific needed their labor to mine the coal that kept their trains running, and had lied to get their way. The furious Chinese refused to return to the mines. The White miners re-formed their mobs and threatened to kill any Chinese who did return because there were more Chinese working below ground and for less pay. The governor who'd brokered the first peace took the coward's way out and returned to the territorial capital of Cheyenne, saying the standoff was a labor issue between Union Pacific and its workers.

Over the next few days, Crane's and Colt's patients improved but the situation in town deteriorated. The Chinese refused to leave the boxcars and in retaliation the company stores stopped selling them food, hoping to starve them into surrendering. The White miners went on strike and stationed their armed mobs at the mouths of the mines. There'd been a similar strike in 1871 when the railroad bosses hired in Scandinavians at a lower wage, but the Scandinavians, English, and Welsh were now united against the Chinese. The U.S. government sent in more troops to keep the peace, but the jeering and threats continued. When the Chinese demanded back pay as a condition to return to work, Union Pacific refused and threatened to evict them from the boxcars. The mines at Rock Springs were the company's largest producers and the stoppage was negatively impacting their profits.

In the end, Union Pacific won by threatening to fire any worker, Chinese or White, who didn't return to work, and promised that those who refused would be barred from working for the company for the rest of their life. A handful of Chinese remained adamant and left town. The rest, needing to accumulate enough money to return to their families in China, were forced back into laboring for a company that had lied to them, and in a place where their countrymen had been burned out and slaughtered.

Colt packed up his belongings in preparation to return. He felt good about helping Crane and his people but he was physically and mentally exhausted. He missed his family and the comforts of home.

Crane walked up as Colt hefted his bedroll onto the back of his horse. "Thank you for your help, Dr. Lee."

"You're welcome. What are your plans?"

"Maybe return to Green River. Maybe go home to China. The American government is talking of limiting how many of our people can enter in the future, so I'm not sure."

Colt understood his uncertainty. "May I ask you a question?"

He nodded.

"Is Crane your real name?"

For the first time since they'd met ten days ago, the doctor smiled. "No. I refuse to allow my true name to be in the mouths of these savages so it could be mocked and denigrated. I chose Crane because the birds are revered and the ignorant here could pronounce it."

Colt chuckled.

"I was born . . ." And he offered his name.

Humbled by the honor, Colt said, "Thank you.

I've enjoyed our partnership. If there's ever anything I can do, let me know."

Crane nodded and walked back into the tent to continue his service to the few remaining patients.

At the train station, Colt joined Whit and the others and led his horses into the boxcar.

"Glad to be heading home," Whit said, sounding as tired as Colt felt. He'd been with the soldiers during the stay.

"Me too. Miss my daughter and Regan."

"Dr. Lee. May I speak with you for a moment?"

Colt turned and looked up into the somber face of the mounted Lieutenant Levi Spalding.

Whit went on ahead and Colt waited to see what the man had to say.

"I just want to thank you for helping out."

Colt nodded and waited.

Spalding appeared uncomfortable. "Look. Just tell Regan, I'm sorry I lied to her."

Colt held his look for a moment, offered no response, and walked away.

Chapter Eighteen

"*W*hen is Papa coming home?" Anna asked petulantly during breakfast. "I miss him."

Regan was seated with her at the table. "Hopefully soon, sweetie. I do miss him, too."

"He never goes away this long."

He'd left for Rock Springs ten days ago. Regan had been keeping up with the volatile situation there as best she could via the Laramie and Cheyenne newspapers, and tried not to worry about his safety in the midst of all the violence. "How about we ride into town and see if the supplies for the school have arrived?"

She twirled her spoon in her oatmeal. "Okay," she said gloomily.

Regan smiled inwardly at the little brown face. She missed her papa a lot and Regan knew exactly how she felt. Colt being away was like missing a part of herself.

In the meeting with the ladies group, the day after his leaving, they took a vote and decided to focus on raising money to better outfit the school rather than fund a lending library. A trip to the building the next day revealed that Mr. Adams had stripped the school of everything from readers to pencils. He'd even taken the paper from the outhouse. If they were to open again with Regan as the teacher they'd have to start from scratch. And they did. For the past eight days, with the help of Mr. Nelson, the men of the Ranchers Association, and other members of the community, the interior of the schoolhouse was cleaned, the warped and aging floorboards replaced, and the walls painted. Ed Prescott donated a new stove to keep the students warm once winter settled in. Regan and Glenda paid for new books and all the rest of the supplies. Odell and his checkers buddies donated wood for the stove. Spring sent away for a new handle for the pump, and undertaker Lyman Beck had his carpenter install new benches with trestle tabletops so the children could sit and do their work. Although there were fewer than ten students on the rolls, the people of Paradise began embracing the school as their own and the names on the petition the council had requested began to add up.

Regan thought about all this as she and Anna drove to town. She felt good about playing a role in the effort. After helping to paint and sand and dig a new walkway to the school's newly painted front door, she was no longer looked upon as an outsider.

Her attire of denims and men's shirts no longer drew stares and she was no longer introduced as Doc's new wife, but by her name or as Mrs. Doc, which she enjoyed.

Rolling into town, the sight of her husband's shuttered office dampened her mood a bit, but she knew he'd be home as soon as he was able and that his presence in Rock Springs was a help to the people there. She parked the wagon in front of the telegraph office and she and Anna went inside.

As usual there was a game of checkers under way. Odell was seated across the board from saloon owner, Heath Leary. Regan didn't know if the Irishman had made any more overtures to win Dovie's heart, but if he had she'd not shared it with Regan or Glenda.

Upon seeing her and Anna, Odell nodded and Leary said, "Ah, the lovely Mrs. Doc and the lovely lassie Anna."

While Leary was charming them, Odell kinged him and hopped across the board and took four of the gambler's men. "Hey!" Leary yelled.

Odell smiled. "You need to pay more attention to the board and less to the lovely lassies. Aren't you supposed to be a gambler?"

His buddies laughed. Heath hung his head.

Odell asked Regan, "What can I do for you lovely lassies?"

Smiling, she replied, "We came to see if you have anything for us? We're still waiting on the new schoolbooks."

He stood. "It's your lucky day. Moss Denby brought them in last night on his run from Cheyenne."

Elated, Regan waited while he unearthed the large crate from the rest of the delivered mail and crates.

Heath said, "Since these old codgers would probably keel over trying to lift something of that size, I'll help you load it."

He received catcalls and jeers for his remark and Regan told him, "Thanks."

Once the crate was in the back of the wagon, she thanked him again and he went back inside. "Let's stop by and see Wallace Jr.'s mama before we head home."

They crossed the street and entered Dovie's shop to the tinkle of the bell above the door. The small interior had dress forms wearing the latest fashions and shelves holding neatly folded fabric lined one wall. There was also a small sitting area where customers could view pattern books or discuss what kind of services they wanted.

The tall blonde Dovie came out of the back and smiled at the sight of Regan and Anna. "If school doesn't start back soon, I may have to sell my son to the zoo. I love him dearly but he has enough energy for six boys. How are you two doing?"

"We're fine." Regan laughed. Dovie and her son lived over the shop. She assumed the sounds of running feet coming from above was Wallace Jr. at play.

Dovie asked Anna, "Anna, how about we make a trade? Wallace Jr. can live with your mama and you come live with me? I'd love to have a nice quiet little girl."

Anna shook her head. "I want to keep my mama."

"I don't blame you. So, what brings you two by?"

Regan told her about the school supplies, adding, "Which means, you won't have to give your son to the zoo. As long as everything we ordered is in the crate, we should be able to start school in the next couple of days."

"Thank the Lord."

"I also stopped by to see if you have any patterns Anna and I can look at. She needs some new things, dresses mostly, a nightgown or two."

Dovie's face lit up. "I would love to sew some things for her. I rarely get to sew for little girls. Take a seat and I'll get my books and tape."

Measurements were taken, pattern books were pored over, and selections made. An hour later, a very happy Anna and her mama walked back to their wagon and drove towards home.

On the way, they were discussing the dresses and other garments Dovie would be making when Regan noticed a rider in the middle of the road. As they neared the man, his familiar face stoked both wariness and disgust. It was Dun Bailey. When he didn't move out of the road to let them pass, Regan stopped the team.

"Afternoon," he said.

She nodded.

"Heard the doc's out of town."

Regan didn't respond.

He gave her a serpent's smile. "Just wanted to let you know I'll be watching your back while he's away. Wouldn't want you to get shot like my brother, Jeb, did."

It was a threat and he didn't bother veiling it.

"Thank you for your concern," she responded coldly. "Now let us pass so we can be on our way."

"Pretty little girl you got there. I'll be watching her, too."

Regan kept her anger from her face. She knew he was trying to provoke her and he'd done a good job. Were her rifle within reach, she would've blown him to Tucson.

Smiling, he touched his hat and moved out of the way. She drove past him without a glance.

After they cleared him, Anna asked in a soft voice, "Who was that?"

"Vermin."

"I don't like vermin."

"Neither do I." She'd be sharing the encounter with Colt and Whit when they returned. In the meantime, she'd keep an eye out for him and on Anna.

That evening as they were eating dinner, Colt came in. Anna screamed, "Papa!" She ran to him and climbed like a squirrel up a tree. "I missed you!"

Laughing, he hugged her tight. "I missed you, too. Have you been good?"

"Yes. I'm so glad you're home."

Still carrying her, he walked to the table and gave the equally happy Regan a warm kiss. "Welcome home," she said. "Are you hungry?"

"As a bear, and so tired I'm surprised my eyes are still open."

"Sit. I'll fix you a plate."

She returned with a plate groaning with large slabs of ham, yams, collards, and three biscuits. "I dreamt about a meal like this."

Anna asked, "You didn't have food?"

"Not a lot, no."

Regan could see his exhaustion and that he'd lost weight. Eating, he asked, "How have you two been?"

"We've been well," Regan replied and told him about the school renovations.

"You all did a lot while I've been gone."

"We want to open in a few days."

"Are you still going to teach?"

"I am. Mr. Nelson said he may have found a prospect in Laramie. He's waiting to hear back."

He asked Anna, "What do you think about your mama being your teacher?"

She shrugged. "It's okay I guess. We saw a man named Vermin today."

He paused. "Vermin?"

She nodded. "He said he was watching over me and Mama while you were gone."

This was not how Regan wanted the topic introduced but the cat was out of the bag now. "Dun

Bailey. He was on the road. I'll tell you about it later."

His eyes flashed to hers.

Anna continued. "I told Mama I didn't like vermin. She said she didn't either."

"Finish eating, Colton," she encouraged her husband gently. "We're fine. He can wait."

She could tell he wanted to have the conversation right then but he grudgingly acquiesced and returned to his food.

After eating, he stayed awake long enough to tuck Anna into bed, and when he and Regan left her bedroom, Regan asked, "Do you want me to run you a bath?"

"No, I'll probably fall asleep and drown. I just want to lie down, preferably with my wife but I'd sleep through that as well."

She walked with him to his room and watched as he fell facedown onto the bed.

"After ten days of sleeping on the ground, this feels so good. Too tired to even take my boots off."

"Here. I'll help."

Once they were removed, she asked, "Anything else you need?"

"Besides you?" he mumbled, still facedown and fully dressed.

She was so happy to have him home where he belonged. "I'll turn out the lamps so you don't forget and burn the house down."

The room plunged into darkness. "Good night, doctor man."

Snoring was his reply.

Chuckling, she left him to his dreams and closed the door softly behind her.

The next morning, while Colt slept like the dead, Regan and Anna were having breakfast when Spring stopped by.

"I'm on my way to town to get feed for the piglets. Wanted to see if Anna would like to go with me."

Her brown eyes sparkled with excitement. "May I go, Mama, please? I like feeding the piglets."

Regan said, "Yes, you may, but finish your eggs, then you can get dressed."

While Anna finished her breakfast, Regan said, "Colt came back yesterday."

"Good. I was starting to worry."

"He was so tired, he'll probably sleep until Christmas."

Anna took her now clean plate into the kitchen and hurried off to get dressed.

Spring asked, "Shall I tell her those little piggies that she adores will be on her plate as bacon one day soon?"

Regan laughed. "Don't you dare."

"I'm just teasing. When my father told me the truth, I was probably just a bit older than she is now. I didn't eat bacon for months."

Regan told her about the arrival of the school supplies and the encounter with Dun Bailey.

Spring went still. "If that bastard even looks at

Anna when I'm around, I'll geld him and watch him bleed to death on the ground. How dare he threaten you two that way. Does Colt know?"

"A little of it. I'll tell him the rest when he gets up."

Spring was still fuming when Anna appeared, but brightened. "Are you ready?"

"Yes."

"Then let's head out. We'll be back around suppertime. That okay with you, Anna?"

"Yes."

They started for the door and Anna called back, "Mama, tell Papa I love him and that I'm still glad he's home."

"I will, sweetheart. Have fun."

Around noon, Regan was on the back porch leafing through one of the readers she'd taken from the crate of school items when Colt stepped outside. "Good afternoon, lazybones," she said to him.

"I woke up with all my clothes on."

He looked so confused, she stifled her grin. "You went to sleep that way."

"I don't remember taking off my boots though."

"That's because I did the honors."

He shook his head and ran his hand down his unshaven face.

"Did you sleep well?"

"I did. Still tired though." He still looked tired, too.

"You were snoring before I left the room."

"Sorry."

"No apologies needed. Hungry?"

"Very. Where's Anna?"

"With her beloved Aunt Spring. They went into town for piglet feed. She'll bring her back by suppertime. Anna said to tell you she loves you and is still glad you're home."

He smiled. "She's something."

"Yes, she is."

Regan cooked him a hearty breakfast and sat with him while he ate. "Tell me about Dun," he said.

She gave him the details and saw his anger as he asked, "Does he think talking about Anna that way is something we'd laugh about?"

"He was deliberately trying to provoke me."

"I'll kill him if even looks at her."

"I let Spring know before she and Anna left."

"Good."

"I don't think he wants to tangle with any of us."

"No, he doesn't."

To take his mind off Dun for the moment, she said, "Tell me about Rock Springs."

"Lieutenant Levi Spalding was there."

She stilled. "Did you use your scalpel on him?"

He grinned. "No. Told me to tell you he was sorry he lied."

She rolled her eyes. "Forget him, tell me the rest."

He did, and she was moved by how the Chinese suffered. He told her about Dr. Crane and finished with how the Union Pacific Railroad tricked the Chinese miners. She was speechless for a few moments. "That's unconscionable."

He nodded. "Yes, it was and they were furious to find themselves in Rock Springs. Reminded me of the government's broken treaties with the Native tribes. Promise something knowing it's a lie."

Regan was outdone, but pulled her mind away from the railroad's atrocious actions. "I put all your mail in your study."

"Thank you. I'm going to sit and enjoy being home. With any luck, no one will break a leg, fall off a horse, or get eaten by One Eye for the next day or two."

"And I will leave you alone, for today at least. I've missed you. Been a while since I've made you run amok."

He gave her a grin.

She paused at what she saw reflected there.

He stood, walked over, and picked her up. She laughed. "What are you doing?"

He carried her purposefully to his bedroom and set her down on her feet. "Time to run amok, Mrs. Lee. Kindly take off your clothes, so I can determine how much you really missed me."

Laughing, she said demurely, "Yes, Doctor."

*T*wo days later, the school officially reopened and Regan surveyed the faces of her students. They looked skeptical, including Lucky the dog lying at the feet of his owner, Silas Taylor. She cleared her throat. "So, how did Mr. Adams usually start the day?"

Anna said, "He'd collect the work we did at home."

"Ah." Since there wasn't any, she plunged ahead. "Then what?"

Wallace Jr.'s hand shot up.

"Yes."

"We'd get recess for the rest of the day."

His classmates snickered.

Regan smiled. "Since we know Wallace Jr. is pulling my leg, who can name the current president of the United States?"

Livy raised her hand.

"Livy?"

"Mr. Grover Cleveland."

"Very good. Who knows the name of the country's very first president?"

Livy's hand went up again.

"Let's give someone else a chance, Olivia, okay?"

She looked disappointed but nodded.

Regan looked to other children but no one volunteered to respond. "Silas?"

"George Washington," he groused. "I'm nine years old, Mrs. Lee, why do I have to answer baby questions?"

Regan was thrown by that. "I'm sorry. What's twelve multiplied by nine?"

He didn't hesitate. "108."

She was impressed. "Very good. Do you know all the tables of multiplication?"

"Yes. Lucky and I know everything," he replied proudly. "Don't we, Lucky?" The dog barked in agreement.

Regan stifled an eye roll and wondered where Silas had gotten the preposterous notion. Her first thought was to ask him how many people lived in China, but wasn't sure teachers were supposed to snatch the rug from under their students on the first day. "I've never met anyone who knows everything."

He puffed up. "I do."

The other children were viewing the conversation eagerly as if enjoying the new teacher being challenged, even Anna. *Traitor!*

"Did Mr. Adams know that?"

He blinked and turned slightly red. "No, ma'am."

"How about your parents? Do they know they're wasting your time and their money sending you to school?"

He shook his head.

"Okay, then let's make a deal. Pretend you don't know everything, and I'll pretend to know more than you."

He nodded.

She smiled.

In the month that followed, Regan grew more comfortable standing at the front of the classroom and the students grew more comfortable with her being there. She worked reading and spelling one-syllable words with the children in Anna's age group, and three- and four-syllables with self-proclaimed genius Silas Taylor. They went for hikes to look at nature, laid in the grass during recess to find cloud shapes, and held spelling bees. She made Wallace Jr. sit in the corner at least once a day for terrorizing the girls; Felicity seemed to be his favorite target because she'd cry instead of socking him the way Livy had when he slipped a tiny frog down the back of her dress. Each day at two, Regan went home exhausted, but pleased by the growth of the young minds she was helping to mold.

The town council meeting held during the last week of July was packed. On the agenda was the hiring of the new teacher, Mr. Irving Dunbar, a recent graduate of an Illinois college and the nephew of one of the members of the Ranchers Association. People turned out to watch Regan and the ladies turn in the petition the council had asked for, holding twice the number of needed names, to make sure the mayor and the other members kept their word about paying the new teacher a decent wage.

And when all went well and the meeting was adjourned by the sour-faced Arnold Cale, the roars of approval shook the walls of his bank.

That evening on the back porch, Regan sat cuddled in her husband's lap. "So now that you're no longer the teacher, how are you feeling?"

"Sad. Teaching was exhausting but I'll miss being with the children."

"Even Wallace Jr.?"

"Even Wallace Jr."

The rumble of his chuckle played against her ear on his chest.

"So, what are you going to do with yourself all day now?"

"I don't know. Maybe Odell will let me deliver the mail."

"If I get a vote, I say no."

"Then it's good you don't get one."

Again, the rumble of amusement.

She sat up. "I have an idea. How about I come to your office every day, slip beneath your desk, and make you run amok."

He laughed. "No."

"No one will know. They may wonder why you're having trouble breathing and why your eyes have rolled back into your head, but I'll be very quiet. Promise. Let me show you."

She slid to her knees and as she demonstrated, he had lots of trouble breathing. His eyes rolled so far back into his head it was a wonder they didn't jump free and spin around in the darkness of the porch floor, but she kept her promise. She was very quiet.

Chapter Nineteen

$\mathcal{A}$ few days later, Regan dropped Anna off at school. After waving good-bye and watching her enter the building, she decided to drop in on Spring and invite her to dinner. She was about halfway there when the crack of a rifle broke the early morning silence and pain exploded in her back and shoulders. Her first thought was to get off the seat, find cover, but another crack followed, and she screamed as the next bullet brought even more pain. She tried to pick up the reins because the horses had panicked and were running, but her back was on fire, her vision hazy. She pitched forward. It was the last thing she remembered.

$\mathcal{G}$lad that one of Ed Prescott's new foals was finally responding to the colic medicine he'd prescribed last week, Colt headed home to see if he could steal a few kisses from his wife before riding to his office. He didn't see the wagon, so he assumed she hadn't made it back from the school yet. He'd just dismounted and was on his way to the door when the sound of thundering horses made him stop and look back at the road. It was his wagon but where was Regan? He ran to intercept the team, and that was when he saw her slumped over the footboard, caught in the reins, bobbing like a bloody rag doll. "Regan!"

Frantic, he stopped the horses, climbed onto the seat, and attempted to visually assess the damage even as he threw open his bag and grabbed a scalpel to cut her free from the leads. She moaned while he worked. "I'm sorry, darlin', but I have to get you inside so I can see how bad this is. Don't you dare die on me, Mrs. Lee."

It took him only a few minutes, but it felt like a lifetime to get her from the wagon to the house. He wanted to run but forced himself to walk so as not to jostle her. Once inside, he carried her into his room and gently laid her down on her stomach on his bed. Scalpel in hand, he quickly made a cut that split the back of her bloody shirt open from collar to tail and did the same thing with her blood-soaked shift. Using a pad of clean gauze, he gently wiped at the blood so he could see the source of the bleeding while she moaned and shrank away from his touch. "I'm sorry I'm hurting you." He found two bullets. One just below her shoulder. The second, low on her back, just to the left of her spine. Cursing the unknown person responsible, he left her for a moment and hurried to the kitchen. The new stove had a hot water receptacle that held three gallons of water. He placed his hand against it and found it still warm from breakfast. He opened it, placed the surgical instruments he'd be needing inside, and added more wood to the stove to bring the water back up to a boil. He needed to tell Whit what happened, and later, Anna would need to be picked up from school but he refused to worry about any of that now. His only concern was Regan, and with that in mind, he buried the part of himself that loved her and became the emotionless detached doctor who'd been trained to save lives.

"*How* is she?" Spring asked Colt as he stepped out of his bedroom. She'd come by an hour or so ago to drop off Regan's weekly supply of bacon not knowing Regan had been shot.

"I got the bullets out. She lost a fair amount of blood. Had the bullet in her upper back been a few inches lower it would've pierced her heart, and the one in her lower back was only inches from her spine, so she was lucky in that sense, but there's some internal bleeding. The next day or so will be critical."

Spring rubbed his arm consolingly. "She'll pull through. She's tough."

He hoped she was right. "I need to go back in and check on her. Can you do me a few favors?"

"Whatever you need."

"Go into town and let Whit know what's happened. Tell him the shells were from a Springfield just like the last time. And later, would you pick up Anna from school? I may need her to stay with you a few days until I'm sure Regan's recovery is going the way it should."

"I'd love to have her, but prepare yourself, she may balk about being away from Regan. That little girl loves her mama."

"Yes, she does and so do I."

Spring studied him. "I've noticed. Glad you figured it out."

"I've come a long way since that night I came to you for advice." Regan held his heart, which is why he needed her to live.

"Have you told her how much she means to you?"

"Every chance I get."

"Good for you. There's hope for you yet." She threw her arms around him and gave him a strong hug. "You two have earned your happiness."

Colt couldn't remember the last time they'd shared a hug, but it felt good.

When they parted, she said, "You go see about my sister-in-law and I'll ride into town. Is there anything you need from your office or from Miller's?"

"Not that I can think of."

"Okay. I'll be back as soon as I can."

He was thankful for her. Her visit turned out to be a godsend. With her shouldering some of the load, he could focus all his energies on Regan.

Back in his bedroom, he looked down at his sleeping wife. He'd given her a steeped mixture of plants and bark he'd learned to make from Ed's grandmother early in his career. It aided sleep and more importantly dulled pain. Back East doctors often ridiculed Native remedies, but Colt knew better. Healers like Ed's grandmother had been keeping their people alive for centuries. He placed a light hand on Regan's brow. Her temperature was slightly elevated, which was to be expected after what she'd endured, but not high enough to cause him concern. His earlier rush of anxiety and worry had faded, leaving behind the sense of how tired he was, but now was not the time to sleep. Instead, he brought a chair over to her bedside and sat to watch and wait.

Spring had been correct about Anna. When his sister brought her home from school, Colt sat down with her and quietly explained what happened. Taking her hand, he led her into the room where Regan lay sleeping. Anna viewed her silently and the tears that ran down her cheeks broke his heart. "Is she going to die?"

"I don't think so, but I want you to spend the next few days with Aunt Spring so I can take care of her."

"No. I want to stay." She glanced up. "Please."

Not wanting to disturb Regan he said, "Come. Let's talk about this outside."

Giving her mama a backwards glance of concern, she let herself be led out.

They sat in the parlor and he again explained his position, and she again refused. "I want to stay. I can help."

"Sweet, I can't take care of you and your mama at the same time."

"I'll take care of myself, I promise. I want to stay. Please, Papa."

"No, Anna."

"Please! If I leave, she'll die." He pulled her onto his lap and she wept. "Please, Papa. Don't make me go."

There were tears in his eyes now, too. "This is hard, Anna. Help me by doing as I ask, please."

"But I don't want to leave Mama."

He held her close. "I know, honey. But you can help her best by staying with Aunt Spring." He glanced up to see his sister standing in the doorway.

Spring said, "Anna, I promise to bring you to see your mama every day. Let your Papa help her get better."

"She's going to die," she cried.

"No, she won't," Colt said reassuringly. "She loves you too much to leave you."

"Please," she pleaded softly. "Please, let me stay here."

Spring walked over and picked her up from Colt's lap. "Come on, baby. Let's get your things."

Anna put her arms around Spring's neck and sobbed as if her heart was breaking and Colt closed his eyes against the pain her distress set off inside.

Spring and Anna drove away a short time later. Anna didn't come to him to say good-bye.

That evening, Whit and Odell stopped by.

"How is she?" Whit asked.

"Holding her own for now."

"Good. I went by Dun's place, but he's not there. Didn't see the dogs either. Put out a poster on him saying he's wanted for questioning. We'll see if he turns up."

"He's the one who did this," Colt insisted. "I know it's him."

"I understand but the court's going to need evidence, and right now, we don't have anything but gut feelings."

"What happened with the court case for Jeb's friends after we left?"

"Judge Jinks sent them to trial. It's scheduled to be held over in Cheyenne in a few weeks."

Odell asked, "How's Anna?"

"I sent her home with Spring, but she didn't want to go. She's scared Regan will die if she's not here."

Odell shook his head in sympathy. "She loves her mother a lot."

"I know." He could still hear her sobs.

"Let me know if there's anything I can do."

"I will."

Colt walked them to the porch. "Let me know if Dun turns up."

Whit nodded. "By the way, Minnie's place looks deserted. I knocked but she didn't come to the door."

"She was here a few evenings ago and said she was moving back East."

"Oh," Whit said, appearing confused. "She never

said anything to me about moving. I'll keep an eye on her place until we hear something definitive."

Colt thanked him. He and Odell left and Colt went back inside to Regan.

For the next few days, the draft kept her asleep. Colt kept an eye on her around the clock and was pleased that she seemed to be sleeping less fitfully. The bleeding had stopped and he didn't see any signs that she was still bleeding internally. A steady stream of visitors stopped by to ask about her progress. Glenda, Lacy, Lucretia, and Dovie brought food and did laundry, for which he was extremely grateful because lying on clean bedding lessened the chance of her wounds becoming infected. True to her word, Spring drove Anna over every day and while Anna sat silently by her mama's bedside, Spring took her mare, Star, out for a run.

*R*egan opened her eyes. Her vision was hazy, her mouth felt as if she'd eaten cotton. Closing her eyes again, hoping it would help her focus and clear the cobwebs in her mind, she laid still a moment. Breathing hurt, so she took in small breaths. The fog lifted just enough to let her know she was lying in a bed, but not where.

"Welcome back, Mrs. Lee."

She turned her head and croaked, "Colton?" His features were difficult to make out, so she tried to sit up but pain sharp as shards of glass ripped through her back and she cried out.

"Lie still," he said. His hands touched her gently.

A moan rose from her.

"Just lie still."

She drew in little puffs of air until the hurt faded. When it finally did, she asked, "Where am I?"

"In my bed. Here, take a few sips of water."

Scared of setting off the pain again, she raised her head just enough to feel the cup against her lips, then took a few sips. Lowering herself again, she drew in a few breaths. She was exhausted. "What happened to me?"

"You were shot."

She had trouble remembering at first, but soon pieces of the event rose in her mind. "I was going to visit Spring and . . . Two bullets," she whispered.

"I took them out."

"Anna?"

"With Spring, but she's been here to see you every day."

"How long have I been like this?"

"This is the afternoon of the fifth day."

"Aunt Eddy got shot once, too." But before she could explain, she drifted back into sleep.

The next time she opened her eyes, Anna was sitting in a chair beside her. Regan smiled, or at least she thought she was smiling. "Hi, honey," she said softly. "How are you?"

"I'm fine, Mama. How are you?"

"I've been better but I'll be up and around soon."

"You're not going to die?"

"No. It'll take more than a couple of lousy bullets

to do that. Besides I have your love to help me get better and your papa is the best doctor in the Territory."

Anna smiled.

By the eighth day, Regan could sit up without much pain, if she didn't do it for long periods of time, and by day ten, she was sick of lying in bed.

"I want to get up, Colton."

"You need to heal up a bit more."

"I'm tired of lying around and doing nothing."

"And here I thought you enjoyed my scintillating company."

"In small doses, yes. Not all day, all the time."

"You wound me."

She rolled her eyes.

"How about I carry you outside?"

"How about I walk on my two good legs."

"You're not as strong as you think you are, Mrs. Lee."

And because Regan never met a challenge she could ignore, she swung her legs over the side of the bed and stood up. They immediately turned to water, and had he not quickly caught her and lifted her up into his arms, she would've ended up in a heap on the floor.

Amused, he looked down into her scowling face and asked, "Will you listen to your doctor now?"

The scowl deepened and he sat down on the bed with her in his lap. "You'll be able to go back to being the Queen of Lee House soon. For now, I need you to go slow just a little longer."

She leaned against him. "I detest this."

"I noticed."

"I'm sorry for being such a poor patient."

"Once you're all healed up you can show me how good a patient you can really be."

She raised up and thought back on their memorable lovemaking on the porch, in his study, in the stand of trees on the day they visited Ed Prescott's horse ranch, and the night on her knees when she was very quiet.

"Making love to you will be better if you're fully healed, so do us both a favor, okay?"

"Yes, Doctor."

"Now, give me a kiss and I'll get your lunch."

She complied and as he left the room, she imagined all the ways she planned to be a good patient once she was better.

In the weeks that followed, Whit's search for her shooter turned up nothing, and no one had seen Dun Bailey. Meanwhile Regan had healed enough to ride Star again and she was in heaven. She also resumed attending the Paradise Ladies Society meetings, enjoying Anna's company, and cooking on the new stove. She also got to jump up and down on the bed with her husband as Anna so hilariously described lovemaking and that pleased Regan the most.

She, Anna, Spring, Dovie, and Glenda Cale took the train to Cheyenne and went shopping. Regan purchased lots of clothes for Anna to go with the things Dovie made for her. She also ordered new furniture, bought a few things for herself, and new shirts for Colt. They'd had a wonderful time. Upon their return, she consulted with Adele about ridding the house of the stuffy old furniture to make room for the new.

A month after the shooting, carpenter Porter James returned to Paradise, and he and his men finished the repairs on Regan's bedroom. From daybreak to dark the air rang with the sounds of their work. The scent of fresh paint filled the air. Since the carpenters were already there, Colt and Regan had them begin the work on Anna's room, too. The plan was to remove the back wall to make the room larger, and add a door that led to a small porch because Regan believed every little girl should be able to sit outside, look up at the stars, and dream.

Colt and Regan wanted her new room to be a surprise, so while the work was being done, they sent her to spend a week with Aunt Spring. She was due home later that day.

"Do you think she'll like it?" Colt asked Regan as they stood in the now finished room.

"I think she will."

The walls were robin egg blue. The blue-and-white patterned curtains sewn up by Dovie added the perfect touch. Her new bed and bedding ordered from a store in Cheyenne was in place, too.

Colt put his arm around her waist and gave her a squeeze. "Thank you for this."

"You're welcome. She's a sweet girl. She deserves nice things."

"Have you spent yourself into the poorhouse yet?"

She chuckled. "No. I am getting low though, so I wired Uncle Rhine yesterday about replenishing the well. He wired back that he'd take care of it." She looked up at Colt. "In addition to the new furniture I ordered, we need new lamps, and carpets, and next year—a larger kitchen so Portia and I can stop running into each other."

"Lord," he voiced, amused.

"You give your life's blood to the people around here, Colton. Sometimes you're away two and three days at a time, and you were in Rock Springs what, ten days? The least I can do is make sure you have a comfortable place to come home to. Like Anna, you deserve it." Her doctor man worked himself to the bone and all without complaint for people who often couldn't pay. He didn't grouse, call it unfair, or deny anyone his services. If he was needed, no matter day or night, he saddled up and rode out. She admired that, but the woman who loved him wished they had more time together. It seemed as if every time she turned around, someone had fallen off a roof, been injured in a rock slide, or a rancher's animal was in distress.

"Did Spring say what time she planned to bring Anna home?" he asked.

"In time for supper."

"It's only noon. Do you want me to help you move into your new room now that it's done?"

"That would be wonderful. Mr. James brought my bed yesterday while you were gone." He'd been overseeing the birth of one of Lucretia's cows and had gotten in so late, he'd gone straight to bed.

"Lead the way."

When they brought in the first load he looked around. "I'm impressed."

"Do you like it?"

"I do. It looks nothing like it did before."

She liked it as well; from the soft yellow paint on the walls to the ivory drapes made by Dovie to the lovely ivory-and-gold bedding she'd ordered, it was as nice as her bedroom back in Arizona. She'd had a door and a porch added to the space as well.

"Couldn't find a bigger bed?" he asked, scanning the new oversized four-poster with its ivory brocade canopy.

She smiled. "I wanted it to be large enough to accommodate my doctor when he makes his house calls."

He walked over and tested the give on the mattress. "I may have to make a series of calls to judge it correctly. Will tonight be soon enough for you, Mrs. Lee?"

The look he gave her made her senses flare. "I believe so."

He walked over to where she stood. "Are you sure?"

Her body was already calling to him. "Yes."

He slid a finger down her cheek, then brushed it gently over her bottom lip, before moving it slowly over her already budded breasts, and her eyes slid shut. "Afterwards," he said, kissing her. "I should probably evaluate your new tub, too. We'll use that fancy soap I missed out on the last time I was invited."

She was ready to be undressed and evaluated there and then. "I look forward to it."

It took a while but her large amount of hat boxes, shoes, gowns, and the rest were all moved in. Now she just had to put everything away. "Thank you."

"You're welcome. Figure it'll take you a while to put all this stuff away, so I'm going to my study. See you in a year or so."

"Out!" She laughed.

He left, and as she looked around, she thought it might take more than two years.

Later, Regan was in the kitchen preparing for dinner when Spring entered via the back door.

"Hello," Spring said, "why does your kitchen always smell so much better than mine?"

Regan knew she was teasing because Spring was an excellent cook. "Where's my daughter?"

"Outside. And she has a surprise. Will you get Colt and meet us out front?"

Wondering what this was about, she said, "Sure. Let me get him."

She and Colt stepped out onto the porch and seeing Anna perched happily on the back of a smoke gray pony made their jaws drop. They stared at the smiling Spring.

Anna said, "Watch." She and the pony rode a

short distance before she turned him around and trotted back.

Regan and Colt left the porch to get closer. He said, "I'm so proud of you, Anna."

"And I haven't fallen off and broke my neck, not even once."

"Look at you," Regan said, laughing. "Is the pony yours?"

She nodded. "His name is Shadow. Aunt Spring got him for me, and she taught me how not to be scared. Now me and Livy can ride together."

Regan gave Aunt Spring a big hug. Colt did, too.

Spring said, "We've had fun. And she knows how to care for Shadow, too. Right, Anna?"

"Yes." And she rattled off a litany of things she had to do to keep Shadow safe, well, and clean.

Regan's eyes were misty. Anna had come so far.

Colt looked moved, too. "That is one big surprise, Anna, but guess what?"

"What?"

"If you want to come into the house for a minute your mama and I have a surprise for you, too."

Anna slid off Shadow's back, tied him to the post, gave his neck a squeeze that Regan found so endearing, and followed them inside. The door to her bedroom was closed. Colt said, "Close your eyes."

She did and they took her hands and led her in. "Now, open them," Regan said.

Anna glanced around. Her eyes widened and she began to cry.

Concern filled Colt's face and he bent down. "What's wrong?"

"It's so pretty," she whispered through her tears. With her hands steepled over her mouth, she took it in again: the bed, drapes, the new wardrobe holding all her new clothes. There was even an easel and a stool so she could draw to her heart's content. She ran to her father and gave him a big hug, then did the same thing to Regan, who said, "There's one last thing we want you to see."

Colt opened the door and they all stepped out onto the little porch.

"Is this mine, too?" Anna asked excitedly.

"All yours."

She took a seat on the bench. "I like this."

Spring replied, "I do, too. I think I may sell my place and move in with you, Anna. What do you think?"

"Can I have it to myself for a little while first?"

Spring laughed. "If you must."

That evening, after Anna went to bed, Regan's doctor made a house call. She was stripped, teased, left breathless, and filled so much she forgot her name. When he asked her to lean up against her headboard, she said, "Yes, Doctor." When he took a seat on her new vanity bench and invited her to ride, she said, "Yes, Doctor." And later in the tub, when they washed each other slowly with a fresh bar of her lavender-scented soap, there were no questions or answers—just his growls and her soft soaring cries.

Chapter Twenty

$\mathcal{R}$egan was searching through her bedroom's chaos for her favorite hairbrush. She thought she'd left it on her vanity, but after moving aside an armful of nightgowns, three pairs of black stockings, and a pile of books to get to the surface below, the brush wasn't there.

She was on her knees peering beneath her bed when she heard Colton ask, "Lose something?"

Still on all fours, she replied, "Yes. My best hairbrush." She spent a few more seconds trying to spot the brush in the dimness, but spied only a shadow-shrouded boot, a handbag, and a pair of gloves she'd been searching for for the past few days. Straining to reach the gloves, it occurred to her that she was offering him a very nice look at her behind and she smiled inwardly.

"It's a wonder you can find anything in here."

She turned her head to view him over her

shoulder. He raised his eyes smoothly from her be-hind and in them she saw—*heat*. Response coursed through her sinuously. She got to her feet.

But then, he was slowly gauging the turmoil of her bedroom and she knew the moment was gone. Regan had always kept a messy bedroom. She made sure it was picked up when he paid his house calls, but he'd been in Denver at a medical convention for the past four days and just returned last night. While he was gone, the clutter had gotten away from her.

"Regan, I love you, but if there was a fire or some other catastrophe, you'd trip and possibly kill yourself before you could get out."

"You sound like my aunt and my sister."

"Obviously two smart women."

Regan knew she didn't have a leg to stand on; never had her entire life. Her usual way of dealing with the lectures about her messiness was to promise to do better, and she would. However, as time passed, she reverted to her old ways as did her room.

"Consider this. Our daughter believes you walk on water."

Regan smiled. "You know how much I love her."

"I do. She's beginning to mimic the way you walk, talk, ride. Anna is six. Suppose she begins to mimic—this?" He gestured towards the room. "At her age, if there was a fire, she'd never get out."

Regan froze. The idea of Anna losing her life in such a horrendous manner would be heartbreaking and no doubt kill her and Colt. "You're right."

"I'm heading over to Odell's. His gout's acting up."

"Okay." After his departure, she cleaned her room.

When he returned a few hours later, he stuck his head in to let her know he was back and she asked, "Better?"

"Yes. I just worry about your safety."

"I know, and you're right about what might happen during a fire."

"I wasn't trying to patronize you or speak to you like a child."

"I know but I'd keep this room much cleaner if you moved in with me. And if you say something plumb dumb about husbands and wives not sharing bedrooms, I will—not sure what I'll do—but it will be something."

He smiled.

"My aunt and uncle share their bedroom, so it's not a far-fetched idea. I like waking up with you beside me, Colt."

"I like that, too, and I've wanted to ask you about moving in, but it isn't something I'm familiar with. My mother and father never shared this room. Adele and I never shared a bedroom."

"Why didn't Adele move in here?"

He sighed.

"I'm sorry, I don't mean to pry."

"The problem was Minnie. She thought Adele might catch my mother's cancer."

"Can you catch cancer?"

He shook his head. "No, but Minnie was convinced it was in the walls, the floors, and rather than be browbeaten about it, Adele slept in the other room."

"I'm glad Minnie's gone."

"So am I. It's curious that she didn't leave any instructions about her house though. No one seems to know if she wants it sold or rented out or what."

Regan didn't care about Minnie. "Back to you sharing this room with me. Will you?"

"I'd love to." He looked around. "Is there space for my wardrobe, or will it have to be outside on the porch? You do own enough things to start your own store."

"Be nice. We can put it over by the fireplace or by the door to the washroom, or wherever suits you."

He glanced around. "I'll give it some thought."

"I'm meeting with the ladies after supper this evening. We'll be making our final plans for the Founders Day new school fund-raiser." It was only a few days away.

"Okay. Anna and I have a date to go riding after supper, but we'll be here by the time you return. She loves that pony."

"Yes, she does and to quote her: she hasn't fell off and broke her neck not even once. Take that, Minnie—wherever you are."

Colt's face turned serious. "Please be careful."

"I will and I'll keep my eyes open. Promise."

Her shooter still hadn't been unearthed, and although he never expressed it, she knew he worried each time she left the house, particularly alone. She did, too, but she refused to quake in fear, afraid of venturing out.

The meeting went well. They met again at Glenda's home. Everyone knew what they were bringing for the bake sale, and Glenda roped Odell and Porter James into being judges for the ladies' horseshoe tournament.

Lucretia asked Regan, "Are you going to enter?"

"Of course. How about you?"

"Of course. May the best woman win."

Colleen Enright looked disgusted but she was ignored.

Lacy said, "I'm entering, too, and plan on beating the drawers off both of you."

The meeting broke up soon after, and as Regan went to the door to mount Star and ride home, she was waylaid by Glenda's husband and banker mayor. "Uh, Mrs. Lee, may I speak with you? Privately in my study, please."

"Sure."

He led her into his study that was filled with furniture that reminded her of the old pieces she'd recently discarded.

"Have a seat, please."

Once she did, he said, "I received a deposit from your Uncle Rhine Fontaine for you, and I just wanted to let you know it arrived."

"Thank you."

"It's a substantial amount."

She didn't respond.

He looked uncomfortable, then said, "Well, I'm

wondering if he might be amenable to some invest-
ments I'm considering."

"I'm told you wired my Uncle Andrew in San
Francisco."

His face reddened. "Uh, yes, I did. And he responded, immediately."

"And very succinctly, too, from what I gathered."

He cleared his throat. "Yes."

"My Uncle Rhine won't be interested in your in-
vestments."

"But you haven't even asked him."

"And I won't be because the money he trans-
ferred to you under his name is mine, solely."

He stared. "Yours?"

She nodded. "Yes, and I'm a stickler about ac-
counting. If I learn that even one penny has been
diverted or gone astray, I'll be alerting them both to
have your institution investigated." Regan trusted
him about as far as she could toss him.

"Well, I—I, it's been nice speaking with you."

She stood. "Same here."

After breakfast, the Lees loaded up their wagon
with Regan's contributions for the bake sale and
headed into town for the Founders Day celebration. Main Street was as crowded with vehicles
and people as Regan had ever seen. Red, white,
and blue bunting decorated the buildings along
with small American flags. Paradise was celebrating Founders Day in a big way. The popping sound

of firecrackers punctuated the air and drivers held on to the reins of their horses and teams to keep the animals steady. Anna said, "I'm glad we left Shadow at home. I don't think he'd like the firecrackers."

"I don't think so either."

"I hope he doesn't get too lonely while I'm gone."

Regan gave her a hug. "I think he'll be okay."

Colt drove the wagon to the field behind Miller's store. Because of the parade, people were being encouraged to use the field for parking instead of lining the street. After finding a spot, they walked the short distance back to Main Street. Regan asked Anna, "Where's your favorite place to watch the parade?"

"In front of Papa's office."

"Then look for us there."

She nodded.

The schoolchildren would be marching in the parade, too, so Anna was left at the bank with their teacher, Mr. Dunbar, and the children who'd already arrived. Regan and Colt walked to claim a spot in front of his office.

"How long is the parade usually?"

"Ten minutes."

She laughed. "Ten minutes?"

"Small town. Small parade."

And to her amusement, he was correct. Marching first was Odell and his trapper friends decked out in snarling bear hides, complete with heads, teeth, and claws. She'd never seen anything like it, but she joined the bystanders in applauding and cheering. Next came buggies driven by the Paradise business owners: banker Arnold Cale and Glenda; store owners Chauncey and Lacy Miller; undertaker Mr. Beck, Heath Leary, and smaller establishment owners like Dovie. Regan wondered if her friend and the gambler would ever work things out between them.

Regan asked Colt, "Why aren't you marching?"

"Not much of a parade man."

The business owners were followed by the mounted men of the Ranchers Association. A few of the earlier marchers like Odell had circled the block to be with them thus earning the opportunity to be cheered twice.

Last but not least were the children along with the proudly marching Lucky, who received a rousing cheer of his own. The smiling children waved the tiny flags they'd made in school. Regan didn't see Felicity, but put her absence out of mind. She and Colt cheered loudly when Anna walked by and their daughter turned their way and grinned.

And that was that.

Colt looked at his pocket watch. "Twelve minutes."

Regan laughed, put her arm in his, and they left for the field behind the store where the activities would take place.

It was a day of games, food, and fun. The ladies' horseshoe tournament put on by the Paradise Ladies Society was a big hit. There were only four competitors, but many people bought tickets and everyone gathered around to watch Regan battle it out with Lucretia Watson as the final pair. Lacy lost in the first round to Lucretia. Bets were placed while good-natured taunts flew back and forth.

It was a tense fight. The women were tied until the final throw. Regan's shoe stopped just short of the stake and her supporters groaned. Lucretia's shoe hit the stake, circled it for the win, and the onlookers cheered. Regan walked over and lifted Lucretia's hand high in the air and the adulation soared.

As the bets were paid off, Regan walked to her husband's side.

He asked quietly, "Why'd you do that?"

She asked innocently, "Do what?"

"Shorten your throw on purpose."

"Lucretia won fair and square."

"And my name is Matilda."

She laughed. "Let's go find Anna so we can eat."

There was grilled corn, baked beans, and lots of chicken, ribs, steaks, and Spring's special pork link sausage. Dessert was courtesy of the Paradise Ladies Society and between the funds brought in by the horseshoe tournament and the desserts they had a good start on their dream to build a beautiful new school.

As dusk fell, everyone began settling in for the fireworks and Colt went to find Anna so she could watch with her family. For most of the day, the children had been playing on their own, and after dinner had gone back to their fun. She and Colt, like the other parents, had looked up every now and then to make sure they were okay. But Colt was gone so long Regan began to worry.

She searched the crowded field and finally saw him talking to Livy's mother, Julia. Beside them stood her husband, Paul, her parents, and Livy. Even from her distant spot, Regan saw it was an earnest conversation and knew instinctively something was wrong. She did a frantic search of the crowd for Anna's face but didn't see her. She made her way through the throng as quickly as she could to find out what had happened.

"Anna left with Minnie a few minutes ago," he said, visibly upset.

Regan was certain she'd misunderstood him. "What?"

Julia explained, "She told Anna she had a surprise for Shadow that you and Mr. Lee wanted Anna to have and they had to leave quickly."

Regan's knees went weak.

Julia said, "Dr. Lee just told me why I shouldn't have allowed her to go, but I didn't know Minnie was a threat. She's her aunt, and Anna didn't balk. I'm so sorry, I love Anna like my own. If anything happens to her . . ." Tears flowed down her cheeks. Her husband took her into his arms.

Regan rubbed her back. "It's okay, Julia. We'll find her. Don't worry."

"It's going to be dark soon," Colt said. "Regan, get the wagon. I'll find Whit and gather a search party."

She ran.

Everyone volunteered to help search and went out in small groups. When Julia was asked which way the buggy had gone, she said east, but it was impossible to know if they were still traveling in that direction. She also said there was a man driving but the buggy's canopy was raised so she hadn't gotten a clear look at his face. Whit and Odell hurried off to send a telegram to alert the sheriffs in both Laramie and Cheyenne in case Minnie tried to board the eastbound train.

When it became too dark to see well, the search was called off. After receiving reassurances and prayers from their neighbors, Regan and Colt reluctantly headed home. With any luck Minnie and the mystery would be foiled by the darkness, too, and be forced to hole up somewhere until dawn.

As they entered the house, they worried that Minnie might somehow succeed in escaping with Anna and they'd never see their daughter again. Guilt ate at them, too.

"If I hadn't been distracted by the bake sale cleanup, maybe I could've stopped her."

"And if I hadn't been tending to Chauncey Miller's sprained ankle, I might have been able to step in, too." Miller injured himself during one of the sack races.

"Poor Julia. If we're wrestling with guilt I can only imagine how she feels."

He nodded and eased her into his arms. "We'll find her." He kissed her brow. "Go on to bed."

She left and went to their room. He doused the lamps and joined her.

Neither of them slept.

*A*t dawn, they wearily drank their coffee and were outside walking to their mounts when they stopped at the sight of the wagon rolling slowly in their direction. It was Ben and on the seat beside him wrapped in what looked like a bearskin was Anna! Paying little attention to the buggy and team trailing the wagon, they took off at a run. Regan could barely see through her grateful tears. Colt got there first and swung her off the seat and into his arms. Anna held on tight and Colt rocked her with joy. He then eyed her like a doctor. "Are you all right? Are you hurt anyplace?"

"No, Papa. Vermin choked Minnie and then he got eaten by One Eye!"

They froze. *Vermin?* Regan instantly thought of Dun Bailey. Had he been involved?

Ben said, "Minnie's body's in the buggy. Regan, take Anna inside."

Colt put Anna down and rounded the wagon to the buggy. Regan turned to the familiar-looking vehicle. "Isn't that Colleen's?"

Ben said quietly, "Go on, Regan. You take care of Anna. Colt and I will be in shortly."

Setting aside her many questions, Regan picked Anna up and carried her towards the porch. "I'm so glad to see you," she said, hugging her child tightly. She was so grateful Anna was safe. "Are you hungry?"

"No. But can I see Shadow and then go to bed? I'm sleepy."

"You sure can."

After a short visit with the pony, Regan took her inside, washed her up, helped her into her night-clothes, and was tucking her in when Colt joined them. "Are you certain you're not hurt, Anna?"

"I'm sure. I was real scared though, Papa."

He sat beside Regan on the edge of the bed and ran a fatherly caress over her hair, currently pulled into twin pigtails. "We were scared, too, but you're home now and safe."

"Aunt Minnie tricked me, didn't she?"

Regan responded, "Yes, she did."

"I kept asking her about Shadow's surprise, but she wouldn't tell me what it was. Am I in trouble for going with her?"

Her father said, "Of course not. We're glad you're home and want you to get some rest. That's all. Okay?"

She nodded and went silent for a moment before asking, "Is Aunt Minnie in heaven now with my other mama?"

Not wanting to speak ill of the dead, not even Minnie, Regan nodded.

"I've never seen a dead person before."

She went silent again and Regan wondered if the terrible incident would give Anna nightmares.

Colt asked, "Do you want to talk about it?"

She shook her head and said softly, "No."

"If you think you might later on, just let me and your mama know."

"I will. I want to go to sleep now."

"Okay, honey."

They gave her one last hug and a kiss, then left her to sleep off the ordeal.

"I hope she doesn't have nightmares," Colt said with concern.

"Me either."

They joined Ben at the dining room table and because she assumed he and Colt had already discussed some of the details she asked, "So Dun Bailey killed her?"

"Yes. From what Anna said, Dun and Minnie got into an argument because Minnie didn't have the money she owed him."

"Money for what?" Regan asked.

"For shooting you."

Colt slapped the table. "I knew it!"

Regan was glad the mystery was finally solved.

"Anna said he put his hands around Minnie's throat and choked her until she fell over."

Regan thought that an ill-fitting end, even for someone as unlikeable as Minnie Gore. "How was One Eye involved?"

"Not sure what Bailey planned to do with Anna after he killed Minnie, but he tried to take the buggy up the Old Trapper trail."

"You can barely get a horse up that trail," Colt pointed out.

"I know. I figure maybe he was looking for some place to hide out for the night. Anyway, Anna said they ran over something or something got caught in the wheel. Dun lit a lantern and got out to investigate. One Eye came out of the darkness and chose Dun for dinner. I was close by checking traps when I heard what sounded like a man tangling with a cat. He was yelling, the cat was snarling and yowling, and a child was screaming."

Regan's heart broke. Anna had to have been terrified.

"When I got there, I swung my lantern towards the buggy and saw One Eye feasting on a body on the ground. The cat looked up. I saw it was Dun, so I let him have his meal, and he dragged the body off into the dark. Inside the buggy I saw Minnie slumped over and then Anna."

"Thank you for bringing her home," Colt said.

"Why was Anna with them to begin with?" Ben asked.

Colt told him about Minnie wanting to take Anna back East, and how she'd tricked Anna into leaving the Founders Day gathering.

Ben said, "Minnie needed a better plan and a better partner."

Regan said, "I'm glad she had neither."

"But Dun and Minnie having Colleen's buggy worries me," Colt said. "I don't believe she'd play a part in Anna's abduction, but I'm going to ride over to her place to see what I can find out. I'm hoping he didn't harm her or Felicity."

Regan wanted answers, too, and hoped he was right about Colleen not being involved, and that she and her daughter were safe.

"I'll go with you," Ben said. "Then I'll take Minnie's body into town and turn her over to Beck."

"Tell him I'll pay for the burial," Colt said and looked to Regan for approval and she nodded in agreement. The old woman needed to be buried and she was family.

Ben said, "You're a better man than me, Colton, but then you always were."

Their eyes met and a silent moment passed between them.

Ben rose to his feet and Regan said, "Thank you for saving Anna. You're still welcome here, Mr. Lee. You always will be."

He responded by heading to the door and leaving.

Regan shook her head in frustration and asked Colt, "Do you think he'll ever bend?"

He shrugged and placed a kiss on her brow. "Time will tell. I'll be back as soon as I can."

*N*o one answered Colt's knock at the Enrights' small cabin.

"Try the latch," Ben said.

Colt did and the door opened. In the small front parlor, a gagged and tied-up Colleen was seated on the floor, her back against the wall. Felicity, tied and gagged as well, lay sleeping with her head in her mother's lap.

Grateful tears sprang to Colleen's eyes as they moved quickly to her side. Felicity awakened and Ben's hunting knife made short work of the ropes binding their wrists and ankles.

Colt untied the bandanas in their mouths and a tearful Colleen grabbed him around the neck and sobbed, "Oh thank you for finding us. Thank you!"

He patted her back consolingly and let her hold on for a few moments longer before gently prying himself loose. "Are you injured anywhere?"

"I don't think so," she whispered.

"How about you, Felicity?" he asked.

"My hands and ankles hurt."

"It's from being tied up. You should get the feeling back shortly. Are you hurting anywhere else?"

She shook her head.

Ben said, "Do you want water?"

Colleen nodded. "Please."

Ben withdrew the canteen from his pack and held it to her mouth and then her daughter's.

Once they were done, Colt said, "Tell us what happened."

"Dun Bailey came by as we were leaving for the Founders Day parade."

"Why?"

"Because Minnie asked him to."

Colt was confused.

"Minnie's been staying here since the night we had cake at your place. She wouldn't let me take her back to town."

"Why didn't you just drive her anyway?"

"She's an old woman, Colton. She said she was afraid being in her house alone. I was trying to be kind."

Felicity said, "Miss Minnie said she was going to tell everybody about the men who come to see Mama at night."

Colt stared. Ben's lips thinned.

Colleen snapped, "Hush, Felicity! It was a lie, but I thought people might believe her, so I allowed her to stay."

Colt didn't know what to make of that, so he moved past it. "Did you know she and Dun were going to abduct Anna?"

Colleen's eyes went wide. "No! Oh my goodness. Is that why they wanted my buggy? I kept telling him he couldn't take it, but he said he'd shoot us both if I kept refusing, then tied us up. They took your daughter?"

He nodded. "At the celebration, yesterday. Ben found her last night, but Minnie and Dun are dead."

Colleen turned to Felicity. "How are your legs feeling?"

"Better."

"Then go to your room and change your clothes. I'll be there once we're done talking here."

Felicity complied and once she was gone, Colt filled her in on yesterday's events. When he finished, she said, "Poor Anna must've been scared to death. Personally, I'm glad they're dead."

"Do you know when Minnie and Dun made their plans?"

"No, but she had me drive her to his place a few days ago. She said she wanted to pay him for fixing some loose boards on her porch. She went inside but I stayed in the buggy. I got the impression that he'd been working for her on and off since the spring."

Colt said, "Regan arrived late spring. And the first time he shot at her was just a short time after that." That Minnie might have been planning to kill Regan from the day she arrived made his anger rise. Dun must have gone into hiding after the second attempt on Regan's life then slipped back home. Had he ridden out the storm at Minnie's empty place in town, knowing Whit wouldn't look there?

"Did you know Dun was wanted for questioning after Regan was shot?" Colt asked.

"I did."

"But you didn't tell Whit or anyone else that you'd driven Minnie to see him at his place a few days ago?"

"No. I told you what Minnie threatened. I had my reputation to think about."

"What reputation?" Ben shouted.

Colleen jumped.

"Miller's bragging about rutting with you, and so has Cale. You could've cost Anna her life!"

Her lip quivered and tears filled her eyes. "I have to feed myself. I have a child. I need gowns!"

"To hell with your gowns!" he roared. "Had you done what was right, Dun would've been in jail,

Anna wouldn't have been taken, and you and your daughter wouldn't have been trussed up like chickens, pissing on yourselves."

Colt said, "Ben—"

"I know. I'm leaving. I'll take Minnie's body to town and let everyone know Anna's been found. You ride on home when you're done here." And he left.

As she sobbed, Colt, like Ben, was angry that her pride had placed Anna in danger, but he was also sorry that circumstances had become so dire she'd chosen to use her body as a way out. "People would've helped you, Colleen. All you had to do was ask."

She spat angrily, "I was tired of charity. Do you have any idea how I felt being reduced to a common laundress? I deserved better! I was the one you were supposed to marry after Adele died, Colton Lee! Me! Not your precious uncouth Regan Carmichael."

Sympathy gone, Colt picked up his bag and headed to the door. On the way, he saw a teary-eyed Felicity watching from the threshold of the bedroom. He wanted to pick her up and take her with him, but he knew that was impossible.

At home, Colt found Regan in the kitchen browning beef for tortillas. "How's Anna?" he asked.

"Still sleeping. Colleen and Felicity okay?"

He told her about the visit, then asked, "Did you know she's been prostituting herself?"

"Sort of." And explained what she meant.

"You could've knocked me over with a feather when Felicity spoke up."

"That poor child."

The memory of her watching him as he left rose in his mind. "I know. They might be better off moving elsewhere and starting over."

Regan nodded her agreement and stuck a spoon into the sizzling meat. "Taste this. Does it need more seasoning?"

He let her feed him the spicy concoction and he groaned with pleasure. "Perfect. Just like the chef."

"Are you trying to butter me up, Dr. Lee?"

He linked his arms around her apron-covered waist and, after placing a soft kiss against her lips, replied, "Every chance I get."

"Would you mind if I invite my family out for a visit before the weather changes?"

He studied her. "No. I've been wanting to meet them and I know how much you've missed them."

"Then I'll send a wire tomorrow and see if they can come and when. Thank you, Colt," she said sincerely and hugged him tight.

He kissed the top of her hair. "You're welcome."

A month later, when a large buggy pulled up in front of the house, Regan, on her knees planting the tulip bulbs she'd ordered, looked up. When her sister, Portia, stepped out, followed by her husband, Kent, Aunt Eddy, and Uncle Rhine, Regan screamed and ran. The reunion was filled with rocking hugs, cheek kisses, and many tears.

"I can't believe you're here!"

Aunt Eddy, as dark and beautiful as Regan and her sister, said, "I can't believe it either. Why does this doctor you married live in the middle of the wilderness? Took us an eternity to get here."

Uncle Rhine said, "Hush, Eddy, we made it."

Regan, still in disbelief that they were in Wyoming, looked at the people she loved with all her heart and said, "Come in. I want you to meet my family."

Introductions were made. Anna first.

Her aunt and uncle smiled fondly. "We've heard a lot about you, Anna. We're pleased to finally meet you."

"I'm glad to meet you, too."

Regan said, "Anna, this is my sister, Portia, and her husband, Kent."

They both offered smiles and hellos.

Then it was Colt's turn. "Pleased to meet you all," he said. "Welcome to Wyoming."

Regan smiled inwardly at the skeptical look on her aunt's face as she looked Colt up and down. Eddy asked, "Is she keeping her bedroom clean?"

"Aunt Eddy!" Regan yelled,

Colt laughed so hard, Regan thought he might fall over. "Traitor. Stop laughing."

By then, everyone was laughing, even Anna.

Her family stayed for five days. There were nightly dinners filled with food, laughter, and tales of the past. They took rides around the countryside to meet Spring and Ed Prescott who loaned the family horses. They saw Anna's school, went into town to see Colt's office, and felt the coming of winter as the temperature cooled and the first leaves began to turn red and gold on the trees.

And then came the morning they were scheduled to head home. The hired coach that would be taking them back to Cheyenne to the train depot arrived at dawn. Shivering in the cool morning air, Regan hugged each of them tight. Anna received farewell kisses from her great Aunt Eddy and great Uncle Rhine, and tight hugs from her Aunt Portia and Uncle Kent.

As Regan and Portia shared a final parting hug, they whispered their love for each other and their wishes that both be happy. "Take care of my niece," Regan said, wiping her tears. Portia would be having a baby after the new year, and when Portia shared the news, Regan had cried with joy and reminded her sister that growing up, they'd pledged to have only girls. Now she was shedding tears of farewell.

Eddy said, "Colton, I hope you and Regan and my Anna will come to Arizona when the weather warms."

"Yes, ma'am. We will."

They piled into the coach and Colt put his arm around the teary Regan and gave her a soft kiss on her cheek. "We'll see them again, soon. Promise."

As the wagon rolled away, Regan and her family watched until they were out of sight.

Three days later, Regan and Colt were cuddled together on the bench outside their bedroom watching the moon rise.

"Still missing your family?"

"Yes, but it was wonderful to see them." She wished they all lived closer but she knew Colt would never leave the Territory and now that it was in her blood, she wouldn't want to live anywhere else either.

"Ben stopped by my office today. He and Odell found One Eye's body up near his cabin. Said the way the cat's stomach was distended, he must've eaten some bad meat."

Regan chuckled softly at the awful joke. "Dun Bailey had to be rancid." She then told him, "Anna said Felicity and her mother are moving back East next week."

"Hopefully, for Felicity's sake, they can make a new start."

"And hopefully, one day, I'll forgive Colleen for keeping Dun's whereabouts a secret."

"Me too. Did your sister share any further news about your mother?"

"Yes. Our mother sent a note by the Pinkerton Aunt Eddy hired and it said she had a new life now, didn't want further contact, and not to bother her again."

"How'd your sister take it?"

"Not well. She said she wept. But I'm hoping now that she and Kent have a baby coming, she'll let go of the past and focus on their child and the future."

"And you? How do you feel?"

"I'm just glad the door is closed. I've already gone on with my life. Speaking of which, can I share a good secret?"

"Yes."

"I'm having a baby."

"Truly?" he asked excitedly.

"Truly. Sometime in the spring I'm guessing."

He hugged her closer. "That's grand news!"

"All those doctor visits, I'm thinking."

"You're probably right."

"The day we met, did you think we'd wind up this way?"

"The day you shot me?"

She poked him gently with her elbow.

"No, I didn't. I just wanted you for Anna. I didn't know I'd come to want you for myself so very much."

She turned to him, moved by the emotion in his tone. "I'm glad we went forward. Had we not, we would have missed this."

"I know."

She whispered, "I love you so."

"I love you, too."

As she resettled herself in the comfort of his arms, she admitted her mail-order bride adventure may not have begun well, but it was ending just fine.

Dear Reader,

Tempest brings us to the end of the Old West/ Rhine Fontaine series, and I hope you enjoyed this final installment. Many of you were concerned about Regan heading off to Wyoming alone, and how she'd fare as a mail-order bride. I was, too, but she found love with Dr. Colt Lee and his daughter, Anna, and now, all is well.

Tempest touched on more than a few historical notes. For me, one of the most compelling and heartbreaking was the incident at Rock Springs. The events told through Colt's participation are true. In the end, the Chinese did return to work but it took an act of Congress to award them their back pay. The U.S. Army built Camp Pilot Butte in Rock Springs to keep the peace, and stationed soldiers there for the next thirteen years.

Another interesting aspect was my brief mention of Dr. Alexander Augusta. Born free in Virginia in 1825, he was the highest ranking Black officer in the Union Army, and went on to become the first African-American professor of medicine. Every African-American physician in the nation owes him tribute for his perseverance and determination. It is my hope that by highlighting him in *Tempest*, he and his accomplishments will no longer be unsung.

So, for further study, your homework: please research and share

1. Rock Springs Massacre.
2. Dr. Alexander T. Augusta.
3. Dr. Joseph Lister.

In closing, my thanks to my editor, agent, and the Avon production team members for their patience and care. Readers, you can thank my editor for the Fontaine reunion at the end of *Tempest*. The first draft didn't contain one, much to her disappointment.

And as always, a huge Bevy thanks to you, my readers, for your love of *Forbidden*, *Breathless*, and now *Tempest*. This series has been fun. I've no idea where we'll travel next or who we'll meet, but I hope you'll come along.

You're the best!

B

We hope you enjoyed
Regan's story in *Tempest*.
If you've missed where it all began,
turn the page for a peek at
Forbidden (Eddy's story) and
Breathless (Portia's story).

Forbidden

"It's possible that no one sets the scene for romance better than Beverly Jenkins . . . This is historical romance at its very best."
—Sarah MacLean for *The Washington Post*

Rhine entered his shadowy bedroom and gently placed Eddy in the center of his large four-poster bed. Another man might fret over her and her dirty clothing being laid on the clean sheets, but he was more concerned with her well-being. Her breathing was so shallow and her skin still so hot he worried that she might not pull through. Taking a hasty look back at her over his shoulder, he quickly grabbed a basin and hurried down the hall to the washroom to fill it with water so he could continue wiping her down.

Luckily, it was a Sunday and the saloon was

closed. Otherwise she might've been disturbed by the noise and revelry of drunk miners and card players from the floor below. He stuck the large sponge into the water-filled basin and slowly and gently slid it over her face, throat, and the tops of her breasts above the shabby shift. That she wasn't wearing a corset was a plus. More than likely she would've died in the heat had she been. To his thinking, she'd be better off nude and immersed in a tub of cool water, but he needed to wait for Jim to return with Sylvie—as she was affectionately called—or Doc. The questions surrounding Eddy's plight continued to plague Rhine, but they had to be set aside until she was strong enough to answer.

A short while later, Jim entered with Sylvie and both came to the bedside. Concern filled Sylvie's face. "Sorry I wasn't home. I was out at the orphanage. Jim said you found her in the desert?" The middle-aged boardinghouse owner was a trusted friend.

Rhine stopped his ministrations for a moment. "Yes. And her skin's iron hot."

Sylvie placed her palm on her forehead. "She is very warm. Poor thing. I'd suggest a tub, but until she's fully awake I'm scared she'll slip beneath the water."

"I can hold her up if you think that will help."

She studied Rhine as if thinking that over. "It might. Do you know who she is?"

"No."

"Okay. Do you have a shirt or something for her to wear?"

"Yes." He walked to his wardrobe and took down a shirt. "Jim, were you able to find Doc?"

"He's in Reno. He'll be back in a day or two."

Rhine saw the exasperation on Sylvie's face. She had been a nurse for the Colored troops during the war and served in that capacity now for the city's Colored community. According to the rumors, she and Doc Randolph had been at odds for decades, but Rhine had no idea why.

Sylvie took the shirt from his hand. "Let me get her undressed and I'll call you in to carry her to the tub. In the meantime start filling it with water."

Eddy thought she was dreaming about being carried down a dark tunnel. She knew a man was carrying her but she had yet to see his face. He eased her into a pool of water and she leaned back against his strong shoulder. The water lapped over her like a balm, magically erasing all her hurts and soothing her everywhere: throat, arms, breasts. It felt so glorious, she sighed with pleasure. Languidly opening her eyes, she stared into the deep green gaze of a White man. For some reason, she wasn't alarmed. His jet black hair and handsome, ivory-skinned features seemed familiar somehow. She gently cupped his unshaven cheek—something she'd never done to any man before—and he smiled softly. She smiled in return, and that was the last thing she remembered.

"I trust you'll be gentlemen if I leave her in your care for the night?"

Jim nodded.

"Of course," Rhine added, eyeing the woman sleeping peacefully in yet another one of his clean shirts beneath a light blanket.

"My cook, Felix," Sylvie said, "left to go back East yesterday, so I'll have to listen to my boarders complaining about my serving them burnt breakfast before I can come back here to check on her in the morning."

Rhine smiled. Everyone in town knew Sylvie had no cooking skills at all. He pitied her boarders. "Do you have a replacement for Felix in mind?"

"Not yet. Nor do I have a place for this young woman to stay, at the moment. One of the men will be leaving in a few days and she can finish her recovery with me. Will you mind looking after her until then?"

Rhine glanced over at Jim, who shrugged, so Rhine replied, "No." His fiancée Natalie probably wouldn't approve if she knew, but he'd cross that bridge if and when the time came.

"Okay good. I'll bring some aloe for her sunburn tomorrow. When she wakes up, encourage her to drink, but not a lot all at once. Jim, cook her light food. Eggs, maybe some toast, and we'll see how things go. Let's hope she'll be in better shape after she rests up."

Rhine agreed.

Jim asked, "Do you want me to drive you back?"

Sylvie nodded. After glancing down at the young woman a final time, she said, "Keep an eye on her."

After their departure, Rhine surveyed his sleeping guest. He ran his eyes over the clear-as-glass ebony skin, the long sweep of her lashes, and her perfect mouth. While in the tub, she'd taken him by surprise when she opened her eyes, looked deeply into his own, and cupped his cheek as if they'd been lovers. The urge to turn her hand and place his lips against her damp palm had also taken him by surprise. He had a fiancée and was due to be married before year's end. He had no business thinking about kissing another woman. Deciding what he'd felt was nothing more than concern, he set the incident aside and took a seat to watch over her as promised and await Jim's return.

Eddy awakened in a four-poster in a large room barely lit by a turned down lamp. Having no idea where she was or how she came to be there, she shook the cobwebs dulling her thinking and noticed she was wearing a man's shirt! Perplexed, her eyes moved around the room to a well-appointed sitting area and then to the face of a White man watching her from one of the chairs. Panic flared. She snatched the blanket to her neck and she drew back fearfully.

"Don't be afraid. You're safe. I'm Rhine Fontaine. My friend Jim and I found you in the desert."

Confused, she tried to force herself to calm down so she could make some sense of this, but she couldn't. Watching him warily, she asked, "Where am I?" Her throat was dry as sand. She wanted water badly, but needed to solve the mystery of this first.

"Virginia City."

"And this place is?"

"My bedroom."

Her eyes went wide. "I need to go, I can't stay here."

"Maybe in a few days, but right now—"

Alarmed, she didn't let him finish. She swung her legs over the side of the bed. Her mind was so foggy she wasn't sure what was happening, but she knew she had to get away.

He stood and said urgently, "No! You'll fall!"

He was right. The moment she stood, she was hit by a wave of weakness so strong, her legs folded as if they were made out of cards. She cried out involuntarily as she hit the floor.

He walked over to her. "As I said, maybe in a few days. Are you okay?"

Drawing away again, she looked up and recognized the face of the man from her dream. She stilled. Had it been a dream? "I'll scream!"

He sighed. "If you feel that's necessary, go right ahead, but I'm not going to hurt you—in any way. When you're done, I can help you back into bed, or carry you to the facilities, whichever you'd prefer."

Heated embarrassment burned her cheeks. Her needs were not something she talked about to a stranger, and especially not a White man stranger. "I can walk."

"No, you can't, but if you want to try, I'll wait."

At that moment she saw her bare legs sticking out from beneath the long-tailed shirt, and also realized she had on no underthings! No drawers. No shift. As quickly as her weakened state allowed, she reached up and pulled the blanket down. Ignoring him as best she could, she covered her bare legs. This was getting worse and worse.

"As I said, my name's Rhine. And yours?"

"Eddy. Eddy Carmichael."

"Pleased to meet you, Miss Carmichael. You gave my partner Jim and I quite a scare out there in the desert, but I'm pleased to see you are recovering."

Then her muddled brain remembered Nash's perfidy and her walk across the desert, but nothing else. "How long have I been here?"

"Four or five hours."

Lord, she was thirsty. "May I have some water please?" she croaked. She felt so weak. It was not a state she was accustomed to.

He poured her a glass from a pitcher on the nightstand and handed it to her. "Slowly," he advised softly. "Just a little for now."

She nodded and took a few short swallows. The water tasted so good and she was so thirsty she wanted to down the entire offering, but heeding his advice, she took only a few more slow pulls. Done, she handed the glass back and her parched throat savored the relief. "Why am I so weak?"

"Walking the Forty Mile Desert under a full sun takes its toll. So, Miss Eddy—facilities or back to bed?"

She hated to admit it but she really needed choice number one. Thoroughly scandalized, she confessed softly, "The facilities, but I can walk. Just point me in the right direction." Looking around, she didn't see a screen of any kind.

"It's at the end of the hallway."

"Oh," she said disappointedly. Still bent on getting there under her own power, though, she wrestled with the blanket in an attempt to fashion it around her waist. Trying to get it out from under her hips and secured without treating him to another show of her legs was a struggle, however. He'd seen more of them than any man ever before.

"Do you want to go today?" he asked in a tone of muted amusement.

She shot him a glare. Reasonably certain the blanket was secured, she said, "Yes." Now she just had to get up. No small task. The fullness of the blanket made it difficult to get her feet planted so she could stand. She decided she'd use the side of the bed to give her the leverage she needed. She scooted closer.

"You always this stubborn, Miss Carmichael?"

"It's called determination, Mr. Fontaine."

"I stand corrected."

Giving him another withering glare, she grabbed hold of the bed's wooden side panel and began working herself to her knees. She made a bit of progress, but her weakened state conspired against her efforts. Refusing to surrender and breathing harshly, she slowly inched herself to a standing position, careful not to get her feet fouled by the swath of blanket, and promptly keeled face forward onto the mattress.

Chuckling softly, he picked her up from behind

and placed her gently into the cradle of his strong arms. He smiled softly. "It's called stubbornness."

Rolling her eyes, she allowed herself to be carried from the room.

Rhine came from a long line of determined women, and the little lady presently in his washroom could have been one of them. While he stood waiting in the hallway a short distance away from the closed door to give her the privacy she needed, he had nothing but admiration for Miss Eddy Carmichael. He wondered again what she'd be like at full strength. Those withering looks she kept shooting him had probably brought more than one man to his knees, but he was finding them amusing.

The door opened and there she stood, upright but panting from the exertion. She appeared to be wobbly on her pins and on the verge of toppling, so he went to her and picked her up. She didn't protest but he could tell by her tight face that she wasn't enjoying being carried as much as he seemed to be enjoying offering the assistance.

He set her gently back in the center of his bed. "Would you like more water?"

She nodded.

He poured again from the pitcher.

When she'd had her fill she handed the glass back with a shaking hand. "Thank you."

"You're welcome."

"And thank you and your friend for rescuing me."

"You're welcome for that, too."

"I had a carpetbag with me. Did you find it?"

"Yes."

"Can you bring it to me?" No matter her condition, she wasn't going to go without underwear.

"Yes, I will. Now, lie back."

Again a nod. He waited while she undid her cocoon. From the slow pace of her movements, she obviously had very little strength, but rather than offer to help and draw her ire, he let her handle it alone. Finally free of the blanket confines, she slowly spread it out, seemingly careful to keep her lovely legs hidden from his sight. Content, she snuggled in. If she had any lingering worries or misgivings about being in the room with him, she didn't voice them. "Rest now," he told her quietly. A blink of an eye later she was asleep. Shaking his head at her determination, he went back to his chair for some rest of his own.

 *Breathless*

"This heartfelt story and its endearing characters and gratifying ending will leave readers breathing a sigh of pure contentment."
—*Publishers Weekly* (starred review)

Santa Catalina Mountains,
Arizona Territory
Spring 1885

"*I* wonder how it feels to be that much in love."

In response to the question, Portia Carmichael glanced up from the ledger she was working on to look over at her sister, Regan, standing at the window. "I've no idea," she replied as she refocused on the column of numbers she was adding. Regan was gazing cow-eyed out at what Portia assumed were their aunt Eddy and uncle Rhine Fontaine.

The sisters were in the business office of the Fontaine Hotel and although the twenty-five-year-old Regan longed for love and children, Portia, two years older, wanted neither. Being the manager of the family's successful hotel was more than enough to make Portia's life complete.

"To have someone look at you that way and know you are their entire world—oh my."

"Please don't swoon, or at least do it elsewhere," Portia teased. She didn't have to look up to know Regan responded with a shake of her head that held equal parts amusement and pity.

"Numbers won't keep you warm at night, sister mine."

"That's what quilts are for."

"One of these days, Cupid's going to hit you with an arrow right between the eyes. I just hope I'm around to see it."

Smiling, Portia ignored the prediction only to hear Regan gush, "Oh my, they're sharing a kiss."

Portia sighed audibly. "Why don't you step away from the window and let them have their privacy."

"They're having a picnic by the gazebo. If they wanted privacy they'd be in their suite behind closed doors."

She supposed Regan was right. The couple's love was legendary and they didn't keep their mutual affection a secret. At any moment of the day one could round a corner and find them stealing a kiss, holding hands as if still courting, or drowning in each other's eyes. Not that Portia found their affection unseemly; she was glad they were in love and that it extended to their nieces.

Regan vowed, "When I find someone to marry I want that type of love."

Their mother, Corinne, had been in love, and when her intended demanded she cast her daughters aside because they weren't his progeny, Corinne put the then twelve-year-old Portia and ten-year-old Regan on a train to their aunt Eddy in Virginia City and never looked back. In the fifteen years since, they'd not heard a word. Portia wanted no part of something that could cause such irreparable harm. She planned to remain unmarried and immerse herself in work. Work didn't break hearts.

"Don't you want to marry, Portia?"

"Not particularly, but if I do, he'll have to be an exceptional fellow who loves me for my intelligence and business acumen, not for how I perform on my knees. I'm not Mama."

Regan turned from the window, her voice thoughtful. "Do you ever wonder where she is?"

"Sometimes." Portia would never admit how much her heart still ached from being abandoned so callously or how often she thought about her.

"Do you think she wonders about us?"

"I don't know."

Corinne had been a whore, and the hardship of their life with her still held a pain they rarely discussed. Thanks to Aunt Eddy and Uncle Rhine they'd survived though and were still together.

Regan's attention returned to the scene outside

the window. "I would love to be as happy as they are."

"I added this column wrong," Portia muttered, and began searching for her mistake. She blamed the error on being distracted by her sister's chatter.

"Thoughts of being in love can do that."

"No, your going on and on about love can do that," she replied, humor in her voice.

"Don't you want a man you can sneak off into a corner with and who will kiss you so passionately you don't care if the whole territory is watching?"

Portia shook her head with amusement. Regan changed beaus as frequently as some women changed their gloves but never stayed with any of them very long. "You're so shameless."

"I know, but somewhere there's a man who'll appreciate that part of me. I have no intentions of relying on quilts to keep me warm at night and neither should you, sister."

"Don't you have mail to deliver or something?" In addition to his vast business holdings, their uncle Rhine owned the government mail contract, and the unconventional Regan had talked him into letting her take charge of delivery. Twice a week she and her mule, Josephine, drove the five miles to Tucson to see to its distribution. As far as Portia knew there'd been no complaints about Regan's race or gender; folks just wanted their mail.

"Not until the day after tomorrow, which you'd remember if you weren't so focused on your duties."

"I take my position very seriously."

"I know."

The tone made Portia look up.

Regan said sincerely, "I don't claim to know a lot about life but there has to be more to it than work. When was the last time you spent the day sitting in the meadow listening to bird songs or riding out to the canyon to take in the waterfalls?"

"I don't have time for that, Regan. A lot goes into keeping this hotel running. There's staff to manage and menus to approve, guests to oversee . . ."

"Which is why you have a staff. This place won't fall to pieces if you left your desk every now and again."

"You sound like Aunt Eddy."

"Good. She loves you, too, and we worry about you."

"No need. I'm fine."

Regan showed her exasperation and moved away from the window. "Am I to assume you don't need my help for the anniversary dinner this evening?"

"You're correct. Everything is in order." They'd be celebrating their aunt and uncle's fifteen years of marriage in the hotel's main ballroom.

"Okay. Then I'm going over to Old Man Blanchard's. He has a package for me to take to his daughter in Tucson."

"Okay." Mr. Blanchard lived on a ranch a short distance west of the hotel. "Make sure he's coming tonight. Aunt Eddy will be disappointed if he chooses to stay home and play checkers with Farley and Buck." Farley and Buck were his ranch hands.

"Will do," Regan promised, and she left the office.

Sitting alone, Portia knew her sister's gentle chastisement about the long hours she put in at her desk came from her heart, but there were those who thought the Fontaines mad for placing their niece in charge of their hotel—thoughts that never would have risen had Portia been a *nephew*. She wanted to prove she was as capable of the job as any man and so kept her nose to the grindstone. They were now living in the Arizona Territory in a beautiful, temperate area at the base of the Catalina Mountains a few miles north and east of the town of Tucson. Rhine and Eddy built the hotel from the ground up in '73 upon a large open swath of land originally owned by a mine president. When the mine went dry, his funds did, too, and her uncle Rhine and aunt Eddy were able to buy it and the hundreds of acres of open range surrounding it from the bank for a pittance. Over the years, the Fontaine Hotel became famous for its fine food and luxurious accommodations. Lately it also served as a magnet for well-to-do Europeans and Easterners wanting a taste of the Wild West; a new phenomenon Uncle Rhine called Dude Ranch Fever. Ranchers from the Rockies to the Mexican border were opening their doors to wealthy guests who wanted to hunt, fish, and ride the open ranges to take in the meadows, lakes, and canyon waterfalls. Some came strictly to view the myriad species of birds while others wanted to tour old silver mines or pretend to pan for gold. The Fontaine Hotel, in partnership with Mr. Blanchard's ranch, also offered guests the opportunity to watch cattle being branded, take roping lessons, and in the evening gather around a roaring campfire to eat and listen to Buck and Farley tell exaggerated stories of ghost towns, deadly outlaws, and dangerous Indians. The guests could then ride back to the hotel for the night or remain at the Blanchard place to sleep in tents or on bedrolls under the stars. It was a lucrative trade for both establishments, so much so that it was necessary for guests to make reservations a year in advance if they wanted to be accommodated. Coordinating all the details took a clear head and a steady hand, and with so much to do, there was no time for Portia to take leisurely trips to view waterfalls.

A soft knock on the open door broke her reverie and she looked up to see her aunt Eddy standing on the threshold. Like her nieces, Eddy Carmichael Fontaine was a dark-skinned, dark-eyed beauty and she wore her forty-plus years well.

Portia asked, "So are you ready for your grand affair?"

"I suppose. You know how much I dislike all this fuss. I would've been content to celebrate with a nice quiet supper, maybe a few musicians and a cake, but your uncle loves fanfare."

"So you tolerate it."

"Barely, but only because I love him so much."

"Regan was spying on you two in the gazebo. Says she wants the kind of love you and Uncle Rhine share."

"That's not a bad goal. Although it took me a while to see it."

Portia knew that when Aunt Eddy and Uncle Rhine first met, he'd still been passing as a White man. Eddy hadn't wanted to fall in love with him because of the societal dangers tied to such unions. "But you did."

"Yes, and sometimes, like with this anniversary business, I have to remind myself of that because only for him would I endure the torture of being fitted for a new gown."

Portia never failed to be amused by her aunt's aversion to dressmakers. "You have armoires stuffed with gowns yet you always say that."

"Because it's the truth. All the pin sticks, measurements, and having to stand still." She waved a hand dismissively. "A woman should be able to go into a dress shop, find something to her liking, and leave with it."

"You can." Ready-to-wear gowns were becoming quite popular.

"But they all seem to be made for someone taller and they're never the right color. It's as maddening as the fittings." She sighed with exasperation and asked, "Is everything ready for the dinner tonight?"

"Yes, so no harassing the staff about what's being done or not being done." Her aunt and uncle had run the hotel as a team since its founding, but now Portia mostly held the reins. Although Eddy refused to relinquish control of the hotel's kitchen, Portia had relieved her of all duties related to the preparation of the anniversary dinner. She'd initially balked of course, then reluctantly agreed.

"Is Janie still baking the cake? Does she have enough eggs, flour?"

"Aunt Eddy," Portia chided. "Everything is being taken care of."

"But I feel so useless."

"I understand, but you aren't allowed to do anything except get gussied up and enjoy the party."

Eddy didn't like it and it showed on her face. She finally sighed audibly in surrender. "Okay, I suppose."

Portia almost felt sorry for her. Almost. Her aunt was the hardest-working woman she'd ever met and one of the reasons for the hotel's great success. Not being able to direct this event was threatening to send her around the bend. "If you want to do something, you can go over to the Wilson place and check on your centerpieces."

"I get to pick the flowers? Oh, be still my heart."

Portia laughed. "Or I could send Regan."

"Lord, no. She'd stick a bunch of saguaro on a plate and call it done. I'll go."

"Good."

There was silence for a moment as they viewed each other, and then Eddy asked, "Have I told you how proud I am of all you've grown up to be?"

Emotion filled Portia's throat. "Numerous times."

"I'm glad Corinne sent you and Regan to me."

"As are we." Had she not, both Portia and Regan would've had their virginity sold for a pittance and grown to adulthood with little knowledge of the world beyond the walls of their mother's shack. They most certainly wouldn't have attended Oberlin to complete their education, nor would Portia have been given the opportunity to hone her bookkeeping skills at the San Francisco bank owned by Uncle Rhine's half-brother, Andrew. Portia was grateful every day for being given a home by Eddy and Rhine.

"I'll ride over and check on the flowers in a bit," her aunt said.

"Okay, and no worrying allowed."

With a roll of her eyes, Aunt Eddy departed.

By late afternoon, Portia was done with her ledgers. Realizing she'd missed lunch, she pushed her chair back from the desk and left the office for the kitchen. The hotel was spread out over five, white adobe, one-story buildings with red tiled roofs. One housed staff and the business offices. The others held guest rooms, the family quarters, dining spaces, and kitchens. All the buildings were connected by covered breezeways. As she stepped out into the sunshine to walk to the kitchen she was brought up short by the unexpected sight of a brown-skinned cowboy seated on the broad back of a beautiful blue roan stallion. She couldn't make out the man's features beneath the black felt hat, so shading her eyes against the bright sunlight, she asked, "May I help you?"

He pushed back the hat. "Is this the Fontaine place?"

"It is."

For a moment he didn't say anything else, simply stared down at her from his perch before fluidly dismounting to stand facing her. "Hello, Duchess."

Portia froze. She scanned the unshaven features, trying to place him. *Duchess?* Only one person had ever called her that. Suddenly recognition solved the mystery. "Kent Randolph?"

He nodded and a glint of amusement lit his eyes. "How've you been?"

She found herself slightly mesmerized by his handsome face and teasing gaze. "I've been well. You?"

"Can't complain. Good seeing you again."

"Same here." When she first came to live with Rhine and Eddy in Virginia City, she'd been twelve years old. He been six years older and the bartender at Rhine's saloon. She hadn't paid him much attention, except when he called her Duchess, which annoyed her to no end. The passage of fifteen years had turned him into a man taller than she by at least a foot and with shoulders wide enough to block the sun. Her eyes strayed over the worn gun belt strapped around his waist and the butt of the Colt it held. Snug denims on muscular legs were covered with trail dust as were his boots, single-breasted gray shirt, and black leather vest. She heard he'd gone back East to medical school. With such rugged good looks, he certainly didn't resemble any doctor she'd ever met.

"You've grown up." His soft tone grabbed her attention and touched her in a way that made her feel warm, female.

She blinked. "Um, yes."

"Is your uncle here?"

Realizing she was staring, she shook herself free of whatever his eyes were doing to befuddle her so totally. "Yes. He's inside. This way, please."

She waited while he tied the roan to the post and reached for his saddlebag. Tossing it easily over his shoulder, they set out, his heeled boots echoing against the wooden walk. She got the feeling that he was eyeing the sway of her blue skirt, but she was so overwhelmed by the air of maleness he exuded, she kept walking and tried to ignore his effects on her usually unflappable self.

Her uncle's office was in the same building that housed her own, so she led Kent back to the breezeway and past the giant oaks and flowers enhancing the landscaping.

"Nice place you have here," he remarked as he looked around.

"Thank you. We like it."

"When the man in Tucson gave me directions to the hotel, I expected something more like the hotels back East or in Virginia City, not a spread like this. Looks more like a ranch."

They approached the door. He reached around her to open it. His arm gently grazed her shoulder and Portia jumped nervously.

"Sorry. Not trying to scare you," he said apologetically. "Just wanted to get the door for you."

"Thank you," she said, looking up into his face. She wondered if he remembered how uneasy and fearful she'd been around men when she and her sister first came to Virginia City. Because of Corinne's way of life, Portia had imagined herself fair game to any man in a pair of trousers, and as a result she'd been as afraid as a tiny mouse in a world filled with large feral cats.

He held the door aside. "After you."

She inclined her head and entered.

The coolness of the interior's air always offered relief from the blazing Arizona heat. "My uncle's office is this way."

She led him past the large sitting room filled with elegant dark wood furniture. The white adobe walls were adorned with framed brightly hued paintings and plants stood in large colorful floor pots.

"Feels like Mexico," he said.

"We're not that far from the border." She stopped at her uncle's closed door and knocked.

He called, "Come on in."

Kent entered behind her and when Rhine, who was seated behind a big fancy desk, saw him, his jaw dropped and he slowly got to his feet. "Where in the hell did you find him?" There was a smile of wonder on his face.

"Outside on a horse," she said with a grin. "I'll leave you two to your visit."

Kent turned to her and said in the same soft tone he'd used earlier, "Thanks, Duchess."

"You're welcome." Forcing herself to break his captivating gaze, she turned and exited.

*Next month, don't miss these exciting
new love stories only from
Avon Books*

The Duke's Daughters: Lady Be Reckless
by Megan Frampton

Lady Olivia refuses to repeat her siblings' scandalous mistakes. Instead, she'll marry the lord rejected by her sister. When he resists, Olivia forms another plan: win his lordship's admiration by helping his best friend find a bride. How difficult can it be to transform the rakish Edward Wolcott into a gentleman? To ignore his good looks? To not kiss him in a moment of madness? Apparently, very difficult.

A Princess in Theory by Alyssa Cole

Between grad school and multiple jobs, Naledi Smith doesn't have time for fairy tales . . . or patience for the constant e-mails claiming she's betrothed to an African prince. *Delete!* As a former foster kid, she's learned that the only one she can depend on is herself. But when the real Prince Thabiso tracks her down, she mistakes him for a pauper and finds herself falling for the first time.

My Once and Future Duke by Caroline Linden

Sophie Campbell is determined to be mistress of her own fate. Surviving on her skill at cards, she never risks what she can't afford to lose. Yet when the Duke of Ware proposes a scandalous wager, she can't resist. If she wins, she'll get five thousand pounds, enough to secure her independence. And if she loses . . . she'll have to spend a week with the duke.

Discover great authors, exclusive offers,
and more at hc.com.

REL 0218

NEW YORK TIMES BESTSELLING AUTHOR

LYNSAY SANDS

The Highlander Takes a Bride
978-0-06-227359-8

Raised among seven boisterous brothers, comely Saidh
Buchanan has a warrior's temper and little interest in
saddling herself with a husband . . . until she glimpses
the new Laird MacDonnell bathing naked in the loch.
Though she's far from a proper lady, the brawny
Highlander makes Saidh feel every inch a woman.

Always
978-0-06-201956-1

Bastard daughter to the king, Rosamunde was raised
in a convent and wholly prepared to take the veil . . .
until King Henry declared she would wed Aric, one of
his most valiant knights. While Rosamunde's spirited
nature often put her at odds with her new husband,
his mastery in seduction was quickly melting her
resolve—and capturing her heart.

Lady Pirate
978-0-06-201973-8

Valoree has been named heir to Ainsley Castle. But
no executor would ever hand over the estate to an
unmarried pirate wench and her infamous crew.
Upon learning that the will states that in order to
inherit, Valoree must be married to a nobleman—and
pregnant—she's ready to return to the seas. But
her crew has other ideas . . .

LYS8 1016

Discover great authors, exclusive offers, and more at hc.com.

At Avon Books, we know your passion for romance—once you finish one of our novels, you find yourself wanting more.

May we tempt you with . . .

- **Excerpts** from our upcoming releases.

- Entertaining **extras**, including authors' personal photo albums and book lists.

- Behind-the-scenes **scoop** on your favorite characters and series.

- **Sweepstakes** for the chance to win free books, romantic getaways, and other fun prizes.

- Writing **tips** from our authors and editors.

- **Blog** with our authors and find out why they love to write romance.

- **Exclusive content** that's not contained within the pages of our novels.

Join us at
www.avonbooks.com

AVON *An Imprint of* HarperCollins*Publishers*
www.avonromance.com

Available wherever books are sold or please call 1-800-331-3761 to order.

FTH 1013

Give in to your Impulses!

These unforgettable stories only take a second to buy and give you hours of reading pleasure!

Go to *www.AvonImpulse.com* and see what we have to offer.
Available wherever e-books are sold.

AVONIMPULSE

IMP 0811